# The Cornish Village School – Breaking the Rules

KITTY WILSON

# The Cornish Village School

BREAKING THE RULES

CANELO

First published in the United Kingdom in 2018 by Canelo

This edition published in the United Kingdom in 2019 by

Canelo Digital Publishing Limited
57 Shepherds Lane
Beaconsfield, Bucks HP9 2DU
United Kingdom

A CIP catalogue record for this book is available from the British Library.

Print ISBN 978 1 78863 342 0
Ebook ISBN 978 1 78863 116 7

Look for more great books at www.canelo.co

Printed and bound in Great Britain by Clays Ltd, Elcograf S.p.A.

*For Jack, Katharine, Timmy and Tatters*

# Chapter One

Rosy jumped into her car and sped through the village as quickly as she could without knocking over small children, trying to maintain as professional a look as possible in case she was seen. Headteachers were not allowed to scowl in public, and vehicular manslaughter was obviously a no-no. She whizzed past the last stragglers from school and the thirteenth-century church on the corner, its Grade One listing and historical importance ignored by the teenagers getting off the secondary school bus and sneaking into the graveyard to have one last cigarette before reaching home.

The rows of cottages all jumbled together and daubed with the pastel colours of sage green, baby pink and ice-cream yellow – colours of Cornwall in the summer – receded into the distance as she passed the central hub of the village. The local shop, recently revamped, was now a pale slate grey and stocked with halloumi, hummus and miso paste, a nod to the gentrification of the village as Cornwall had become fashionable again and property prices had shot through the roof. It was at complete odds with its tatty neighbour, the butcher's, which hadn't been repainted since the nineties and had a window chock-full of community posters, yellowing and curled at the edges, inviting residents to events long since passed.

She careered past the pub and then the beach, heaving in the summer months but empty at this time of year, and the ice-cream shop, boarded up until Easter when hordes of barefooted families would suddenly appear, snaking all the way back to the sands.

Nearly home and with minutes to spare, she just had to get past the final row of fishermen's cottages and she could pull up in her driveway and grab the one book she had forgotten this morning.

Her cottage came into sight, the late winter sun bouncing off the granite, lending warmth and making the quartz deep in the stone sparkle. The exposed walls were different from many homes in the village, most of which were prettily painted and as fresh as gin and tonic as the sun sets. Rosy's cottage was more of a well-loved local ale, one with bits bobbing in it. Its neighbour was the same, both boldly joined together in their rebellion.

As she turned into her drive, Rosy caught sight of the higgledy-piggledyness of the roof, all uneven tiling and indents, and the stunted, windblown cherry tree in the front that exuded character and never, ever failed to make her smile. She had spent many hours wondering how the tree had become windblown, protected as it was by walls all around the front garden. There was just a little space that had been taken out to make way for a drive, and a small gate embedded in the front with its promise of a secret garden.

For her the cottage summed up Cornwall; sometimes wild and grim and grey but, in the right light, welcoming, quirky and warm. The cottage seemed honest, somehow, more in keeping with Cornwall's past.

Rosy was fairly sure that the fishermen and smugglers of yesteryear weren't big on sage green or baby pink.

Today, though, was one of those rare days where Rosy didn't have the time to smile at her cottage's eccentricities and meander slowly up the drive, drinking them all in. Indeed, this time she ran from her car, falling over her feet and then through the door, hallway and into the kitchen, her heart pounding, slowing only as she spied Rufus Marksharp's writing book on the kitchen table.

The day had already been difficult, filled with staff absences, glitter-dough vomit, hijacked lunch boxes and World War Three breaking out over the school hamster, but at least she would no longer be mauled into itty-bitty pieces by Rufus's mother at the after-school meeting she had recently demanded. She was a woman who never failed to make Rosy think of a velociraptor, stalking the playgrounds, hunting in the hallways and watching, always watching. That woman could drape herself in as much Cath Kidston as she liked; she was fooling no one.

Rosy now had only ten minutes to get back to the school so she could listen to just how gifted Rufus was. She was going to have to keep herself in check, be professional and a little bit less of a grouch. She knew that her mood today had been tetchy – she had even scowled at four-year-old Billy during maths when she had to firmly remind him, twice, that in school one kept one's trousers on.

Heading towards the kitchen door, book in hand, Rosy spied a small metal tin on the worktop. Her smile returned. That was just what she needed. A nutty millionaire's slice. She flipped the lid and snatched a piece, ramming it into her mouth before it crumbled into nothingness and the caramel wrapped around her fingers. Perhaps one more bit, maybe two.

Now she really did have to move! She raced to her car, hopped in and started to reverse down the drive.

*Screech!* She was forced to jam the brakes on, a peanut falling from her mouth onto her dress as she was jolted forward. Where on earth had that come from? Blocking her drive was a removal lorry, big enough to house a circus and not showing any signs of moving. That had definitely not been here when she had arrived. With only a few minutes left before she was due to sit in a teeny-tiny chair with a woman reputed to down entire careers with one glance – rumour had it she could take out small island nations in less than three minutes – she was going to need to move fast.

She blared her horn as hard as she could. No movement. She needed to get out of the car and track the removal men down. Up until now she had been curious as to who her new neighbours were going to be, but now, at this moment, she wasn't fussed about finding out. She just wanted them to move their truck so she could get back to school. The last thing she needed was Mrs pain-in-the-arse Marksharp kicking off about her reliability. Oh, for goodness' sake! Where was that lorry driver? *Beep! Beep!*

With the truck clearly empty and no patter of removal men's feet, she jumped back out of the car, dark hair flipping up and down against her shoulders, and stalked down the drive towards the cottage attached to hers. What were they playing at? Honestly, upsetting your new neighbour before you had even unpacked was a stupid thing to do.

*As is shouting at your neighbour on their moving day,* her sensible voice pointed out from the back of her mind.

*No one is doing this on purpose. It's just life. Be nice. Get the lorry out of the way and then be on yours. Do not cause a scene with people you have to live alongside for years.* Imagine if someone drove past and witnessed her screeching like a banshee. The embarrassment may kill her. The village would be agog to hear that Rosy Winter had lost the plot.

Rosy paused on her driveway to take a deep breath. As she stood there she noticed a silhouette just by her wall. She raced towards the road and spotted someone in front of her tree, holding onto something presumably from the lorry. It was hard to distinguish what it was in this light, and she squinted to see if that helped. It didn't. More importantly, the minutes were whizzing by. A groan escaped her lips as she pictured Mrs Marksharp arching an eyebrow and checking her watch. She scrunched her nose and practised her best caring-new-neighbour face but it seemed that today not even her face was prepared to be obedient. She could feel her eyes thinning and her mouth dropping as her features seemed determined to rest in their most resolute do-as-you're-told teacher face.

Realizing that wrestling with her face was not getting her back to school any quicker, Rosy approached the removal man standing by her wall, who was as oblivious to her presence as he had been her car, chattering away on his phone. Uh-huh, so that's why he hadn't responded to her beeping. Thankfully, Sensible Voice was dominant in her head, calmly but forcefully repeating 'more flies with honey than vinegar', although Cross Voice had also popped up, whispering about people on phones and social deterioration in pure 1950s BBC tones. As she got closer she realized that the previously unidentifiable shape she had spied by her tree was some kind of rolled–up rug, balanced on the upper part of his body.

She came closer still and, as he remained absorbed, stood on tiptoes to tap the man on the back of his rug-free shoulder.

There was no response as he nodded and made 'hmm' noises into his handset. Was her tap too light? She could feel her teeth clench. Maybe she needed to punch him? She could almost hear Marion Marksharp's fingers tapping at breakneck speed on a desk. She should definitely punch him.

She most definitely should not! Although as she uncurled her fist, a glimmer of a smile crossed her face. It was a pleasing thought, but as a headmistress and infant teacher, she wasn't going to damage her hard–won reputation by hitting men in the village. Or anybody, anywhere. Tap, yes, she would just tap him again. But a little bit harder this time. Tiptoes up, fingers out, there, and again. Perfect.

'Excuse me.' Rosy used her firmest tone.

'Yep, yep, just keep him for me until tomorrow... I know... look, I have to go.' The man, with a voice so deep it jolted Rosy's core, spun around to see her standing there and broke into a million-kilowatt smile. Rosy's desperation to get back to her classroom and her fervid hopes of Rufus's mother's approval were suddenly blown to bits, completely forgotten. She smiled back so widely that her ears hurt and she sensed the warmth of a massive blush flush up her cheeks.

'Hello.'

'Hello,' said Rosy, really aware of her face. And not quite sure what she was supposed to say next. Oh my goodness! Then she remembered how cross she was about her car being blocked in, and how, as she had learnt rather forcefully at nineteen, one did not trust men that exuded sex quite as blatantly as this. Damn her fickle soul! However, she still wasn't actually speaking, just standing there. Like a lemon. But clearly not as sharp.

'How can...' Ravishing deep-voiced sex-radiating man, who she couldn't help but notice had rather broad shoulders, paused and rapped his fingers on his forehead and then smiled even wider. 'You're from next door. And I've blocked your driveway. I'm so sorry, just give me a few minutes and I'll move it.'

'Um, I don't have a few minutes.' Rosy surprised herself at the slight snap of her tone, but she was frustrated both at her inability to articulate moments earlier and her shallowness in the face of equally superficial beauty. Particularly as she had thought she had learnt – aced – that lesson. 'I have an appointment at work in ten, no five, minutes flat, please could you move it now? Like right now?'

Great, she had gone from mute to overly aggressive. No, no she hadn't. She'd stood her ground. Her shoulders rose and a confident – sort of – smile returned to her face, the blushing gone.

'Of course, I'll go and get it done now, right now,' he teased. 'It's just there's something magical about this place, isn't there? Calming. It's as if the sea breeze, and the history...' He waved his arm at the cottages and widened its scope to take in the picture that lay before them: the houses almost layered on top of each other, the narrowness of the streets and their downwards tilt towards the sea. '...they seem to slow everything down.'

'Well, yes, they do but...'

'You wouldn't believe how tricky it was getting through the lanes with this thing.' Again he gestured but this time towards the van. 'But with the windows open and the breeze whooshing in you kinda feel as if everything will just be OK. I had to stop at the top of the main road, by the turn off to Penmenna, at the brow of the hill that looks across the bay. I'd seen it before but still the beauty takes your breath away. It's almost like a dragon resting his head between his paws, the shape of the peninsula, I mean. I don't actually see dragons everywhere. I'm not that sort of person, but still it just struck me. I supposed you're used to it, living here.'

Rosy was split in two; she was still in a hurry but never before had she heard anyone vocalize the sleeping dragon theory. It had always been how she described the shape of the promontory in her head. And that place at the brow of the hill – that was one of her absolute favourites, filling her with that safety-of-home feeling as she saw the fields rolling down gently to the coast. Of course, up close, the coastline was far more ragged than tranquil, jagged rocks and secret pathways leading to hidden coves and dangerous riptides. The sleeping dragon, serene from afar but perilous when explored.

'I don't think you ever get used to it. The beauty of the coastline still takes my breath away and I've been here years and years now. And time does seem to move slower down here. Whenever I visit anywhere else my head spins with the speed at which everything rushes past – I've got used to Cornish time, that's for sure.'

'And it's not just the coastline – the whole county is like a different world, certainly different to the rest of the country, don't you think? They say the light in St Ives is magical, but I think that the whole of Cornwall seems to have that magical sense to it, as if nothing can go wrong here; all your ills will be cured. You must think I'm being naive but really I just can't believe I get to live here. And in this village, too. It's so picturesque, postcard perfect, like someone envisioned the most idyllic place they could and *pop*, it appeared. I know I'm meant to be unpacking the van but I keep getting sidetracked. Every time I grab a box something else catches my eye and before I know it I'm just stood here staring at beauty. Oh, I'm sorry. You're in some kind of mad rush and I'm banging on about scenery – I apologize.'

'It is beautiful, and any other time I would be happy to chat but I'm just in such a hurry. I'm sorry.'

'No, all my fault. I'll move the van now, right now, promise. No more interruptions.' And with a broad smile, and added eye sparkle, he wandered off towards the house. In the opposite direction of the lorry.

'Wow! Really?' Rosy muttered and ran her hands through her hair, shaking her head. She may as well just set up a camp bed right here and accept that Mrs Marksharp was going to be waiting all night. Clearly this removal man was a perfect fit for the Cornish pace of life.

'I'm fetching the keys,' said the removal man over his shoulder. His words hung heavy with amusement but were accompanied by a crashing tinkle as the rug he was carrying knocked a terracotta plant pot from her wall.

The dried-out earth and dead stick it had contained lay on the pavement between them, the baked clay spread into chunks and shards. Rosy just stared, eyebrows almost shooting from the top of her head and fighting to keep her hands off her hips, as the removal man knelt on the pavement and slowly swept it into a little pile with his hands, the rug now lying at his side.

She had kept the pot there on the wall for the last couple of years with the full intention of clearing it out and replanting something a little less dead. Probably this weekend. What was this man going to do next? Moving the van quickly didn't seem to be on the agenda.

'I'm sorry. I'll sort it out properly in a moment. This really is not a great start, is it? But don't you worry about it, I'll have it as good as new before you can blink.'

'Don't worry about the pot, please could you just move the van?' Desperation had replaced that fleeting misplaced spark of lust. 'I'm going to go and wait in my car.' Perhaps a final winsome smile would help. 'Please, thank you. Please?'

'Be right with you, promise.' He beamed, moving with a bit more speed towards the cottage.

And Rosy headed back to her car to wait, wondering if she was ever going to make this meeting and really hoping that no one had noticed her stamp her foot.

–

A few minutes later and Rosy was inside her classroom, thankful that Marion's tendency to wander around the school causing trouble meant that her own tardiness had gone unnoticed. Not so lucky was the Class Two teacher, Harmony Rivers, currently being harangued by Mrs Marksharp as she attempted to cross the playground.

Harmony relied upon conflict resolution techniques that nodded to New-Age theory to defuse situations between seven-year-olds, but a smudge of lavender oil and a talk about doing unto others was not going to appease Marion. Rosy, for kindness' sake, was going to need to intervene, but as she stood up Mrs Marksharp turned and headed to the classroom.

Rosy let her breath fill her chest before gently exhaling and letting the air slowly play on her bottom lip as the head of the PTA wandered into her room. It wasn't that she was physically intimidating as such... well, she was a bit: all that perfect blondness and skin that looked as if it were stretched a little too taut. Very thin and as quivery as a racehorse, she was one of those women who was constantly looking over your shoulder for someone slightly more important to talk to – which was fine because it meant that after a minute or so of insincere chit-chat she would be heading off to buttonhole someone else. What was frightening was when you were the number one person she wanted to see; then there was no hope of escape.

That overdone beam was now heading her way, eyes lit with a determined glow as she approached. It took all of Rosy's professionalism to maintain eye contact and not visibly gulp.

'Hello, it's soooo good of you to fit me in, Rosy.' Mrs Marksharp addressed all the staff by their first names. She had confided to Lynne, the teacher Rosy shared her class with and friend, that she thought it created a strong bond. Lynne, in turn, confided in Rosy that as far as bonds went, she'd be more comfortable with masked men, rope and some gaffer tape, but didn't want to give Monster Marksharp ideas.

'Now the thing is, I really need to talk to you about Rufus. You see, he is so gifted and I'm very worried about the absence of challenge.' She drew back the tiny plastic chair and sat herself down, motioning to Rosy to do the same. 'Well, as a mother, you see, who wouldn't be? Why, only the other day he was trying to make olive oil in the conservatory using our olives and a screwdriver. Obviously he didn't mean to smash the glass, but that's the price you pay for having such a bright boy. And then last week he fed the chickens Miracle-Gro – such a lateral thinker!'

Forty-five minutes later – all of which were devoted to how special Marion's three boys were – Rosy managed to escape, but only after promising to sufficiently stretch Rufus, despite her own doubts about his natural genius.

The more surprising aspect of the conversation was Marion confiding that she had heard whispers that the Local Authority had bought a large tract of land on the outskirts of Roscarrock. If this were the case it could have ramifications for the school. Roscarrock was where most of the Penmenna children went for the next step of their education so if it was for a new secondary school that would mean a shiny new school for them once they became eleven, but if it were for a new primary then it could impact negatively on Penmenna's future numbers. Either way, she made a note for Sheila to see if she could find out more.

Sheila was the school secretary and Rosy's PA and was teetering on the brink of retirement – teetering being the key word. Sheila was lovely, the most supportive and compassionate woman Rosy had ever met and surely on a list somewhere for potential sainthood. It was just that if anyone had given Sheila that list, she would have promptly lost it, or scrunched it up, or run it under water and used it to dab a grazed knee. She reminded Rosy of a little dormouse behind her desk – petite, smiley, oh-so-cute and just as effective. Dormice may have no role in the running of an efficient school, but Sheila had been at Penmenna since the year dot, and was as much an institution of the school as the Nativity play, so it was a matter of just riding it out until retirement rolled around. And making sure she wasn't allowed near any of the important stuff. This job should be safe with her, though.

Dropping a note on Sheila's desk, Rosy crossed her fingers and headed back to the office to tackle another new government directive to increase efficiency and standards. Then, four hours after the supposed end of school, she set the alarm, turned the key in the lock and headed home to a large glass of wine and a little bit more caramel shortbread.

–

The windows shook for the full length of the five-minute journey back to the cottage as Rosy sang along with the radio and the smile returned to her face.

'Ricooooochet… da da da da da da… titaaaaniuuuum!' Maybe she had been a tad rude to the removal man? It wasn't his fault she'd had a crappy day and left Rufus's book at home. The last time she had felt such an instant, visceral attraction as she had this afternoon was upon meeting Josh, and that hadn't ended well. Perhaps her snappiness was her subconscious trying to protect her? Regardless of the reason, she should apologize when she got home. Yes, that's what she'd do, make a cup of tea and apologize.

But when she pulled up in the drive, there was no sign of the removal van, either responsibly or irresponsibly parked, although the lights sparkled in the cottage next door for the first time in ages. She wondered if the new neighbours would have children. A couple more on the roll was always a good thing in a rural school.

Tomorrow was Saturday so she could bake them something yummy and go around to introduce herself, and hope her reputation wasn't tarnished forever because of her uncharacteristic snappiness with their removal guy. Perhaps she could ask them to pass on an apology for her? Perhaps she could make another cake for them to pass on with it? Everyone liked chocolate cake, didn't they? Perhaps she should just stop worrying and not be so neurotic? She was self-confident and in control. She had just been assertive – that was good. Plus the man had been quite smiley; he hadn't seem perturbed by her foul temper. And he had broken her plant pot – that was quite remiss of him. Yes, she'd just leave it.

As she parked the car and headed towards her cottage, something on the doorstep caught her eye. What was that? The late January evening was pierced by the glare of her outdoor light, making it impossible to define what was sitting upon the step. She walked up to the shape to find it was another terracotta pot, but this one didn't have a dead stick in it; no stick at all. She picked it up to take it inside and have a better look.

The light showed that it was certainly in better condition than that which had been broken. The pot itself was full of rich-looking compost and had a note attached. Kicking her shoes off, she headed to flick the kettle on as she unfolded it. There, in what she could only term as a creative scrawl, were the words *Sorry about the pot, and the van, here's something for spring.*

What a lovely thought. It certainly went above and beyond all expectations. Damn! Now she doubly wished she had asked his name, and not been so rude. She would have to say something to her neighbours in the morning. There was no way she could let a kindness like this go unremarked.

Rosy hugged a smile to herself. The day hadn't been that bad; she had survived Marksharp, and then to finish it was her lovely doorstep gift. As she curled up, slippers on, remote in one hand, tub of ice cream in another, she popped the TV on and prepared to relax. But all night that smile stayed on her face, and broadened every time she looked up at her promise of spring on the window sill.

## Chapter Two

The next day Rosy was determined to have a long laze under the covers, read a book and drink two cups of tea before getting up properly. Her mind may have been awake far too early (it didn't seem to understand weekends) but there was no way she was going to let her body comply.

One cup of tea and a couple of chapters down and a *thump thump thump* on the door jolted her from her Saturday morning idyll. Popping her head out of the bedroom window, she spotted that it was for her new neighbours instead. It was going to be weird having people next door, because despite years of decoding the bumps and bangs of her previous neighbour, she had been used to complete silence for several months now. And liked it. It meant she could sing as loud (and it was loud) as she wanted, into hairbrushes and wine bottles, without any shame.

Their visitor was very glamorous, draped in a fake fur coat, balancing upon heels higher than any ever seen in the village before, and hair so perfectly styled she must've risen at dawn. As Rosy examined the top of the woman's head she could almost hear the twitter of small birds embedded within the pyramid of blonde hair à la pre-revolutionary French court.

This vision of perfection was tarnished by the dog accompanying her. The woman was gripping the lead fiercely and glaring at the dog as if she didn't trust him one iota. Which, given the look of him, was probably wise. He was the scruffiest dog Rosy had ever seen, a great big tangle of dark grey with a very naughty look on his face. Rosy's profession meant she was well versed in Very Naughty Faces and this one was glowing with mischief. Glowing with mischief as he jumbled around his owner's feet, looking as if he would topple her any minute and quite deliberately so. Rosy's heart melted a little bit.

Having knocked at the door again, the woman was now trying to stop the dog's antics by whipping the end of the lead at him. Rosy tried to stifle a giggle; she knew that the dog was going to love this game.

Perfect Hair glanced up at Rosy's window, after a poorly aimed kick caused the dog to speed up the circles he was gleefully running in, and tutted loudly. Which, combined with the sneer she shot at the same time, was a pretty impressive skill. Rosy had a quick try, but it wasn't as easy as Perfect Hair made it look.

However it seemed neither sneering nor tutting was persuading the dog to obedience. He was now snapping at her ankles, darting in and out as he did so and increasing Perfect Hair's bad temper. She knocked again, but less glamour-puss, more police raid this time, loud enough for the dog to pause in its tumble and look startled.

'Honestly, you didn't need to lock the bloody—' Her voice, loud and a combination of rage and drawling enti-tlement, was cut off mid-sentence as the door opened. Then, with another high level of skill, she managed to deliver two killer looks consecutively, one at the door-opener, who was hidden from view and Rosy was itching to see, and an even more brutal one up at Rosy's window.

Normally remorse over snooping would have made Rosy duck back behind the window. She wasn't a natural curtain-twitcher, but the dog's antics had been so compelling she hadn't realized she was still staring until Perfect Hair's second pointed glance of evil.

The hairs on the back of her neck fizzed and then her arm jerked up, but instead of pulling the curtains shut and bowing her head in shame, her fingers waggled in greeting, a grin – as mischievous as the dog's – on her face in the split second before her second new neighbour stormed into the house. She supposed that was two apologies she owed them now!

More irritatingly, there was no way Rosy was going to be able to get comfy back in bed now. It was almost as if having been seen up she was duty-bound to actually get up. She knew it wasn't pleasant to judge people, especially not at first glance, but she had a feeling that she and the next-door neighbours might not get on. Fancy not being able to be nice to something as cute and fluffy as that dog! She wondered what the husband was going to be like. Was he also going to be a perfectly coiffed city type that kicked small animals?

Enough with the judgements. Power of positive thought (Harmony would be proud) – her new neighbours were bound to be lovely and she should know better. She was going to stop assuming the worst and do some baking. That way she could get a welcome-to-the-neighbourhood-sorry-I-was-peeping cake made, race through her chores and maybe take a quick, reaffirming walk on the beach.

Two hours later there was a lemon drizzle cake cooling on the side, the house had been cleaned, albeit in a fairly slapdash way, top to bottom, her wellies were on and a chocolate cake was in her hands. She was all ready to head next door. Mean preconceptions were forced out of her head, and gratitude for the sweet plant pot by their removal man was at the fore. She gave a little shake, reminding herself not to stare evilly at Perfect Hair, and to make a point of passing on her gratitude for the plant whilst looking as welcoming as possible. Beam, beam, beam.

—

The winter sun was streaming through the breaks in the cloud as she wandered down her path and through the country-cottage gate that took her, in turn, to their gate and path, the clouds of pink flowers cascading down the drystone walls as was typical of the county. Balancing the plate on her hand carefully, she knocked loudly on the door and, biting her lower lip, braced herself to meet the family that would be living next door to her for the foreseeable future.

Her heart sank as the woman from earlier answered the door. Fake smile plastered on Rosy's face, she proffered the cake.

'I thought I'd come and say hello, and welcome to the village. I live—'

'It's not me you want,' snapped Perfect Hair.

*Thank the Lord for that, just keep smiling.*

'Stay here!' the horror barked as she spun on her vertigo-causing heels and headed back into the cottage. She was swiftly replaced by the four-legged ball of wool that came bowling down the hallway and started jumping up at Rosy.

Kneeling down with her plate held high, she made a fuss of the little thing. He really was the cutest dog ever, like a big old ball of tumbleweed. He started jumping up, licking her face and sniffing for cake, presumably desperate for affection if Perfect Hair was what he was used to.

'Scramble, get down. Leave her alone, here, let me take that,' came a familiar male voice suddenly standing over her and removing the plate.

Rosy looked up to see the smiling face of the removal man from yesterday and once again could feel a flush seeping from the roots of her hair down to her toes. Oh, bloody hell!

'And let me help you up.' He reached out his free hand to her. 'Scramble, get back! I'm so sorry, but if it makes you feel any better he's a good judge of character. He just never really got the hang of puppy school.'

'He's OK. I don't mind. Really, I don't. He's just saying hello.' *Please stop blushing, please stop blushing, don't say that out loud.* She noticed he was holding the cake. Oh God, what was it she had wanted to say?

'I thought, since I'm your new neighbour, I'd better come and say hello properly and bring you cake to welcome you officially to the village and so on. Everyone is pretty lovely here really, I'm sure you'll settle in just fine.' Great, now she was prattling. What was happening to her?

'That's really kind of you, especially after I messed you about last night. My name's Matt, by the way, and it's a pleasure to meet you – officially, that is.' He stretched out his hand and twinkled his eyes. Rosy hadn't realized that 'twinkled' was something you could do before now. But she was learning.

Oh yes, hand, um, shake. She remembered what she was actually meant to do, as opposed to just staring at said eyes. She stretched her hand out towards his and as their palms touched a shock tingled all up her arm and through her body. Oh, this was delicious. No! No. Not delicious, ridiculous, that's what this was. *Behave yourself*, she chastised her disobedient body. *For God's sake, woman! You've got to live next door to him.*

*Besides which, look at his girlfriend. He is not going to be interested in someone whose idea of style is anything that can be achieved in less than five minutes.* Actually, thank God for Perfect Hair, otherwise she could have been tempted to break her cardinal rule of dating. And this was exactly the sort of man that her rule had been designed to insure against.

She realized this handshake was going on a bit too long. She dropped his hand and forced herself to look at his face. Eye to eye, like a normal person making contact the first, oh all right, second time. Oh, bloody hell, maybe not the eyes! Now what was it he had said? Of course, that was right…

'Um, Rosy, and it's a pleasure to meet you properly.' She managed to control her urge to drop a curtsy, and congratulated herself for beginning to sound more like a lucid adult. 'And I'm sorry I was a tad grumpy last night but I had had a difficult day.'

'Grumpy? Not at all. We had blocked you in, and then I broke your pot. I reckon I should thank my lucky stars you didn't troop around brandishing a pitchfork.'

Rosy giggled, relatively normally. 'No, I find poisoned chocolate cake is a far more discreet method. It's funny though, I was going to ask my new neighbours to thank you. I should know not to make assumptions and I had assumed you were the removal guy. I'm pleased I was wrong and that you are my new neighbour so I get to thank you in person. Thank you. That was a lovely thing you did. That plant pot is so much nicer than my grotty old one. And it looks like you planted something in it too. I was really touched. In fact, despite my day, your gift meant that, come the end of the evening, I was smiling.'

'Well, I'm a man with lots of plant pots and I do like the thought of making you smile. Be warned, I may besiege you with them.' Twinkle repeated twinkle.

'You're welcome to,' she replied. Was this exquisite man flirting with her? Were her initial instincts right? He clearly wasn't to be trusted. Dear God, did she just think the word 'exquisite'? Hmmm. She needed help! Rosy blushed again, but this time she thought the warmth flooding her body was less feverish than before. With any luck it was a dainty pink rather than the unattractive beet-root glare of earlier. Somehow she managed to maintain eye contact and keep talking.

'Be warned though, I'm rubbish with plants, they seem to wither and die the minute I look at them. I wouldn't want you to waste your efforts.' Her head was exploding with the effort of normal conversation. She seemed to have developed some kind of split personality with half her brain filled with a hallelujah-ing chorus of angels and the other half occupied by her tearful, traumatized nineteen-year-old self shaking her head furiously at her adult self.

'Oh, I don't think they'd be wasted, I'll just have to show you what to do.'

*Yes please*, thought the naughty part of Rosy joyfully, shutting down her own whispers of warning. They stood and looked at each other for a millisecond longer than was normal and she swore her tummy squirmed. Actually squirmed.

A high-pitched shriek from Perfect Hair, a room away, smashed their momentary silence.

'Matt. Matt! Will you please put her down so we can get on with our day!'

'I'm sorry about that, she's intolerably rude!' responded Matt, eyes rolling like a surly fifteen-year-old.

'No, that's fine. I have to get on with my day too. Anyway, it's a pleasure to meet you properly.'

'It was. An absolute pleasure. I'll see you soon.'

Adrenalin still pumping, she offered up a quick prayer of thanks to the girlfriend, feeling that she had been saved from a weakness she had thought no longer existed. She switched right back to neighbourly and gave him a final smile as he showed her out.

–

As Matt shut the door his smile dropped. He turned and headed into the kitchen where his earlier guest was waiting for him.

'For Christ's sake, Ange, do you have to be so rude? I've just moved in – she's my neighbour. Could you try not to upset her, or anyone else in the village, just for the first day or two, perhaps?'

His guest yawned and flicked a pistachio shell across the kitchen counter.

'She's dowdy and a peeping Tom, *and* who gets up and bakes a bloody cake? On a Saturday! That's what Waitrose is for. Silly cow. Silly cow in a stupid primitive county.'

'This county is one of the most beautiful places in the country – beaches, moors, sunshine, peace and quiet. And not so primitive that it's prevented you from jumping in my car at the crack of dawn to drop the dog off before I'm settled in!'

Angelina smiled, stood up and pulled Matt into a massive hug.

'You're welcome. Besides, who the hell else would put up with me? And for that matter who would have helped you with Scramble? Honestly, he's a nightmare. I couldn't keep him any longer. Do you know he chewed one of my Louboutins last night? I'm billing you.'

Matt gave in to the cuddle and grinned at his difficult, pain-in-the-arse baby sister. 'I'm not paying until I actually see the damage. And stop eyeing that cake with evil intent, it's mine and you don't eat cake anyway, you freak. And what do you mean a peeping Tom? I think she's cute. Do you know that last night she actually stamped her foot at me? I don't think she even realized she had done it.'

'Hmmm, I bet she does it all the time. I was standing on the doorstep, waiting and waiting for you to answer, and she was spying on me from her upstairs window. On top of which, people who stamp their feet clearly have emotional issues. Demanding narcissists. You can't spend time with those sorts of people, it'll bring you down.'

Matt's eyes widened and he blinked slowly before speaking. 'Your lack of self-awareness never fails to amaze me. As for spying? I don't think so.'

'My what? Honestly, you talk such rubbish! And what else do you call someone watching someone else? When I saw her, she shot back behind the curtains quicker than a wink and then, get this, had the cheek to come back out again and taunt me. She did.' Angelina's head was nodding fast, emphasizing the truth of her statement.

'She probably heard poor Scramble's cries for help, desperately calling for rescue from your dastardly clutches. You're lucky she didn't come racing out of her house and wallop you with her rolling pin so she could set him free.' Scramble jumped up high onto Matt's lap and curled his lip at Angelina in agreement. Matt loved this dog. Angelina remained oblivious.

'Yeah, I bet she has a rolling pin too, and one of those poncey cake stands, and watches *Bake Off*.'

'Everyone loves *Bake Off*. What is wrong with you? I'm serious. You are not normal, you know.'

'Pfft. You've been saying that for years. But you still love me.'

'True, but I don't really have a choice. Look, stop being such a cat and help me work out how to get that beautiful brown-haired domestic goddess interested in her slightly scruffy neighbour.'

'No, I cannot. You said you weren't interested in dating for a while. And you know I have the perfect friend lined up for you. You're going to love her. Much better for your career and she's got this season's Birkin.'

'Oh please, not again!'

# Chapter Three

Rosy had fled down her neighbour's path and marched as quick as her legs could take her to the coast, pausing only for breath once the familiar kick of salt and seaweed hit her senses. Storming along the coastal path, framed by gorse and bracken, she soon left the wide open sands of Penmenna and reached her favourite cove, smaller and more intense than the beaches that the tourists sought. Enclosed by rocks and far more darkly Cornish, it provided the perfect escape, only used by locals or hikers stopping for a brief rest, and they were few at this time of year. It was as if someone had tipped her upside down and jiggled her about until everything was loose, and this cove was the perfect place to rebalance herself.

Years of careful compartmentalizing had been smashed down in one quick motion simply because she had had such a physical reaction to her new neighbour. An appreciation of a dishy removal guy was fine, but finding that he had moved in next door was just too much. The fact that his oh-so-sexy-eyes-and-mouth combo had been so reminiscent of Josh's was bad enough, but to have him move in next door, well that was just cruel. And the timing – unbelievable!

She sank onto the slate that covered this particular beach, pushing bits to one side and allowing her fingers to dig deep into the sand that nestled below, resting her aching calves and trying to gain a little perspective. Where to start? The neighbour, Matt, was not Josh. This she had to remember; it would be unfair to assume that he shared the horrendous character traits of that man, just because he had the same stomach-twirling effect on her. She wasn't nineteen years old any more and was far from the impressionable, naive girl she had been at university. She was now an experienced, organized and grown-up grown-up who was not going to make the same mistakes as she had as a teen. This would all be fine. Her breathing, however, was not getting any easier; in fact it was becoming more ragged. *Breathe in, hold for three, breathe out. And repeat. And repeat.*

This was silly, she knew it. One bad experience did not shape your life, not unless you allowed it to. And she had worked so hard at making sure it didn't. She had full control of her life, by having – and keeping – one very simple rule. The Rule (and she liked to refer to it as that in her head, the capital letters highlighting its importance) was that she would never date anyone who lived nearby, hence keeping her private and professional lives completely separate. Completely separate. Completely under control. She would never be embarrassed in that way again.

Yes, Matt may have twinkly eyes that screamed knowledge of all things naughty, and hair as curly as that of Scramble's (she had always had a weakness for curly hair), and he had potted her up a plant for spring (which in itself was the most romantic thing someone had ever done for her) but there were several pertinent facts she had to remember.

Firstly, Matt had a girlfriend, a very high-maintenance girlfriend, and a tendency to flirtation even when said girlfriend was in the next room. Men like that were never to be trusted. Secondly, even if Matt turned out to be the perfect man, he had moved in next door – she would not risk upsetting her life just for sparkly eyes and a nice gesture. That sort of chaos was to be very deliberately avoided. She had The Rule for a reason. This was good; this was almost a whole battalion of red flags waving. The dog was cute, though – she could be friends with the dog. Perhaps if she had a puppy, that would help. She could take it to school, and she'd have company in the evenings, something to cuddle up to.

She snuggled deeper into her scarf as the cold stung her ears and her cheeks. The wind curled the waves into arches, ferociously crashing onto the shoreline, and Rosy repeated to herself: *Matt with the beautiful shoulders and let's-take-our-clothes-off eyes is to be avoided. Avoided at all costs. Matt is not Josh, so don't be mean but definitely don't flirt any more. You are kind, you are nice, you do not bat your lashes at another woman's man. You can be welcoming, you just can't fancy him. At all.*

She let the rhythm of the waves, as they peaked and smashed, take over her thoughts and was soon calm enough to open her book and lose herself in its pages for an hour or so. By the time she left she was feeling a lot more grounded than she had upon arrival.

She was walking back along the coast path when her mobile pinged. Service out here was sketchy so she was surprised to get anything. She checked her phone and bit her lip. How had she forgotten that? With the chaos of yesterday and the sheer force of this morning's sexual attraction/panic, all thought of tonight's date had been pushed out of her mind.

She used the term 'date' loosely. It was, without quibble, a date – a meeting of two single adults with the sole purpose of seeing whether there was the chance of a future relationship. But she knew before she got there that the chances were unlikely.

She had been Internet dating for a little while now – it had worked for a couple of her friends, and with her rural location, her rule about not dating locally and her lack of desire to travel twenty miles to hang out in clubs alongside people she had nothing in common with, Internet dating seemed like it may be the only solution to her unrelenting singledom.

She wasn't sure why she had been single for so long. She may not be as attractive as Perfect Hair but she wasn't a complete troll and every now and again she did get the odd glance on the street. She assumed it wasn't because she had a horned back and webbed feet that she was unaware of. However, glances or not, no one ever asked her out.

On the less superficial side, she was well educated, had a job that she loved, was articulate, passionate even, about certain things, didn't mind watching football or rugby and enjoyed cooking. What more did a man want, for God's sake? Some days she was fairly sure that even if she learnt to play the harmonica whilst juggling fire-lit batons and stripping down to some nipple tassels, she still wouldn't attract a mate.

And it wasn't that she was desperate, but she liked men and was ready for that easy companionship and the cama- raderie that some of her married friends had. Regular sex would also be a bonus. A really enjoyable, almost forgotten bonus. She just had to find someone who was as busy as she was and understood that she needed to be sure before she committed herself and introduced him properly to her life.

Admittedly there were bits of a relationship she could easily do without. Lynne's Dave, for example, piled up musical instrument parts in the kitchen and liked medieval dress. Lucy's husband shouted at the news all night and got arsey whenever she suggested they change channel, and she was fairly sure there was something dodgy going on with Tim, Alice's boyfriend – no one needed to walk the dogs for three hours every evening, did they? So keeping someone at arm's length until she was sure was sensible, not at all weird. She just needed to find someone who agreed with her.

She'd started Internet dating a couple of months ago, and had lost count of the amount of failed dates. All right, she could probably remember them all if she tried hard, but some of them she actively wanted to forget – particularly Tony, who had suggested, three minutes in, with tongue hanging out, that they check sexual compatibility before ordering the starters.

And some of them had been so dull she had considered running to the ladies' and escaping out of the window or painting awake-looking eyes on her eyelids so she could have a quick doze without appearing rude.

Despite this, she was sticking with optimism and was going with the 'if you keep trying then all will come right' view rather than the 'a fool is a person who constantly repeats the same mistakes' that was slowly becoming the more dominant voice in her head.

Hence she had a date lined up for tonight, as she had most Saturday nights since she'd decided that this was her solution. Experience was telling her tonight was not going to be a winner, but her innate (or was that inane?) hopefulness was not letting her give up.

Just because Simon, tonight's candidate, wasn't proving too sparky on their online chats didn't mean he wasn't a good man. Teaching had taught her that if you gave someone a chance, looked a little deeper, real treasure could be found. So she applied it to her dates – give them a proper chance and search for the sparkle.

Lynne said that there was such a thing as being too nice, and sometimes people didn't have hidden depths, just hidden dark, and that a level of discernment was required with this whole thing. Rosy agreed to a point. She was discerning enough to refuse to date the seven – yes, seven – different men who had inboxed her pictures of their willies, but otherwise still stuck to her 'everyone deserves a fair chance' thing.

Which was why she had agreed to meet Simon for drinks in Plymouth later tonight. She had registered only for dates with men from Devon, close enough to get to, far away enough to ensure they didn't know anyone locally, had never heard of Penmenna School and were unlikely to turn up for dinner unannounced.

Simon had started chatting to her a couple of weeks ago, and although he hadn't exactly made her laugh out loud, or even snigger, he did at least seem relatively stable and secure. An all-round nice guy and therefore worthy of a chance.

It was just unfortunate that with his considerate gesture and downright titillating physicality, Matt had made her completely forget about Simon this evening. Should she cancel? Was it fair going on a date with someone when all you really wanted to do was strip your next-door neighbour down to nothing and encourage him to keep his promises about teaching new things? Or, at the very least, spend the evening fantasizing about it. No, all that was surely evidence that she needed to go on the date, and give it her all. There would be no fantasizing about her neighbour; she would not become a laughing stock again.

She looked up to see she was already back in the depths of the village. Her musings meant she had walked back on autopilot, completely oblivious to all around her.

Her musings had, however, reinforced her resolve. She would not allow herself to be fazed by her new neighbour. It was obviously a test she had been given and one she was ready to pass. Looking up, she realized she was at the village shop – she'd nip in and buy herself some chocolate. Maybe a small bar after a late lunch would cheer her up a bit and help her get ready for tonight. Maybe that late lunch should be a Creme Egg?

As she headed back towards her cottage, three large (large) bars of Galaxy and some chocolate eggs rammed in her handbag making the climb up the hill a bit more tricky, she caught a glimpse of Perfect Hair giggling as she slapped Matt on the arm whilst they were walking to his car. Glued to the pavement, she watched as he took a swipe back at her hair – brave man – with those beautifully shaped arms and then dart out of the way. It was an intimate gesture and Rosy could feel her eyes narrow before she forced them back to their normal shape as quick as she could. Life wasn't fair sometimes, but she could do this, she could live next door to the most beautifully perfect physical specimen she had ever seen and try not to care. More importantly, she was going to find that sort of intimacy for herself, that closeness; fear was no longer going to hold her back. She grinned a wide easy grin. *Simon, hang on to your hat, tonight is going to blow your mind!*

# Chapter Four

Rosy took a slug of wine as she looked across the table at her date. As much as she wanted to find The One this evening, she had a feeling there was no way Simon was going to be it. Although he was certainly going to be memorable, just not in the way she had wanted.

She smiled as he shuffled the wad of cue cards that he had brought with him. Her 'looking for the treasure' policy was proving harder than she had anticipated. He was a good ten years older and hundred pounds (OK, maybe not, but she was willing to bet it wasn't far off) heavier than his photo had indicated and her depths were clearly more shallow than she had thought.

'So, Rosy, top five films in ascending order?'

'Um… I don't get to the cinema much. I heard the new *Star Wars* was good.'

He curled his lip and arched an eyebrow. 'Right, so you don't know about films then, hmm?'

'Well, it's just that—'

'Yep, never mind, I can overlook that, you are, after all…' He didn't even disguise the look he shot straight at her chest. Her arms immediately crossed themselves in protection, warding him off. If only she could do something about the waves of body odour emanating off him with such potency. Rosy was amazed they weren't visible.

'Right, another chance then. What's your favourite breed of dog? Quick, quick. No thinking about it. You must know. You're quite slow, aren't you? I thought you said you were a teacher!' All this was shot at her at speed, followed by a bout of burping indicative of some kind of chronic digestive disorder.

'Funny you should ask, I met this adorable little one this morning. All tangly and bumbly. So cute. He made me think about getting one of my own.'

'Yes, but what breed?' He spoke very slowly this time, in contrast to the staccato sentences of earlier.

She could do this, she could be nice, sit here with him for an hour before making her excuses and leaving. Preserving his dignity and keeping her good karma intact.

'Well, I didn't ask, I'm not sure but he—'

'So, you don't know about dogs either.'

Maybe half an hour instead. With only an inch of wine left in her glass, she couldn't even blot out the reality of the date with any more alcohol if she wanted to drive home – and she certainly wouldn't be staying. She excused herself to the loo and wondered how long before he sent a waitress in looking for her. Thank God she had agreed to drinks and not a meal. Maybe half an hour was generous; maybe she'd be kinder by making it clear he didn't stand a chance. Decision made, she strolled out to the bucket chairs they were in, sat down and took her last gulp of wine whilst formulating her excuses.

Suddenly everything moved really fast and a heavy human-shaped form had landed on her lap and oh-my-God! Something wet, slug-like, was on her cheek. Was he licking her? Someone screamed and then a fluster, a flurry of arms and legs were all around her. She felt an elbow – she assumed it was an elbow – whack her in the face and she could feel numbness swell in her tongue as the jolt had caused her to bite down. At least the screaming had stopped.

She could breathe again. The tumult calmed and she could feel air around her again. In and out. In and out. This breathing thing was becoming a pattern! Someone kneeling pressed a glass of water into her hand, and as she turned to thank them she could see the two bouncers hurling her date out.

'Did he… did he… lick me?'

'Um… it did look like he might have.' The young girl by her side scrunched up her face. 'He was kinda going full toad. I've never seen that happen before. Let me grab you some wet wipes.'

No amount of wiping was going to make Rosy's cheek feel saliva-free again, but she was still going to scrub until it was a good red colour. And then a bit more. Rosy and the girl watched as Simon loped off down the road in the opposite direction to Rosy's car, seemingly oblivious to the trauma he had caused. She waited another five minutes, still scrubbing, until deeming it safe, before heading back to her car and home.

But instead of happy thoughts of her sofa and a large tub of praline ice cream, a picture of Perfect Hair canoodling with her neighbour popped into her head. That was a sight she could live without seeing tonight, although she should probably brace herself for millions of sick-inducing glimpses of the pair of them in the future. Probably just at times like these where she was feeling as if she would never have any luck romantically.

Sitting in the car, she took her phone out and sent a text to Lynne, who, fully aware of Rosy's crazy date-every-Saturday-night habit immediately rang back and demanded she stop in on her way home for a debrief. Perfect.

Plus, Lynne would bang on about the perils of online dating, which would mean Rosy, who knew this particular script off by heart, could enjoy her friend's company whilst not listening at the same time.

It wasn't that she was a disloyal friend or didn't respect the wisdom Lynne divulged. It was just knowing what she was going to say meant she knew she fundamentally disagreed with her. Could not be more clear on how much she disagreed with her.

Lynne was of the view that Rosy was a beautiful woman who would meet her Mr Right when she was meant to. Rosy was of the view that one went out looking for opportunities rather than just sitting back and waiting for them to turn up.

Lynne believed that only sociopaths and lunatics signed up for online dating sites. Rosy thought that this may or may not be testament to the fact that she herself was using them. Well, one of them. She accepted this may have once been the case but now it was the normal place busy young professionals went to find love rather than a hunting ground for Norman Bates types. Plus, surely she had met every sociopath or social inept Devon had to offer now? She had to hit the jackpot soon!

And that was another thing Lynne was very vocal about – she did not understand Rosy's policy on dating outside Cornwall. Rosy knew she was at fault for not explaining the full reasons for it, but was aware that a throwaway explanatory comment about a rough experience whilst at university was not just trite but insufficient and would eventually lead to the full story being coerced from her. This in turn would result in an open-mouthed reaction, inevitably followed by hand-stroking and banal nonsense about how it couldn't be that bad, the past was the past, blah, blah, blah – none of which she could stand, and all of which made her want to scream. However, trying to explain that she was just a very private person never seemed to work, and certainly not with Lynne.

Lynne would suggest that a very private person would not go out for dinner or drinks with a stranger every Saturday, and that by doing so she was selling herself short. Rosy didn't quite understand this point of view. Dross and gold, frogs and princes – surely everyone knew how these things worked? And she had to start somewhere.

Then her friend would tentatively pitch the 'nice young farmer down Wherry's Lane' or (God help her) Miles's father or maybe Ellie's dad. Blurring of professional boundaries was not an argument Lynne seemed to understand. But regardless of whatever her friend had to say about this date, it was still going to be nice not to have to go home early, lonely and deflated.

Maybe she should do as her friend suggested, not stop the Saturday night date thing forever, just take a break for a bit? There was only so much weekly disappointment a girl could take. Surely having her face licked by a stranger, and in public, was reason enough to pause?

However, as Lynne answered the door to Rosy, all wrapped up in her dressing gown, with something a bit too fluffy for Rosy's taste on her feet, she didn't look at all prepared to launch into her usual anti-dating rant.

Instead, she grabbed Rosy by the arm and dragged her into the living room.

'Are you all right, Lynne?'

'Yes, yes, sit down. Oh, it's so exciting!' Lynne was pulling her onto the sofa and scrabbling with her finger-tips, like a cat, on Rosy's knee.

'For God's sake, woman! I haven't seen you this hyped up since you saw your fruit bowl in Kirsty Allsop's kitchen.'

'Oh my. Rosy, this is even more exciting!' Lynne pointed to an array of celebrity news magazines spread all over her coffee table. She was completely freaky over such things. She could tell you the details of every single family member of anyone who had ever appeared on *Made in Chelsea*. She could list the nail colours of each woman on *TOWIE* in chronological order, going back a full three months. She could probably tell you the inside leg measurement of the Duchess of Cambridge, if pushed.

Rosy loved her friend, her loyalty, her forthright-ness, her patience, but just didn't understand the celebrity obsession thing. Yes, she too could leaf through a maga-zine and enjoy grimacing at an overdecorated house or a dress that was cut out a bit too much but Lynne, well, Lynne was obsessed. And for the life of her she wasn't sure why.

'Go on, guess. Guess what has happened today?'

'Um, you bumped into Colin Firth in Asda?'

Lynne giggled good-humouredly. 'No, although that would have been amazing! It could happen one day.'

'Probably not!'

'Don't be so negative. That's not like you. Of course it could. It happens all the time. Especially with all the filming down here. Debbie Anderson's mum bumped into the guy from *Poldark* in the pub the other night.'

'Poor bloke.'

'Yeah, I know, he might not come back. But anyway, this is like that. But better.'

'Better than the bloke in *Poldark*?'

'Well, OK, maybe not. But I am a happily married woman so there's not much I could do if I bumped into him anyway,' Lynne said, nodding over at Dave, who was gently snoring in the armchair.

'Dream, Lynne. You could dream. That's what the rest of us do.'

'Oh, I do.' Her friend smirked. 'Anyhow, you've lost focus. Guess what happened today?'

'How on earth can I do that? It's a mile open. The answer could be anything. Did you sell Dave's kidney? You found out Marion Marksharp is an international arms dealer? I don't know. Give me a clue.'

'Oh, I can't, I'd give it away.'

'Well, can I get up and put the kettle on whilst I pretend to guess?'

'No, no. Oh well, yes of course, but I'm going to tell you.' Lynne took a deep breath and clasped Rosy's arm for support. 'I saw Angelina in the village! That's right! Angelina! In this village!'

'Angelina Jolie in Penmenna? Are you sure?'

'Angelina Jolie… No, don't be daft! Just Angelina. You know, Angelina!'

'Lynne, you can say it five times or twenty but no amount of repetition or inane grinning is going to make this clearer to me. If you don't mean the only Angelina I have ever heard of – oh no that's not true, there's the ballerina, of course – then I don't know who you are talking about. Unless you're trying to tell me there's a human-size fictional dancing mouse wandering around the village.'

'Oh my God, you're so useless.'

'Thanks.'

'Well, you are, about the important stuff, I mean.'

'The important stuff? I don't even know where to start with that.'

Lynne bent over and rifled through the ridiculously large pile of magazines on the table.

'Look, here, and here. There she is. She's a model, and got chucked out of *Celebrity Big Brother* this year for being a bitch. But she's had counselling and it's completely changed her and she's the nicest person you could hope to meet now. Everybody says so. And she was in the village today! She was walking past the butcher's, and Pat had the ferret tied up outside again, she didn't even flinch. She's so cool!'

Rosy rolled her eyes, briefly considered if the reverential tone in Lynne's voice was enough to warrant an intervention, and took the magazine off her friend to glance at the figure that was causing so much excitement.

Wouldn't you bloody believe it! There was Perfect Hair smiling at the camera, flicking her oh-so-captivating mane and clinging on to some kind of celebrity beefcake. Great, so not only was she physically perfect, she was super rich, known by millions up and down the country and apparently good with ferrets. Who wouldn't want her as their neighbour?

# Chapter Five

'Look, your bag is there, but I've got to get off now before the train leaves. I love you lots. Try and remember to be human—'.

'Oh, do fuck off!'

'I'm going, but seriously, I'm not around the corner any more. Remember that last anger management woman, she was helpful, what did she say? Try and wait patiently in queues, smile if people ask you for your autograph— Ow!' Matt quickly sidestepped Angelina's swipe at his legs and grinned. 'And try and keep person-to-person violence as low as possible. Nil, ideally!' Laughing now, he started to back away down the train corridor as she swatted at him as if he were a particularly persistent mosquito.

'I don't think you understand how difficult my life is,' his sister shouted after him. He could hear the smirk in her voice.

'Oh, I do! Love you!'

'The world is full of idiots!'

Matt speed-walked away, as years of experience had taught him to. He couldn't help but notice the peaceful nature of the station as he headed for the exit. Posters advertising surfing on the north coast and tours of moors dotted the walls, with a card for Jonny's Mackerel Trips and a mobile phone number. A seagull flew under the cast-iron bridge that straddled the tracks and was followed by three more, cawing messages back and forth, planning their next picnic. If he were in London he would have been menaced by a one-legged, one-eyed psychotic-looking pigeon by now, and the posters would be reminders about unattended luggage and Tube strikes.

He left the platform and headed out of the tiny station, just in time to hear Angelina's squawk outdo even the gulls.

'Seriously, are there no conductors on this bloody train?' Her voice was one that could carry.

He adored his younger sister. She had always been the spoilt baby of the family and that had contributed to the person that she had become. Matt and Angelina had lost their parents when they were still very young. Their mother had been widowed soon after Angelina's birth and then, plagued with grief-induced depression, had eventually taken her own life when Matt had been eighteen. A difficult age at the best of times but to lose his mother in such a fashion had been more than devastating. He was just old enough to take responsibility for his sister but not really old enough to understand the enormity of his choice. It had been a steep learning curve.

He knew that he had a tendency to worry that Angelina may take the same path, and found that throughout her childhood, and still as an adult, he was constantly checking for any signs that she was struggling with mental health issues and was unable to ask him for help. This perpetual fear was his mother's legacy and as yet there was no shred of evidence that Angelina was anything other than over-indulged with a love for the dramatic, but still that worry was there, niggling and ever-present.

Immediately after their bereavement he had retreated into a world of his own creation, finding solace in the allotment his mother had taken on and dragging Angelina there in all kinds of weather. He would lose himself in soil and seedlings, digging and weeding, and Angelina, who had no interest in any of it, would be overindulged by a whole posse of gardeners who showered her with colouring books, cupcakes and adoration. If she hadn't known how to play to an audience before, she very soon did.

Somehow they had managed to grow into well-rounded adults.

Matt smiled again as he pondered this. 'Well-rounded' may be a bit of a stretch for Angelina, but she was a devil of his own making and she did have her good side. As the baby of the family, a cute freckled curly-haired eight-year-old, and all he had left, she had been spoilt rotten by both him and the allotment crew, his grief channelled into making life as easy as possible for her. With the inheritance his mother had left them, Matt had not just been able to feed them and maintain the family home, but he had been able to make sure his baby sister had wanted for nothing. He had overindulged her, laughed at her extremes and failed to chastise her even when she would throw stones at his head. Which she did with frequency.

He had, in fact, created a monster, but a much-loved one. A monster that had gone on to astonishing success as a person famous for being famous and not much else. Terribly short skirts, complicated hair and no apparent cut-off point seemed all that was necessary. And she was pulling in more money than anyone could have dreamt of.

As he approached his car he watched as Scramble, with paws on the driver's-side window, leapt onto the passenger side where he pretended to be snoring. Scramble then did his whole oh-I'll-just-have-a-stretch-after-my-doze routine before yapping a hello as Matt unlocked the door.

'Hmm, despite all your protests I think you and my sister have far too much in common!' As he scuffled the dog's messy head, Matt glimpsed his boots on the floor of the car and decided to head straight to work. Every time he had been to Penmenna Hall it had been full of people. For him to get a solid idea of where he wanted to take things, how he wanted to shape them, he preferred silence, and from there things would begin to make sense.

Working in the allotment after his bereavement hadn't just provided focus for his grief but had gone on to shape his whole adult life. His younger self wouldn't have considered becoming a gardener but that was exactly what he had done, very successfully.

In his early twenties he had won a place as apprentice to the famous French plantsman, Jean-Jacques La Binette, and under his tutelage had been involved in designing gardens across the world: New York, Hong Kong, London. However, leaving Angelina under the care of family friends for extended periods as he worked abroad hadn't felt right so with Jean-Jacques' support and the last of the inheritance he had started his own consultancy – one in which he not only designed but implemented his ideas. Over the years he had, according to magazines, gained a reputation for 'bold new design combined with encyclopaedic knowledge and endless charm'. He wasn't sure about the end bit but the rest he quite liked. The solitary nature of his work appealed deeply but as his reputation grew, a host of wealthy clients scrabbled for his creative stamp on their gardens and he spent less and less time by himself.

Indeed, his clients had developed a tendency to follow him around offering refreshments and, well, all sorts. They seemed to be particularly present, some armed with camera phones, when he was digging. The nature of the work meant he'd have to be all gung-ho and shirtless, and whilst it had amused him when he was in his twenties, as he got older he began to feel resentful and a little bit grubby.

However, his reputation – thanks to both these predatory older women (who all seemed to have remarkably good contacts) and Jean-Jacques – was what had secured him the chance to escape. The husband of one of his biggest clients ran a well-known production company and Matt had been asked to host a TV show, to be aired more or less as it was filmed, based on a Cornish estate that had been recently rediscovered. He wasn't entirely sure whether it was because of his own professional expertise, his relationship to the now famous Angelina, a ploy to get him away from the TV executive's slightly rapacious wife or perhaps an amalgamation of them all – but with an itch to do something new it had come at exactly the right time. Hence his move to this part of the world and this new project. He was expected to develop plans for the gardens that would grow over time to become a spectacle and ensure it was filled with plants that would look equally stunning in the short term whilst the others developed. A Herculean task – but one he was going to love.

He enjoyed projects that seemed insurmountable; his work had made up for all sorts of gaps in his life. Deliberately made gaps in his life. Growing up looking after his sister had left him with a healthy respect and love for women. A healthy respect and love that he didn't mind sharing with lots of women. But a lifetime of Angelina's knickers left in the hallway, make-up all over (all over!) the bathroom and the fact that his sister synchronized menstruation with a full moon had put him off commitment. Angelina was enough. He wasn't writing off marriage and children and all that went with it – he was just going to wait till forty. That way Angelina would be settled by then (surely) and he would have had long enough by himself to accept those female touches all over his house once more. It would be just his luck to have seven daughters and not a son in sight. As lovely as he would find it at the time, he wasn't ready for that risk just yet.

But even with his non-commitment policy, which he determinedly made clear at the start of any dalliance, there always seemed to be fallout. Moving to Cornwall was a break from it all; he would not be getting involved with anyone. No one. Not a soul. Keira Knightley could turn up in her wellies and a negligee and he'd still say a firm no. This year he would be concentrating on work, having some time to himself and not dealing with the messiness that women seemed to bring to life. Besides, he had read somewhere that celibacy was good for creativity, and creativity was mandatory when starting a new project.

Yes, celibacy was the way forward for him for the next little while, and he was going to embrace it.

He pulled up outside Penmenna Hall and took a moment to appreciate the rosy fingers of sunlight dappling the granite of the old house, warming it far more than it should on such a cold February afternoon. He was going to concentrate on developing the old vegetable gardens first, plant them up with heritage vegetables and try and recreate the exact look and feel they would have had when the garden and the house were at their peak.

The programme would need several segments every week to make it into a whole episode, so he thought the vegetable plot could combine historical facts alongside masses of practical help around growing your own produce, and he could aim it at all levels of gardener, from those who had never so much as planted a carrot to those who wanted to experiment with the more difficult types of heirloom vegetables. He could feel those elusive creative juices flowing. Perhaps he should develop a formal rose garden too, something that married complexity with a simple beauty – roses would be just the thing! Actually, that wasn't a bad idea, that should definitely be a segment. And he could explore the seasonal changes too, plants that did best in May, June and so on. This was going to shape up well.

He headed around the house towards the huge old orangery, chock full of seed drawers, old tools and memories of the past. He had made this his base, all sun-glinting glass sitting to the side of the recently renovated Penmenna Hall, and its beauty in the afternoon light still forced the breath from his body.

*Bam!* A foot-stamping brunette jumped into his thoughts, knocking out all his calm just as she had at his front door but a few hours ago. Was that where all this so-called creativity had sprung from? A *rose* garden! His brain was playing with him, determined to pull him from his celibate dedication and convince him into developing a crush on his slightly spiky but very cute neighbour.

He was fairly sure that at thirty-four he was too old for crushes as such. Conquests, maybe, but crushes, no. No way. And as he had just firmly agreed with himself, even simple conquests were a no-no right now anyway. But if his next-door neighbour was going to be popping into his head, potentially influencing his work, then maybe this was going to have to be dealt with, and soon.

Angelina had spotted the signs before he had and had tried hard to dissuade him from any romantic imaginings he may have. She was remarkably single-minded in her belief that she should be the most important female in his life. But even her warnings about Rosy peeking out from the curtains earlier that morning and watching her had made him smile. Quite a lot – certainly far more than it should do.

The fact that she had snapped at him on their first meeting hadn't put him off in the slightest. Used to rich bored housewives slavering over him, awash with the scent of desperation and sexual promise, or Angelina's even more vacuous friends who managed to embody both ennui and entitlement at professional levels, meant that anyone who didn't dribble or pout over him but challenged him instead was the very sort of person he found interesting. He found the I–respect–myself–and–you–can–too–or–sod–off kind of attitude very attractive.

The fact that she wasn't afraid to vocalize her opinions and tempered it with sweetness was so endearing. The baking for her new neighbours was adorable. A kind of country thinking that he could see himself liking. The way she had flushed ever so slightly upon seeing him, in a demure, slightly old-fashioned way, rather than panting at him and encouraging him to remove his clothes, was also captivating. As was her admission that she knew bugger all about gardening, and was pretty rubbish at it when she tried. Honesty rather than bravado was refreshing in his world. Oh, dear God, he needed to get to work!

A whole afternoon of planning, plotting, digging and organizing didn't seem to wear him out, or help reinforce the celibacy equals creativity principle that had been at the forefront of his mind (or so he had thought) this morning. A long shower and a self-administered lecture once he had returned home to his little Cornish cottage didn't lessen his desire to get to know her a little better either. In fact, if anything, knowing she was but a wall away intensified her occupancy in his head.

Scramble, unrepentantly spread out upon the sofa, fixed him with a mournful gaze as Matt put his shoes on again, but without picking up the lead.

'Look, I'm just trying to be neighbourly. You'll be OK here, I won't be long.' He could swear the dog cocked his eyebrow.

'Hmm, I just need a good excuse now...' He cast around the house – what reason could he give for knocking so soon, and on a Saturday night?

Within minutes Matt was wandering up Rosy's path, cake plate in hand and a goofy grin all over his face.

# Chapter Six

Rosy opened one eye just the merest crack. The inside of her head had never felt quite so empty or so tender. Even moving a squillimetre on her pillow seemed to make her brain hurtle from one side to the other and hurt as it bounced.

Ow ow ow.

She decided that the best thing to do was just lie there, really, really still until it all passed. It was Sunday so it didn't matter if it were hours rather than minutes. If she just lay here until she got really bored then the boredom would indicate that she was well enough to move. Problem solved.

She had read somewhere that NASA paid people to stay in bed for seventy days. Maybe if this morning went well she could join them in the summer holidays, top up her finances and see a bit of America. From a window, admittedly, but that was still more than she had seen up to this point.

Hmm, you could do all sorts in bed for seventy days. Keeping her head very still, and thanking God she had duck-feather pillows supporting her in cushioned heaven, she thought of all the books she would read and the ice cream she could eat during that time.

She could take up sewing or needlepoint – after seventy days she could probably have a wall hanging like those littered over Tudor castles and Renaissance palaces. People could come from miles and miles to see her work progressing and bid against each other furiously for each artisanal tapestry. Mind you, she'd have to be careful not to get the ice cream on them.

She was liking this idea the more it developed. What else could she do in bed all day? *Whoosh!* From nowhere and straight into her diminished and sore brain was an image of her new neighbour. Stop it! Imaginary Matt's smile widened. To make things worse the camera eye of her brain started to pan down. No, no, no! She sat bolt upright and shook her head violently to try and disperse the image. That way madness lay!

Ow ow ow ow ow ow ow ow. His image was replaced by a bright white flashing and a spinning bedroom.

For goodness' sake, she and Lynne had only drunk a couple of bottles last night. Bottles, ah! Rosy wasn't a big drinker, partly because she had form for the world's worst hangovers, but mainly because of her active decision after uni to always be aware and alert. Hence The Rule. And she did love The Rule.

But yesterday the combination of Perfect Hair and Matt, and her own godawful hell-date, meant alcohol had seemed like the best way forward. And Lynne was only too happy to help, so much so that they had sung ABBA's whole back catalogue until the early hours when Lynne's husband Dave decided to walk Rosy home.

Lying here hungover and trying to keep images of Matt, naked Matt, out of her head was not how she wanted to spend her day.

She was going to have to take more proactive action. Action that made a difference. Action like Emma Peel would take. Emma Peel was Rosy's role model – a fearless, arse-kicking superspy that always had the answer, and did it all in heels (although Rosy would be quite happy to successfully arse-kick in plimsolls). Emma Peel would not have muddled the words to 'Dancing Queen' quite so tunelessly and then lain here the next morning just whimpering. No, what would she have done?

It would definitely involve a catsuit, but seeing that Rosy didn't have one maybe some paracetamol would be a good start.

She rolled off her bed and onto all fours and padded to the bathroom – this seemed like the best way to do it this morning and had the plus of being dead *Avengers*-like. Once there, she winched herself up onto the sink and scrabbled in the cabinet to find painkillers. Standing properly now, she managed to knock back not just the paracetamol but threw some ibuprofen in at the same time. It was a medical emergency after all. Maybe whilst she was here she should brush her teeth, see if it was possible to do it without moving her head. Look, see, as soon as the pain diminished, today was going to be OK.

Just as she was finishing, there was a loud knock at the door. A very loud knock. Oh, Jesus, the last thing she needed now were visitors. Very, very slowly, muttering just a little bit, she headed down the stairs, pyjama-clad, to answer it.

–

Matt knocked again; he was sure she was in this time. Why was she taking so long? They weren't exactly big houses.

Beautiful but not big. And there had definitely been noises a minute ago, signifying she was awake.

Suddenly he wondered if that was kind of creepy. Had he turned into one of those guys that obsessed about their neighbours, listening to every sound and mapping every movement? Was his next step on the inevitable path to serial killerdom preparing a basement? Perhaps he should step away from the door right now so things didn't escalate.

He'd give her one more minute and then head home. After all, it was quite clear what she – beautiful, sparky, single – would have been doing out last night when he had knocked and why she was now taking her time answering the door on a Sunday morning. Why was he blundering in here? This was madness and he was an idiot.

Mind made up, he turned to go before he embarrassed himself – just as the latch scraped and the door opened. Great! Now for his idiocy to be shown publicly. He turned and smiled, bracing himself for feeling foolish. Yet the sight of her made him glad he had come over. This was ridiculous.

'Oh, hello.' She slowly opened the door, and gave him a weak-looking grin and a 'How are you? How can I help?'

Neither were an invitation in, he noted, but this was no surprise when he had just worked out what he had worked out. But still she looked so adorable in that little shorts set, all wrapped up in a dinky little printed package with hair that was very definitely tousled. It may not be today but maybe, one day, he'd be able to wake up to that exact smile, with that exact hair and that exact pyjama set.

But he was getting a bit ahead of himself. How did he even have time to think all of this? He needed to answer, stop staring and answer quickly. Preferably in a way that didn't make him look like a pervert or the serial killer he was panicking about being just a few minutes ago.

'Hi, I hope it's not too early but I thought I heard you up and um… thought I should return your plate.' He proffered said article and watched as she scrunched her eyes up tight and then moved her hand out very slowly and deliberately to take it.

'Um, thank you, I hope you liked it.'

'Oh God yes, it was delicious. I just thought you had better have it back.' Christ! He was a stammering idiot, she was definitely going to think the worst of him. Where was cool confident charming Matt? The Matt that women swooned at – he knew it happened. He needed him back right now.

'OK, good, right then.' She smiled again and started to close the door.

'Oh, just a minute.' Matt stopped her. 'I was just wondering, um, if you were free later. Maybe? What do you think?'

Momentarily he saw her eyes blink, almost suspicious. Was this an odd thing to do? Weren't people super friendly with their neighbours in rural villages? Then her eyes went back to the full Rosy beam he had experienced yesterday morning, and the smile returned to her face.

'Oh OK, well, um… er, yes. I'm just doing regular Sunday stuff. I'd invite you in but… um … well… I can't at the moment.'

'Oh, that's OK, I wasn't expecting to come in…' *Persevere, man!* 'I was just wondering if you were free because, um… I could really do with some help.'

That should work, and it was true, he did. Did that make him manipulative? Possibly. Or maybe just his inner alpha male was returning, returning to rescue the situation and move things on. Yes, he'd stick with that.

'Ah, um, yes, I can be, this afternoon. What do you need?' Rosy answered, just the hint of pink in her cheeks. Which was a change from the green that had been sweeping across her face seconds earlier.

'Well, I was going to impose on your good nature, maybe ask if you could show me around. I'm completely new and I could do with a guide. Even the lanes around here are a nonsensical warren if you're not local. It was just an idea. It's all so beautiful, and it seems daft that I don't really know where anything is. I mean, I've found the main street obviously, but, well, a little bit of local knowledge could really help me out.' He shrugged his shoulders and smiled in what he hoped was a winning way. 'Maybe we could eat too? You could show me the best local Sunday lunch, if you like, my treat obviously,' Matt continued. She was smiling so he may as well cement the deal if he was in with a chance.

Suddenly Rosy started to wobble. A very strange expression passed across her face and the pink flush had gone, replaced again by the green. Had he gone too far, turning it from neighbourly favour to lunch date? *Don't backtrack, man. Stand firm.*

'Um, Rosy, are you OK?'

'Yes, fine,' she replied in a woozy not-fine-at-all way. 'Umm, come knock for me at about one-ish, look, now is difficult, I can't um… really talk. But just before one should be fine, come back then.'

And then with no further explanation she shut the door in his face.

## Chapter Seven

A couple of hours later and Rosy was feeling much better. She could hold herself upright without needing a friendly wall as support, she no longer felt as if she'd been at sea for a week and her head had diminished its pounding to a gentle knocking that she was choosing to ignore.

Now it was just a matter of wading through the piles of clothes that seemed to have fallen all over her floor in the last twenty minutes and popping some make-up on. Just a smidge; she didn't want to look as if she were trying. This wasn't a date, it was a neighbourly gesture.

Was she going to have to spend the whole time reminding herself he was taken? Or that becoming friendly with a man who lived next door and made her tummy lurch, her fingertips tingle, was against The Rule? No. Because she was a woman of staunch self-will and strong morals. And to prove it she'd limit herself to a pout of sweet honey lip gloss and a wave of mascara and then get her arse downstairs before he knocked.

A light tap on the door scuppered her plan. The man was certainly punctual. She glided down the stairs in film star mode. She did like film star mode. So much more glamorous than her teacher setting. She would make sure she asked about Perfect Hair fairly early on so she could draw a clear boundary line and then they could get on with being amiable and chummy. She could be a good neighbour and everyone would know where they stood. Perfect.

'Hello, come on in.' She smiled in her most platonic manner.

'OK, thanks, sorry for disturbing you earlier.'

'Oh, that's fine, don't worry about it.' They continued to stand in the hallway smiling politely at each other. Little shy half-smiles. Feeling awkward, Rosy lavished lots of attention on Scramble, who was jumping up at her and yapping – he really was adorable – but as she felt Matt's eyes on her she struggled to know what to do with her face. Oh, to have been born elegant!

'Right, come on then. Show me the best roast in the county.' Matt indicated the front door and broke their silence.

'OK, but if I'm taking you out with me you're going to have to practise your Cornish on the way.'

'I think I be quite good at that,' Matt retorted in a broad Somerset accent as he marched alongside her down the path, Scramble tumbling between the two of them.

'I think your dog could do better! That was insulting. If you speak like that, you'll be punched before your pint is poured. We're going to have to start with the basics. Ready? Now, you can refer to men as "me 'ansum" – go on.'

'Do I have to? What if they're not?'

'You say it anyway, so shh and do as you're told.'

'Will you tell me off again if I refuse?' A quick glance at her face made Matt stand up straighter and do as he was told. 'Good day, me 'ansum.'

'No, not like that. "Areet, me 'ansum, how's it to?"'

60

'Howsit what? How does that make sense?'

'Just do it.'

'Woah, schoolmarm voice on much! I like it.'

'I am actually a teacher, you know, a headteacher, so you're getting the real thing. Are you telling me you *want* to hear my strictest schoolmarm voice?' Rosy stopped still at the bottom of the hill that led to their cottages.

'I bet you're an amazing teacher. As to the voice, now I don't know. Half of me is a yes please and the other half is terrified.' Matt arched his brow. He stopped alongside her and gazed out across the fields, pointing towards the sea. 'There's something special about living this close to the sea, you just breathe in the air and feel cleaner somehow. And look...' He turned a full circle slowly, indicating all around him. 'The sea comes lapping in over there, but right here, at this point, all the fields on all sides are rolling down towards us too, like waves of land. All hitting this central point, right here. I don't know if I feel safe, all ensconced in this valley, or whether I should feel scared, at the central point where all the elements meet. Either way it's awesome, isn't it, like in the proper sense of the word.'

Rosy took in the scene as he described it. He was right; just at this point on the corner before they turned into the village was a central meeting point for the landscape surrounding them. She was so used to the beauty all around her she missed the obvious things.

'I'd go with scared if I were you. Doesn't do to get complacent.'

'Are you suggesting that this village isn't the safe haven I expect?'

'Oh, absolutely. Have you lived in a village before? All calm and civil on the surface with a maelstrom of whirling danger and intrigue just a scratch or two under the surface. Trust me, I wouldn't guide you wrong.'

'Hmmm.' Matt attempted a quizzical expression so daft that Rosy couldn't help the giggle that erupted from her lips. 'I don't think I can believe you. I know just around this corner is the most picturesque scene imaginable – you are not going to convince me that there's a hive of wife-swapping and cannibalism going on behind these postcard perfect doors.'

'Well, maybe not cannibalism. Come on, you are far from practised in this accent yet. I don't want you to embarrass yourself once we get to the pub.' Rosy rounded the corner and Matt darted to keep up with her, Scramble just outpacing him.

'Hang on, are we only going to the village pub? Is it not a bit of a coincidence that it happens to be the best in Cornwall? Where are the rooftop terraces, the sea views? If we're staying in the village shouldn't we go to the restaurant on the beach? What's your game, Miss… um… I don't know your surname. Miss Rosy?'

'The restaurant shuts down in January and the first couple of weeks of February so you'd be waiting a while for food. Besides which, I thought you wanted in on the local secrets.'

'Apart from the cannibalism.'

'Yes, apart from the cannibalism. Now stop talking and concentrate. Yes, we're going to the village pub. It's your induction and trust me, it will be an education. Now, to address a woman you can use "maid". Go on.'

'How's it to, me maid.'

'Hmm, better.'

'Does "maid" not imply an age thing? Will I not get arrested?'

'Yes, you will if you keep interrupting. Now, if you want to know where something is, you say "where's it to?" And if you want to know what's happening, it's "wosson?" Got it?'

'No, it's a whole bloody new language.'

'I thought you wanted to be local? Try harder.'

'Yes, miss.' He winked.

'And don't be insolent or you won't get any lunch.'

'Ooh, I think I am enjoying this.' They passed the butcher's and the village shop, the higgledy-piggledy houses in their array of colours watching them from the hillside as they approached the pub.

'You're incorrigible. We're here now.' Rosy leant forward and placed her hand on the big blue door to the pub. Matt quickly glanced at the outside of the building.

'Umm, are you sure?' He looked like he thought he was going to get food poisoning merely by stepping inside. She tutted, loudly. She was enjoying this schoolmistress thing. It almost gave her leave to be as abrasive and rude as she liked; it was a bit of a novelty, and he really didn't seem to mind.

She tried looking at the pub with fresh eyes. Admittedly it was a bit rough-looking. It wasn't just that the paint was faded and flaking, that the hanging baskets were well and truly hung (in a gallows kind of way, not in a flamboyant rioting colour kind of way) and one of the window sills was so rotten it was actually hanging off, attached by no more than a whisper and a splinter. It made her smile; she loved this place. Then she saw him catch a glance of the path by the side of the door and into the pub garden. Scramble followed his gaze and began to bark frantically.

'Rosy, there's a horse in the garden.'

'Uh-huh. Are you coming in?' This was proving more amusing than she had thought. She was so used to the pub that she forgot its ability to make a standout first impression. Matt picked the dog up to calm him.

'Bloody hell, is that a cow next to it? Is dinner really that fresh?'

'Don't be daft.' Rosy pushed on the door and headed inside.

'It's called The Smuggler's Curse, for God's sake! What are you doing? Is this some kind of trap?'

'See you later then, I'll be out after I've eaten,' Rosy called over her shoulder.

'It's got an actual gravestone on its board and you're eating here?' Matt addressed the shut door.

Rosy popped it open from the other side. 'I can still hear you. Man or mouse?'

'Are those the menu choices? OK, OK, I'm coming!'

–

A man stood behind the bar. Wiry with ill-fitting clothes, he reminded Matt immediately of Bean, the gaunt and terrifyingly mean, cider-loving farmer from *Fantastic Mr Fox*. As he got closer he realized he smelt rather like it as well. It didn't seem to bother Rosy one iota as she leaned forward over the bar and gave him a peck on the cheek.

'Alreet, me luvver, you in for the usual?' Matt dreaded to think what 'the usual' was. Although, to be fair, the bar, glasses and bottles behind it seemed cleaner than its external appearance would have you believe. Maybe it wouldn't be so bad. And they didn't seem to bat an eye at him bringing Scramble in.

'Yes, but for the two of us please. Let me introduce Matt – he's just moved into Mary's old house, so I thought I'd best bring him in for lunch.'

'Ar.' The barman gave Matt a cursory look up and down, ignored his outstretched hand and turned his attention back to Rosy. 'From up country is 'ee?'

'Yes. Play nice. I'll have a gin… and Matt?'

'I'll have a pint of…' Matt scanned the pumps and decided to play politics and plump for something local, 'Tribute, please.' Pseudo-Bean's face didn't change as he handed Matt the pint wordlessly, although his eyes could have narrowed a little bit; it was hard to tell. Rosy looked as if she were fighting the urge to laugh. And he couldn't help but smile at her. It would all pan out fine; the locals would eventually accept his family, in seven generations' time.

'Right, we're heading into the other room. Ta, Roger.'

'See 'm in a minute, bird.'

'Yep. Two the same, mind you!' Rosy delivered these last words rather firmly. He really did quite like this schoolteacher voice she kept putting on. He had friends who were married to teachers who constantly complained that their partners spoke to them as if they were six years old. But Rosy managed to make her teacher's voice sound quite dirty. Or maybe it wasn't Rosy, maybe it was him? Maybe he had a whole side to him that he hadn't realized existed? Maybe he should explore this more.

'Um… are you coming?' Rosy called to the accompaniment of Pseudo-Bean-now-called-Roger's sniggering. 'You're in for a treat.'

'Yep, right behind you.' Rosy pushed open yet another door, one that resembled a fire door in a village hall or run-down hotel. Not one that you would place in the middle of a country pub. It led into a big old room with tables and chairs, straight out of an eighties B&B dining room, complete with dark green paper napkins and floral place mats. He thought Cornwall was all mismatched chandeliers, pale blue and slate these days. Not in The Smuggler's Curse, it would appear.

But the decor only took a one-second glance before dismissal; there were far more interesting things in the room. There were the people, for a start. It was busy, far more so than Matt would have ever imagined from the outside. And the customers themselves were a real hodgepodge of people. They appeared to have very little in common, other than, as Matt quickly glanced at their plates, a bloody lovely-looking roast dinner. Yum. Maybe Rosy knew what she was doing after all.

As they weaved through the tables, the smells and sights of Sunday lunch were becoming more and more appealing; he hadn't realized how ravenous he was. At this rate he'd have to wipe the dribble from his chin before he even got to sit down. Always such an appealing look for the ladies. *For God's sake, man!* This was a neighbourly outing, nothing more. Rosy had Mr-Mystery-Saturday-Night and he had commitment issues and a glittering career to build.

'Here OK for you?' His neighbour interrupted his train of thought.

'Commitment issues and a career,' was the answer that fell out of his mouth. Honestly, he was such a fool. It had always got him into trouble when he was younger; his thoughts would often just pop out of his mouth when asked a question with absolutely no bearing or relevance to what was being asked. This was not the time for this to start again. God knows what could come out. Perhaps he should just gaffer tape his mouth up. *No, no, please don't say gaffer tape next*, he begged his brain. It was going to get him locked up at this rate.

'Yup, we all have those but they won't get us lunch, so is this table OK for you?'

'Oh, sorry. I'm an idiot. Of course, although they're reserved.' Matt concentrated really hard and thankfully made sense this time. He drew the chair in front of Rosy out for her to sit, and felt his tummy flip as she smiled up a thank you and carried on talking.

'God, yes. You have to reserve the tables otherwise you don't have a hope in hell's chance on a Sunday. I rang ahead when you left, but I come in most Sundays anyway. I usually squeeze in with some of the regulars, but I didn't want to throw you in at the deep end.'

'Roger McDodger wasn't the deep end?'

'Oh, you've seen nothing yet. Tell you what, we'll eat and then I'll introduce you to some of the locals.'

'OK, sounds like a plan. At least if I die it will be on a full stomach.'

'Oh, don't make such a fuss, they're not a murderous horde.' Rosy paused and looked at him and then, disconcertingly, laughed. 'Well, not most of them.'

Matt slid into his own chair, looping Scramble's lead around it. 'Great, now I am terrified. But I shall combat my fear if you tell me a bit more about this place. It's such a weird setup.'

Rosy's eyes narrowed, bearing a scary similarity to Roger's from earlier – maybe it was a Cornish thing. 'Weird, how?'

'Oh, no, not in a bad way but, well, for example, that drum kit and small stage.' Matt pointed to the items at the end of the room. 'Those are unusual things to have in a dining area, don't you agree? Most restaurants don't have a drum kit in them. Or a harp!'

Rosy broke into a huge smile that reached not just both ears but maybe the tips of her eyes too. 'Well, you might find out later. Unless they've killed you first.'

'If 'ee gonna do that can 'ee take it off the premises, please,' came Roger's voice over Matt's shoulder. 'Last murder took months to shift. Blood's a bugger, you know.' He placed two plates of steamingly hot heaven in front of them and smiled, first at Rosy and then at Matt. 'Now, 'twas the badger you both ordered, weren't it?'

# Chapter Eight

Matt rocked back on his seat. It turned out that the first bite of badger was delicious, remarkably like roast beef and served with horseradish so he was willing to gamble and eat the rest. Not that he was going to let Rosy know this; she was going to get a hard time for pretending he was eating roadkill. Teasing her was so much fun. She flared up a little every time, just until she would see him grin and then she would back down again, occasionally kicking his shins as she did so and then wincing in case she had hit Scramble instead. He chose not to assure her that Scramble was far too quick to be caught out by a foot, and was especially alert when there was a chance of food.

Rosy was easy company; they seemed to spend the whole time giggling at something or other. Lunch was only just starting but he didn't want this afternoon to end for a while yet. He wasn't sure what the rest of the day would bring but he knew he was going to enjoy it. He couldn't remember a time he had felt this relaxed. He knew there must have been one, but right now was perfect. Content silence.

'Make way! Make way!' brayed a voice from across the room, causing Matt's content silence to be punctured and his head to spin around. Not before he noticed Rosy's smirk as she carried on eating.

The door burst open and a gaggle of people, six it seemed, piled through, all in fancy dress and carrying instruments. There were breeches and capes, gowns and headdresses. With them were instruments; some were stringed, one looked like a banjo, and another carried an old-fashioned-looking drum. They whooshed through the dining room like minor celebrities, heading to pop their instruments on the stage at the far end, but stopping and talking to people on the way. They worked the room, nodding, greeting, kissing and occasionally twanging their instruments as they went.

'Aye, aye, my fair maiden, I hope you're behaving as behoves a lady of such grace.' The leader of the group paused at their table, eyeing up Matt, who with a forkful of food to his mouth put it back on his plate and smiled in welcome.

'Don't be daft!' responded Rosy as she leapt to her feet and was enveloped in a whirl of velvet and mwah-y kisses.

'Well, recent evidence suggests you have been playful of late.'

'Oh, for goodness' sake, shut up and meet Matt. He's moved into Mary's house so I thought I'd come and introduce him to the village.'

'Well, in that case, it's a pleasure to make your acquaintance, sire.'

Matt didn't know whether he should answer in medieval, Cornish or just tug a forelock. All of the options seemed a bit ridiculous. Oh, bloody hell, he hated fancy dress. And now it felt like the whole room was watching him, as if there were some subtext he was unaware of. Bloody villages! He shook the man's hand and muttered some pleasantries, as innocuous as he could make them, and breathed a sigh of relief as Rosy sat back down and his new acquaintance continued around the room preening and peacocking at the attention.

'Are they in every Sunday?'

'No, it's every other Sunday. Don't mind Dave, he talks nonsense – you wait, you'll see.'

Matt was not sure he wanted to. Could it have been Dave that Rosy had had in her house earlier? What was all that behaving and behoving nonsense? For goodness' sake, who on earth in the world paraded around dressed as a medieval musician without having serious issues? He bet Dave sat at home in sweatpants spending far too much time on the Internet when he wasn't playing dress-up. What an idiot. Sire! Bloody ridiculous.

Woah! Where had his aggression come from? Was this jealousy? Right, that wasn't happening! Firstly, he was not the jealous type – it was small-minded and ineffective – and secondly, there was no way Rosy would be sleeping with a medieval troubadour, surely not. And if she was, which she wasn't, it was none of his business anyway. He had enough to contend with, concentrating wholly on his career, the gardens and nothing else.

He stopped his internal rant and watched Rosy pull Scramble out from under the table. The dog jumped straight onto her lap and she fed him titbits of fat dipped in gravy from her plate.

'You made my friend Lynne's day yesterday.' Rosy carried on fussing his dog, not looking him in the eye as she spoke.

'I did? Slightly scary. How?'

'Well, OK, not you specifically, sorry. But she was making a great fuss about Angelina being in the village. I think she's a bit of a super-fan.'

'Ah, yeah, she seems to have that effect on people. Slightly beyond me, I must admit. She's a bit of a monster once you get to know her.'

'Oh, I had heard she had therapy and was lovely now.' Rosy gasped a millisecond after she spoke, clearly embarrassed for implying Ange could be anything but a joy.

'I wouldn't believe everything you read in the papers. As much as I love her, Angelina is very much Angelina, and I can't see her ever changing.'

'Oh, OK.' The mood had suddenly shifted to awkward and he wasn't sure why. Something to do with his sister, presumably, but he was determined not to let conversation, and the ease with which they spoke to each other, peter out and die now – not when things had been going so well. He cast around in his mind to find a conversational topic that would relax Rosy again.

'So, you said on the way over you were a headteacher. That's pretty awesome. Are you secretly fifty and just have mad make-up skills or were you some super-smart child prodigy that raced her way up the career ladder really young?'

'Ha. Neither. Just really lucky, I guess.'

'Hmm, I suspect there's more to it than luck. Go on, tell all. Don't hold back.'

'There really isn't that much to tell. I graduated from university and went straight into teaching and worked in a couple of schools around the country before I came down here; right down the other end though, Penzance way. There I was really lucky to be mentored by the most

72

amazing head, Mrs Lindfield. She was remarkable, I love her and owe her such a debt of gratitude. Anyway, she pushed me and pushed me and with her help I became an AST...'

'AST? Astounding Space Tractor? Alarmingly Savage Turtle? Oh, I've got it! Astonishing Super Teacher?'

'Fool. Advanced Skills Teacher. My specialism was in early years.'

Bless her, she blushed again, just a little, as if she were embarrassed of her achievement. It was too cute and so at odds with the Cornish lessons and bossy Rosy from earlier.

'Anyway, before I knew it she was pushing me into the position of deputy head when it opened up and made me take my NPQH – that's the exams you need to do to become a head. I did that and then when this position came up I applied. I'd always wanted to work in a village school so I couldn't believe my luck when I got it, and here I am.'

'Oh wow, so you're the head in this village?'

'Yup. Oh, will you excuse me a minute? I promise I won't be more than a second or two.' She jumped up hurriedly and wandered off.

So, she was headteacher here in Penmenna; that explained so much. All through lunch they had been constantly interrupted by friends and acquaintances of Rosy's. A stream of people all paying testament to how popular and downright lovely she was. Matt could not disagree. She met everyone with a smile and a person-alized comment or anecdote and didn't seem in the least perturbed with the interruptions. He had been introduced so many times that he had lost count and was beginning to fear she might be some kind of cult leader. But now it fell into place. She was obviously widely respected within the community and presumably had impacted all of these people, or their children, in a positive way.

He watched as she wended her way through the room, stopping to kneel at a table occupied by a family group who were clearly getting ready to leave. She was speaking to the young woman, who was pale and with startling red hair, fatigue writ clear on her face even at a distance. And he watched as the whole table lit up as Rosy spoke, the three adults laughing at whatever she had said and the small boy with them nodding frantically. She stopped but a minute or two and then headed back to Matt, who was unable to tear his eyes away as she got closer and closer.

'Sorry about that, I saw they were leaving and just wanted to say hello.'

'Pupil?'

'No, not yet, although hopefully he'll join us next year. I met his mum in Truro a couple of years ago; she used to be a professional ballet dancer. Amazing woman, Sylvie, she teaches self-defence classes now and that's where I met her. She moved back down here, I think she wanted her son to grow up by the sea, and then her mother got ill, so sad. From what I understand her mum hasn't got long left and I just wanted to say hello.'

'I'm sorry. I suppose if there's any positive to be found then at least she's back in Cornwall to support her mother.'

'True. From what I know of her she'll be doing an amazing job as well. She looks so dainty, doesn't she, but my goodness I reckon she could throw an elephant over her shoulder should she need to. I've never seen such strength.'

'Well, ballet is notoriously tough so it doesn't surprise me. Does this mean though that when you were telling me off earlier you could have actually beaten me up if I hadn't done as I was told?'

'You better believe it!' She waved her arms in a faux martial arts style and put on what he assumed was her most threatening face.

Before he knew what he was doing, he leant towards her to scoop a lock of her hair that had fallen forward as she had been gesticulating. Without thinking he placed it behind her ear. They shared a look, and Matt – celibacy and career forgotten in an instant – wanted to sweep her into his arms and out of this crazy pub before any more interruptions, medieval musicians or grumpy landlords got in their path. Instead, he covered her hand with his. She drew her hand away, a little awkwardly, and placed it back on her lap.

'I'm sorry. I didn't mean to do that! That was crossing the line. Really, I apologize.'

He was mortified. What to him was both instinctive and unavoidable was making her ill at ease. Of course she'd pulled away – she was probably already dating and had come out with him out of neighbourly kindness and he had just touched her without even thinking. It had just felt so natural, as if they had been friends for years.

'Oh, yeah, don't worry about it… it's fine. Seriously, I would have hurled you to the floor super-quick if you'd offended me. We're all good.' As she spoke a bizarre twanging filled the room as the Tudors started tuning up in the corner. 'I'm just going to take the plates to the kitchen, save Roger coming in for them. Drink?'

She was flashing him that smile, the one he had seen her bestow on everyone that had stopped at their table. Although this time it didn't quite reach her eyes as the earlier ones had. But still, she had offered another drink, so he wasn't done yet.

'Yes, please.'

–

Three hours later they both fell out of the pub, arms linked and giggling like fools. Matt took back everything he had thought about grown men dressing as medieval musicians. He couldn't believe he had been so bad-tempered and so wrong! They were awesome. Absolutely awesome. Not only did The Smuggler's Curse serve the best bloody roast in the south-west, he would swear to it now, they knew how to put on a party. Never, never in his life had he thought he would enjoy a musical stand-off, but it seemed it was a village tradition. The Penmenna Troupe had a mini battle of the bands every other Sunday, and this week they were challenged by a thrash death metal group from four villages along. But despite it being a battle, or the band being called Blood of your Scrotum or some such thing, there was nothing but bonhomie about it all. They played their own tracks, then they swapped instruments and played each other's. Death metal hair – terribly greasy but still managing to move – flew around as guitars were half killed; jewelled velvet colours mixed in with the black skulls laden with viscera, as they helped teach each other various tricks. No one was precious about who touched what and how, as were most of the musicians Matt had encountered before. In fact, despite it being a supposed battle, people were so friendly and kind Matt wondered if he had suddenly arrived on a different planet entirely. Although, let's face it, it wasn't just the kindness that made him query this.

Non-musical diners were encouraged to have a go, the musicians of both bands played some belters as well as their own genre music, and people were happily singing, dancing, plucking, tooting and drumming. All before the watershed and all oiled by rivers of booze. This was the best Sunday ever.

He had learnt how to pluck a harpsichord, albeit briefly, and he had watched Rosy sing a solo, a traditional verse that Dave accompanied on the lute and made him feel in total awe of her all over again. Was there anything she couldn't do? And best of all, he had discovered that there was no way in the world that Rosy had had Dave back to her house the night before, because it turned out he was married to her best friend Lynne, who only hadn't joined them because, as Rosy let slip with a giggle, she had the mother of all hangovers. He also learnt jealousy, short-lived though it was, truly was a pointless emotion.

# Chapter Nine

Rosy was sitting in her chair – Fridays were office-based days for her whilst Lynne taught their class – swirling as fast as she could. She knew she should be attending to the ream of paperwork on her desk, and she would, but twirling in her chair – just for a second – was one of her favourite things to do, taking her back to an age of pigtails, freckles and home-made perfume. Twirl, swirl, smile.

'Miss Winter, Mr Grant is here for you. Shall I show him in?'

Rosy jumped from the chair as if it had adders swarming up the legs. She looked at the school secretary in abject horror. How had she not known about this? Could she say 'No, thank you, not today'? Edward Grant was the bane of every Cornish headteacher's life, and she needed at least a week of soothing music, meditation and mega-strength mojitos to prepare for their annual meeting. He had always reminded her of Gargamel, the villainous wizard from *The Smurfs*. He wasn't due in for months. Maybe she had misheard.

'Edward Grant, Sheila?'

'Yes, he rang last… oh… oh, oh no… oh, I've done it again, haven't I? Oh, I meant to put it on the system, honestly I did, but well now, what was it that happened? Now… was it… no, that wasn't it.' She furrowed her brow and looked down at the floor, shaking her head all the while. Her O's were rounded with the deep Cornish burr of someone who's never crossed the Tamar and possibly not even left the village. 'Was it… oh, could've been, no, nope. No, you know what, Rosy, I can't remember what it was, but I promise I did mean to put it in the thing. On the… oh, you know. Oh, which reminds me, you've had Mrs Pascoe and Mrs Trewithen on the phone already this morning. I think it was about… now what was – ah! Yes, they phoned about Mr Grant. Now isn't that funny?'

'Right, OK, please show him in. Thank you, Sheila.'

This was not going to be good news. Mr Grant rarely made sudden visits. The only time he visited, outside his annual check, was if he had something alarming to report. This was, it was rumoured, because of the deep joy he took as he delivered bad news, stretching it out in whichever way he could for maximum enjoyment.

'Miss Winter, an absolute pleasure.' Edward Grant, black hair slicked across his forehead and shiny suit far too tight around his midriff, entered her office and came forward to shake her hand. She hated this bit, but proffered her hand with her most professional smile, ensuring the shake was as quick as could be and managing not to wipe her hand down her skirt.

'Mr Grant, do sit down. What a pleasure to see you. How can I help?' How she wasn't struck down on the spot she didn't know.

'Miss Winter. Always a pleasure. Let's get right to it. There are some changes afoot and I felt it only right to talk to you in person.'

'Changes?' Rosy heard her voice lift up at the end, half daring him to continue, half terrified of what came next.

'As you know I'm tasked with overseeing all the primary schools in the area, ensuring standards remain high and—'

'As I'm sure you're aware, we've just been inspected and were deemed outst—'

'Yes, yes, Miss Winter. If you'd be so kind as to let me finish. I'm tasked with overseeing all the primary schools in the area, ensuring standards remain high and budgets remain under control.' He took a deep breath and fiddled with his tie. Was she allowed to speak now? She waited a bit longer, just to make sure. He dropped his tie and looked at her, eyebrow raised, stare bold. OK, so now she should speak. God, she hated him. She had visions of oil pooling around the chair where he sat. She hoped there was a sturdy supply of antibacterial spray in the cleaning closet.

'Well, Mr Gr—'

'*If* you'd let me finish.'

Rosy used all her self-control not to roll her eyes or clench her fists, repeating the mantra 'stay calm' in her head. Along with 'don't give him the satisfaction'. And 'twat'.

'And whilst Penmenna is both on target and on budget I'm afraid not all the schools are and, as a whole, the county needs to do some restructuring in specific areas to reduce costs. I'm sure you're aware that these are lean times, Miss Winter, and we must cut our cloth accordingly.'

*I hate him. Twat. Don't give him the satisfaction.*

'Now, I don't need to bother your little head with too much detail about county financing, ring fencing and budgets...' Did he actually just say that? Clearly he had skipped the training about equality and respect within the workplace. '…but the upshot is that we will be merging five of the village schools in the surrounding area into one large primary in Roscarrock with four-form entry, which obviously will involve a large initial investment but will ensure year to year running costs are substantially reduced.'

'Mr Grant, surely—'

'Miss Winter. I was still talking.'

*I hate him. Twat. Don't give him—* Merging? Rosy felt her heart stop, her body freeze and her mind whirr. Four-form entry. No. No, this couldn't even be a possibility. He was mad. Merge? *Breathe. Breathe and listen. Maybe you misheard.*

'…substantially reduced running costs and a much more streamlined delivery of curriculum. Now, obviously you may be concerned about your position in this new school…'

She wasn't concerned about any such thing! What she was concerned about was the children of Penmenna being uprooted to some kind of soulless, cheap-to-run mega-build, bloody ages away. She took pride in the quality provision Penmenna delivered to all its pupils but especially the children with additional learning needs. Children like Bradley in her own class, whose mum was due in later to discuss how he was doing now he was coming in for full days after an extensive staggered start – the answer was really well, far better than anyone could have hoped.

And not just her own class. Children like Jordan, who really struggled with social interaction and needed the security that a village school can offer so well, sitting in the heart of his community and all that was familiar. Jordan had been selectively mute when he started school and with the help of his specially appointed teaching assistant, Alice, was now able to communicate with his peers and build friendships. Children like Imogen and Jake, both of whom were in Amanda's class and had such an appalling home life that the security of Penmenna school was what was providing them with a much-needed rudder.

And now that Rosy and her staff had got these children settled and happy they wanted to uproot them and he dared think she was only worried about her own position! Rosy was ready to explode but knew she needed to play a more careful game than that.

She had come into teaching and revelled in being a head because of the positive changes she could make, not to play political games. She wasn't sure she had the skills needed to play politics, not at that level. She found it hard enough managing the PTA. She guessed she'd better find the skills, though, and fast. And the first step was to hear this odious man out, then formulate a plan – preferably one that involved people who could play politics, and win.

She looked across at him, still pontificating about the importance of cost-cutting measures to the county and not one single word about the welfare of the children or educational outcomes coming from those nasty little lips, which were still moving at speed and managing to weave remarkable levels of condescension and misogyny in as he spoke.

If he had pitched that they were building an improved school, a school that would better the children's life chances, then she would have been more open. She may have been able to overlook the further references to her inexperience and the fact that she was, apparently, a girl, but not once did he discuss anything other than cost. His eyes glinted as he delivered unacceptable one-liners, as if he knew he was crossing a line, and that his words weren't innocuous but deliberately designed to demonstrate the power he had.

She remembered when she'd first moved down here, seeing him on local news, well before she met him in real life. There had been a spate of closing village schools back then as well. Long-established village schools that were operating with only a handful of children on the roll were being closed down with the pupils sent to neighbouring villages for their education. There had been an outcry at the time and he was wheeled in front of the camera to defend the county's position. Even through the television set he had emanated grease.

Then there was the time he had banned all schools in the county from attending the traditional Christmas pantomime in Truro because he deemed it to have no educational merit. He had also had all the water coolers removed for budgetary reasons, claiming it was not the county's responsibility to keep children hydrated.

Rosy had even had nightmares in which he featured, usually chasing her and her class around the playground, shouting appalling threats about what he intended to do to the school hamster. It was hard, with this combination of facts, to ever see him in a positive light. Today was not helping.

He finally finished up, not asking if she had any questions or concerns, because he quite simply didn't care. He was here to deliver a fait accompli and anyone else's opinion was irrelevant. No wonder Mrs Trewithen and Mrs Pascoe had been calling her; they had obviously had the same visit and were also panicking like mad. Three in one morning. He must be feeling on top of the world.

'Mr Grant, before you go, I wondered if I could ask you some questions about this process.'

He looked at her as if she had just sprouted three heads. 'Miss Winter. My time is rather valuable.'

'Of course, and I do appreciate you coming to see me in person rather than delivering this news over the phone. But can I ask how many schools are looking at potential closure? You said there was to be a four-form entry so I imagine that there will be at least five, possibly six of the smaller schools you're planning to amalgamate. I'm just trying to collect as much information as I can, so I can let the staff know. They're going to be asking these questions later and I wouldn't want to have to disturb you again.'

'Yes, I have a list of six schools that have be deemed the most appropriate to merge.'

Rosy had a lightbulb moment. 'And can I ask if St Ewer is on the list?'

'I really don't see the need to answer that, Miss Winter.'

'So, St Ewer is not on the list then, Mr Grant?'

'As I said, Miss Winter, I really don't have the time to waste on foolish questions. You only need to know that this will be going ahead. There will in all probability be some redundancies and we will keep you updated with what you need to know, when you need to know. Now, if you'll excuse me.' And with that he smiled an oily there's-nothing-you-can-do smile and oozed out of the door.

Rosy sat back in her chair, no twirling this time, just nervous fingers rubbing at her brow. As the adrenalin that had fuelled her through the meeting began to leave her body she felt exhausted; exhausted and defeated. Then, as she closed her eyes and concentrated on her breathing to try and ground herself again, she could feel her true self kicking back in. Defeated? Not a chance. She was going to prepare for battle. Penmenna School would not be closed without a fight. Picking up her pen, she turned to make inroads on the paperwork on her desk. She needed to get this done so she could focus on drawing up a plan of action. She had a staff meeting later today and she was going to need to get as much done as possible before hysteria hit.

–

'Cake? You should put that down right now! I don't understand what bit about not bringing in such… such poison is so hard for everyone to understand. Let me take that, and try this, I made it last night – organic, vegan and sugar-free, you'll find your body much prefers it!'

'Sod off, Harmony!'

'I really must insist, here let me—'

'Touch my cake again and I'm going to blur your chakras into kingdom come.'

'But, look, let me— arrgghhh!'

Rosy smiled as she entered the staffroom. If the children saw what went on in here, they'd put every teacher on the raincloud that the school used for behaviour management.

'Lynne, let go of Harmony!' She used her strictest teacher voice, and a memory of Matt encouraging her for more flooded into her head. This was not the time for that sort of nonsense.

'How dare you! I'm going to phone my union rep as soon as this meeting is finished. This is abuse in the workplace and I will not tolerate it. Rosy, what are you going to do about this?' Harmony rolled up her rainbow jumper to massage her wrist and gave Rosy a look that managed to be both combative and plaintive. Quite a skill.

'Lynne, say sorry to Harmony, you know that's unacceptable! And Harmony, I know you think sugar is the modern-day equivalent to crystal meth, but you cannot, cannot start taking people's food away from them. Lynne can eat what she wants. You can inform, which you frequently do, but you cannot enforce. I heard that last week you nearly knocked Alice to the floor because she had a Werther's Original. This is not some kind of dictatorship!'

'But—'

'But—'

Rosy walked to the chair she usually sat in, pushed up her sleeves and put the iPad she was carrying down as forcefully on the table as she dared.

'No, we have real stuff to deal with today, and I need your full attention. I'm afraid that this meeting may be a lengthy one, and you know I usually keep them as quick as possible so for that I apologize, but we need to get down to work.'

Lynne stopped glaring across the table to where Harmony had retreated and turned her full attention to her friend.

'What's up? I haven't seen you all day.'

Lynne, however, was interrupted by Harmony, who was still on a roll. 'I'm afraid I can't stay late, I have the Festival of the Enlightened Spirit to attend in—'

'Shut up, Harmony!' the rest of the staff chorused in unison before turning their attention back to Rosy.

She looked at them all, this little family of teachers, respected in the community but still a ragbag of everything human: Lynne, loyal to the core, loved by the children andparents alike; Harmony, currently with mouth agape and probably the less said about the better; Amanda, tip-to-toe in pinstripe and the most efficient teacher Rosy had ever worked with; and Sarah, her head cocked to one side like a little bird, glasses halfway down her nose, calm, quiet and with more experience than the rest of them put together. All these women – she was going to have to tell them that their village school, their home-from-home, was hanging by a thread.

'I had a meeting with Edward Grant today and I have to tell you, there's a chance we could be closed by next September. Now the key word here is "chance" – it's not definite but it is probable and the way I see it we have two options. We can let Penmenna School close and the children will be moved into the huge new school they're building in Roscarrock—'

'But that's over ten miles away, they can't do that!'

'Yes, Lynne, and that may work in our favour. They're hoping to get rid of several village schools and pop them all in one larger one, but I'm hoping that, as the school located furthest away, we can use that to give ourselves a fighting chance.'

'But we were classed as outstanding in almost every area.' Amanda shot a quick poisonous glance at Harmony as she spoke; Ofsted hadn't quite understood the relevance of her teachings on the power of the moon. 'Surely it's bad politics to close an outstanding school?'

'Yes, again you're right and we definitely need to use this fact. But we're not alone. A couple of the other schools under consideration are also deemed outstanding. We just need to make sure we have the loudest voice!'

'Well, how do we do that, dear?'

'Sarah, that is exactly what we need to work out. And we need to start working it out today. We need to show people how important Penmenna School is, to the children and to the community. How we do that in a novel and outstanding way is something we need to decide. Can I assume from what you've said that we're in agreement – we take option two, we stand and we fight?'

She didn't dare voice her concerns about how Mr Grant had chosen the schools to close, which had very little to do with performance and all to do with his outdated world view. She needed time to research and get her facts straight, but if what she believed was true that also would give them a much stronger chance of winning this battle.

'Coo-ee! Hope you don't mind me popping in.' Marion, resplendent in a very tightly fitted fuchsia dress printed with hummingbirds, popped her head around the door.

Rosy, all geed up from the staff's positive response to her horrible news, managed to smile. As much as she, and the rest of the team, loathed the woman, she could be a very useful ally. Perhaps she should bring her in on Team Save Our School now? Looking at Lynne shooting the woman looks of pure evil and the other three members of staff who had bowed their heads and were studiously examining the table, she decided against it for the minute. Maybe talk to her about it next week. Yes, that was best.

'The thing is, Mrs Marksharp—'

'Marion, please,' was the inevitable response. Rosy didn't dare look at Lynne.

'The thing is, Marion, we really are having to keep this meeting to teaching staff only today. But having said that, I was hoping to see you. Any chance you're free to come in first thing on Monday?'

'Yes, yes of course. However, Rosy, you did miss the PTA meeting this afternoon about the Valentine's disco. Sheila said you were very busy, but I'm afraid we've had to make some decisions without you.' Marion, disappointment seeping out of her, nodded her head slowly as if she were disciplining a child – clearly not a look she practised on her own offspring.

*Don't look at Lynne, don't look at her!* Rosy told herself, mantra-like.

'So, because I've got a very busy weekend with Richard, very busy, I'm afraid it's fallen on you to cut out the cardboard hearts. We only need five hundred or so, and it's not as if you have family commitments so I knew you wouldn't mind.' And Marion, oblivious to the fury on Lynne's face, placed a thick wad of red card on the table in front of Rosy. 'See you on Monday!'

# Chapter Ten

Matt was also at work. He had spent most of the day with Pete constructing raised beds and ordering seeds. He loved leafing through catalogues and planning ahead for the season and with this new project it was extra exciting. There was an element of risk, because if he got it wrong it wouldn't be a case of a grovelling apology but failure broadcast across the nation in a peak viewing slot. However, there was no reason to fail; he knew what he was doing, he could manage soil conditions in the raised beds perfectly and pests, weather and other gardening niggles were exactly what his years of experience were there for. He was going to send Pete home early and give the big seed-storage drawers they had unearthed a bloody good scour so they would be ready, before getting on with his last job of the day. A rather romantic one at that.

His train of thought was interrupted by his phone ringing. Glancing at the screen he saw it was his agent. So much for a quiet morning pottering. He liked his agent, Susie – she was thorough and supportive whilst being loud and jolly good fun at the same time. They had a great relationship and he had found he could be as honest as he liked with her, without having to couch his words. Nothing fazed her, she'd just laugh and find a way to get things done. But a phone call meant that whatever she had to say was bound to involve him doing something, and he really just wanted to get on with this afternoon's project.

His phone continued to sing. Susie wasn't going away.

'Hey, Susie. How's things?'

'Fabulous, darling. Thank you for asking. But I'm ringing to talk about you!' Matt groaned; it was his least favourite subject. 'Ha, I heard that, you are funny! This is good news, and no, before you ask you don't need to do anything. Well, apart from say yes, obviously I do need you to say yes.'

'I need to know what I have to say yes to and then I'm sure I will.'

'OK, well, great news. I've heard from the production company and they've decided upon a name for the series.'

'OK…' Matt drew the word out. He was fairly sure it would have the word 'gardening' in it, and probably 'Cornwall' – that seemed to sell most things these days – but he wasn't that fussed. It was a gardening show, what was the worst they could do?

'Are you ready? Remember, just say yes!'

That made him nervous. 'Go on.'

'Well, they've gone with… drum roll… *Green-fingered and Gorgeous: The Cornish Edition…* Isn't it fabulous? Women will be tuning in in their thousands and—'

'No.'

'Sorry, I didn't catch that.'

'Susie, I'm very fond of you but no, a big loud not-in-a-million-years, over-my-dead-body no. Just no. No!'

'But, Matt—'

'No. I'll come back to London if I have to and tear the contract up…' He wouldn't; he liked Penmenna too much, but he was playing hardball on this one. What were they thinking? 'There's no way. This is my debut and I know I should do as I'm told, and I'm happy to. But to be packaged up as some kind of gardening sex toy, it's not happening. I'm sorry, Susie, you're going to have to get them to come up with something a little less exploitative.'

'But you know this is how things work, and you're a good-looking man. Where's the harm?'

'I really don't like it, Susie. Please go back and see if they've got anything else.'

'I'll tell you what, I'll tell them and I'll ask them to brainstorm more ideas but I know they're really happy with this and it's the direction they want. I hear what you're saying and I will try, but in return, can you just sit with it for a couple of weeks and see if you feel any better as time goes by? Please.'

'I can't see me changing my mind, but if you promise to try, I'll promise to sit with it and see. How's that?'

'Matt, I love you. Always said you were my favourite client.'

'Well, I haven't been on your books that long!'

Susie laughed and terminated the call. *Green-fingered and Gorgeous*. It was embarrassing. Mind you, he bet it would make Rosy laugh. Which reminded him of his project.

He had been having Rosy flashbacks all week long, although he hadn't so much as caught a glimpse of her in real life since the weekend. Spending Sunday together, despite all his resolutions to keep it neighbourly, had changed the dynamic for him more than he could have thought possible. He was now thinking that celibacy wasn't useful for harnessing creative juices at all, but was just a frustrating state of being that meant he found it increasingly difficult to concentrate on what he should be doing but could while away hours thinking of hair tendrils, big grins and cute little pyjama sets.

He had obviously been looking at this the wrong way and had decided action and declaration was a more sensible path, and with this in mind he had come up with two great plans. One was to make this Sunday as memorable as the last and the other was to prepare a beautiful gift for Valentine's Day, a romantic gesture that would show the best side of him, and hope it trumped anything the guy she was seeing came up with. Failing that, he could tell her about this name thing; she might pity-date him if nothing else. Armed with some black weed-control fabric, some gravel and a glue gun, he was going to start on project number one as soon as those drawers were scrubbed – if he could keep the daft grin off his face long enough to concentrate.

# Chapter Eleven

Sunday came around and, instead of her usual wind-blown walk on the beach or coffee and newspapers in her pyjamas, Rosy was sitting on the floor in the middle of her living room surrounded by millions of red cut-out hearts, several more bits of card and the desperate desire for some light relief.

She padded over on her hands and knees to the laptop to change the music but in that second of silence her ears caught a wisp of something rather bizarre. Frozen, she hovered her finger over the computer, in case she could hear it again. She was most likely imagining things, but she paused to be sure.

*Pling pling pling.*

*Pling pling pling.*

No, that was definitely the same sound. What was going on out there? Getting up off the floor and standing dead still, she listened and then followed the twanging to the front window, peeking out to see what was happening.

No! She couldn't believe her eyes. There was Matt in the front garden, underneath her misshapen tree, with some kind of roughly fashioned velvet pearl-seeded Tudor cap on and a medieval fiddle in his hands, the strings of which he was twanging badly.

'Alas, my lo-ove...' Matt began to sing 'Greensleeves' at her, complete with mournful look in his eye.

Laughing out loud, Rosy threw open the latticed window so she could hear him better. And as he finished the first verse and started the chorus she joined in. Two little voices singing their hearts out together, one slightly more tuneful than the other.

'What are you doing! You're such an idiot.'

Matt stopped twanging and giggled too. 'Well, I thought you might be in withdrawal so I decided to serenade you myself this Sunday. Did you like it?'

'Haha, yes I did. Although I'm not sure I deserve the sentiment. Of the words, that is. The sentiment of being serenaded, I like that very much indeed!'

'It's the only old-fashioned song I know, I remember it from school. We'd be allowed to either butcher it on the recorder or with our voices.'

'Nothing much changes, believe me. Well, actually it does. Do you know what, I don't want to talk about school. You would not believe the week I've had.'

'Well, let's not then. I've got a proposition that may make you smile,' Matt said.

'Hmmm. I bet you have.'

'Sorry, I missed that. What did you say?'

'Um, not to worry. Tell you what, let's stop shouting across the garden – come on in and you can tell me. If it's decent, that is.'

'Oh, if it has to be decent...' Matt shrugged off his cap and pretended to walk away.

Rosy shook her head as she shut the window. Really, the man was so daft! But he did make her giggle. Sadly, though, he wasn't getting any less gorgeous, or living any further away. Thank God she was blessed with a strong moral sense when it came to other women's men and had the self-imposed chastity belt that was The Rule. Not to mention being too exhausted with endless politics, paperwork and poxy hearts. However, she could still be friendly, and who knew – he might join Team Save Our School.

'Come on in then, but still – no insulting my sensibilities with your indecent ideas. Oh, and tell me, where did you get that hat? What on earth is it made from?' Rosy said as she opened the door and led him through to the living room. His face was like a puppy, all happy and bouncy and full. Full largely of naughtiness and irresistibility.

'Well, I think it's quite a good idea rather than an indecent one. I knew you were in and obviously with the Sunday lunch thing not happening this week, I made a hat to fit the mood out of stuff at work and thought it would be nice if we...' Matt paused as he entered the room and took in the scene around him. His little puppy eagerness fell off his face for a minute and he looked, for no apparent reason, as if the world had just kicked him hard and stolen his favourite bone.

'Matt?' Rosy queried, leaning forward and lightly touching his arm.

'Uh?'

'You thought it would be nice...' She watched him shake his head as if to pull himself together and plaster his smile back on.

'Oh yes, that's right. I thought it would be nice to cook you lunch. Just in case you hadn't. I mean, if you have, or have other plans I quite understand, it was a bit of a gamble but I knew you were in and I thought...'

'You've cooked Sunday lunch? For when?'

'Well, it's Sunday and it's lunchtime.'

'You mean now?'

'Yep.'

'What have you cooked?'

'Chicken and potatoes and stuffing, sweet potato, car—'

'For now?'

'Yes, but like I said—'

'Oh my God! Roast chicken! Oh, I think I love you!' Rosy grabbed his arms as tight as tight could be and started jumping up and down on the spot with excitement. Then realized what she'd said, flushed bright red and stopped jumping. But not blushing. So much for iron self-control; she was virtually crumpling over roast chicken!

'So is that a yes? That looks like a yes.' Matt smiled.

Rosy looked at the red hearts sprinkled over her carpet, and the ones still waiting to be cut out.

'Um…'

'Roast parsnips, French peas… Shall I go on?'

Rosy's tummy rumbled as if in encouragement. Bloody typical!

'Oh, it does sound delicious, really good. I didn't mean to appear ungrateful. Let me grab my phone. I'd love to join you and Angelina for lunch.'

'Ange is still in London.'

'Oh…' Rosy paused. How the hell was she going to get out of this now? 'In that case, perhaps…'

'Stop it! It's lunch. There's nothing nefarious going on. You need to eat, and I've cooked, so grab your phone and I shall sing you back to mine, milady. You can wear the hat.'

There was a definite pattern developing, one around yummy Sunday lunches and all sorts of silly giggling. They had talked and talked and talked: politics, fashion, current affairs, gossip, weather, best holidays ever, dreams, ambitions, baby names, Rosy's secret passion for Wotsits, pink wafers and Dairylea – everything. They played each other their top three tracks of all time, with Matt shrieking that she had stolen his when she put on 'Walk on the Wild Side'. She had even told him about the possibility of the school closure, and her doubts that she was political enough to be able to save it. He had listened, said if he could help in any way then he would and reassured her that he had complete faith in her abilities. She wasn't sure how but really appreciated it all the same. And then to top it off she was currently sitting on one of those swingy stool things she had always coveted for herself. Even their furniture choices would be identical, if she had the budget and the time.

However, as comfortable as Rosy was becoming in Matt's company (and house), and as much as she was enjoying today, she was aware she was beginning to develop a proper crush. Trying to remind herself of The Rule was tough when she was so relaxed that she was constantly laughing.

In fact, the laughter she shared with Matt, the light touches and the increasingly long meaningful looks – she could feel her tummy flip just thinking about them – were becoming increasingly flirtatious, and somehow, somehow, she needed to bring Angelina into the conversation. Not that she particularly wanted to talk about the nasty, perfectly plastic, dog-kicking woman, but she did have to remind Matt of his responsibilities and that she really wasn't that sort of girl. She would never, ever even countenance starting something with a man in a relationship, never! She needed to make it clear this was a friendship only thing, and why. She would wait until he came back in from the pantry where he had snuck off to and bring it up then.

But what on earth would she say? How does one tell one's secret crush that they are not harbouring any intention of sleeping with them because a) he has a girlfriend, and b) Rosy herself had a whole baggage-trolley-full of seemingly unresolvable issues? She could hear Lynne's voice saying, 'Yup, just like that', but there was no way in the world Rosy was going to say that. She was all for speaking the truth, but there were degrees.

Maybe she'd just sit here and let the conversation arise organically. Yes, organically, and then the right words would find themselves at the time. That was probably the spiritually awakened way of doing things. Harmony would be proud. She hadn't realized that she was spiritually awakened but obviously that's exactly what she was. That was good. That would help.

'Close your eyes, one... two... three,' came Matt's command from behind the pantry door. She loved this sort of thing so she did exactly that, clapped her hands excitedly, spun around at speed on her chair, and promptly fell off. Bloody typical.

Matt had been holding two glasses of a beautiful-looking cocktail, inviting and layered with colour. However these were abandoned on the counter as he raced over in two big steps to extend his hand and pull her back up from the floor.

'Oh my goodness, are you OK? You're such a fool!'

'Such a fool!' she retorted, holding firm to his hand and allowing herself to be pulled up.

'Yes! You were swinging on that chair like a child.'

'I like it. I do it at work too.' Rosy was standing as close as close could be now she had regained her balance. They were still holding hands and she couldn't resist the urge to stick her tongue out, just very quickly, at him.

'I like that you like it.'

The mood suddenly changed. It was as sudden as a clap of thunder. Rosy stood there awkwardly, not knowing what to do with her hand, apart from praying that it didn't become too clammy, staring at Matt with big eyes. There was no way to mistake this. The sexual chemistry here was even more charged than her first kiss with Ben James in the upper fourth by the bins. And that was a kiss that changed her from girl to woman. Even more intense than her first meeting with Josh at uni, and she hadn't thought that was possible. Good God, she couldn't move. She gulped and wondered what the hell was going on in Matt's head right now.

His eyes hadn't left her face. He didn't seem to be having doubts about sweaty palms or teenage passion. He was just smiling that smile and coming closer and, oh my, she had to stop this, but oh my God, his lips were so close and—

Music blasted out, making Scramble, who was curled in his basket, jerk awake. Rosy used it, and buckets of self will, to take a step back and put some distance between her and Matt. Phew. That was close. The music stopped and then started again. Matt pushed his hand through his hair and looked a little flustered. Or embarrassed. Rosy couldn't tell which but it was definitely one or the other. Maybe a mix of the two.

'I'd better get that.' He turned and picked up his phone from the top of the bread bin where it was singing and vibrating with the energy and determination of a toddler.

'What? Yes, I know… right, calm down, I can hardly hear you… hang on a minute…'

He turned and shrugged at Rosy, no less attractive than he was thirty seconds ago but a little more hassled-looking. 'I'm sorry, let me just deal with this, don't forget your drink…' He nodded at the cocktail on the side, which seemed somehow to have lost its charm, and then wandered into the next room.

Despite the distance between the two rooms, more symbolic than actual, Rosy could clearly hear the gist of the conversation. Even though she couldn't hear Angelina's words, the muffled female screeching on the other end indicated one very upset woman.

'Ange, yes, I can tell how upset you are… yes I know it's Valentine's Day next week, of course I do… I don't really see… right, OK! OK, I'll get the train up as soon as I can…'

Rosy didn't need to hear any more. What the hell was she doing here? How could she? For all her faux morality, all her so-called rules, she knew how badly she had wanted to kiss him just then. Would she have done so had his phone not rung? Had his girlfriend – distressed girlfriend – not rung?

She knocked back the cocktail on the side. After all, she wasn't a complete idiot; she was going to need that to get her through the rest of the day. Cutting blooming hearts out. And possibly ignoring the front door and developing a stronger moral backbone. Oh hell, maybe they'd move soon. Drink drunk, she sneaked out of the front door, ever so quietly but not quite tippy-toes, and headed back to her spinster-like home, leaving Matt trying to calm down the (maybe rightfully) overwrought Angelina.

# Chapter Twelve

Matt heard the door creak shut and let out a sigh before continuing to talk to his sister. He couldn't blame Rosy for leaving. Angelina's voice could sometimes make him want to do the same, and she certainly wouldn't be the first woman his sister had scared off. But he thought Rosy had more to her than to take fright over a phone call. Unless it was him. That might make more sense. He had assumed she felt as he did – all the vibes had been pointing that way – but what if he had read the situation wrong? What if she was being neighbourly and he had come on too strong? Oh God, in that case he owed her an apology. But if she had felt so strongly she had to flee, maybe chasing after her would only make things worse.

'Matt!' His sister barked down the phone at him with that innate skill she had for knowing when he wasn't giving her his full attention. Right. He'd deal with one thing at a time.

'Look, Ange, I've said I understand that you're upset and that it's Valentine's Day soon and that you feel your life is in pieces, and I've said I'll come and visit as soon as I can but I'm in the middle of something and, quite frankly, what more do you want from me?'

'I want you to come and look after me. What do you mean in the middle of something? Well, you just get back to something and leave me here all alone, broken and alone. I don't think' – sob – 'you appreciate' – sob, hiccup – 'quite how much I loved this one.'

Matt resisted all temptation to ask if it was as much as the last one, who also had been her soulmate, love of her life and spiritual twin. He went for a non-committal noise instead. He wished Rosy hadn't left.

'What's that supposed to mean? I need some support here, Mattie.'

'Look, Ange, have you tried ringing that friend of yours, you know, the one you met in group counselling last time?'

'She's not here, is she. She's never here, she's in Thailand or some place having a lovely time. She's not had her heart twisted out of her chest and stomped on...' Angelina changed her tone from desperate hyperventilating and sobbing and went for wheedling instead. 'Please, Matt, you're all I've got and I'm scared. Please...' She paused. Angelina had always known how to get him and it would seem today was no exception.

'OK, OK, I'll get the train up.'

'Now?'

'Now! Are you cr—' Matt managed to stop himself just in time. His sister had always struggled to regulate her emotions, their intensity was often overwhelming and it was he who she had always reached for as she felt things begin to spiral.

He felt that familiar tightening in his chest, a feeling of being trapped, wishing that she would reach out to a professional but knowing she never would. And without professional support who else did she have? He didn't have a choice; he knew it was unlikely but what if the one time he refused to help was the time she took things a step too far? It was a risk that didn't bear thinking about – not considering their family history, not considering their mum.

He wouldn't need to stay for long, a few days at most. His sister's emotions were as fast-moving as they were fierce and once she felt supported would change again in a flash, and then Angelina would be back to her usual self, popping on her shortest skirt and heading out looking for her next celebrity match and his-and-hers Lamborghinis. It seemed an empty, shallow existence to him, and exactly the sort of nonsense he was trying to escape – status-obsessed women driven by dreams of alimony payments and sex with the gardener. However, until she recovered, he didn't like to think of her feeling alone, rejected, desperate. If he could help her, show her she wasn't friendless, that she was loved, then yup, that was exactly what he had to do.

'OK, not right now, but today?' Her voice was plaintive and suddenly drained of all emotion, which was almost scarier than the screaming, shouting Class A bitch behaviour.

'Yep, I'll check the trains and I promise I'll be there by tonight. But, Ange, you have to promise me if I'm catching the train up today you won't do... um... you know... don't do... um... anything stupid, huh?'

Sniffle... sniffle... 'Well, I have already eaten three yum-yums – oh my God, corn syrup and carbs! What was I thinking? I'll throw the rest in the bin. Thank you, Matt, I'll do that now.'

'OK.' He rolled his eyes. 'And then, hang on...' He switched to speakerphone and scrolled down the train times. 'I should be there by eight. Why don't you have a long bath, and then pop on *Gone with the Wind*. I'll be there by the time Rhett gets out his hanky.'

'Yes, that's a good idea, OK, OK.'

'Right, let me just sort some stuff out here and I'll see you in a bit.'

'All right, and, um… thanks, Matt.'

Matt hung up the phone and a bittersweet smile came across his face. *Gone with the Wind* had always been their film. Not particularly masculine, and not something anyone outside his family knew, but it had been their mother's favourite and Matt and Angelina had watched it time and time again as kids. First of all with Mum and then afterwards, using the film to trigger memories of her.

His mum's favourite scene had been the making of the green dress, and she had always hidden behind a cushion from the minute Bonnie got on the horse. Angelina, from the age of four, used to wrap herself in their own curtains and shout, 'Well, I do declare' in a southern accent (they should have known then Angelina was predestined for fame), and Matt had been cushion holder and passer. The film was a comfort blanket now for the two of them, as much in adulthood as after her death.

They knew all the words and would huddle under the blanket mouthing along to all the big scenes. Angelina had, obviously, adored Scarlett and Ashley, whereas Matt had not been so keen, much preferring Melanie, who could always be relied upon to do the right thing, unlike Scarlett and Ashley, who appeared to have no moral compass at all. Watching the film now should calm her down, reassure her and, as a bonus, it was nearly as long as the entire train journey.

He ran up the stairs, slinging things into a bag, Scramble yapping with excitement. He wouldn't be gone for long but before he went, he needed to just whisk around and say goodbye to Rosy, explain why he was racing off. He didn't blame her for leaving, but they had had such a nice afternoon, again. He really could see a lifetime of such afternoons with her. Yikes! That was not part of the original plan for his time in Cornwall. He'd best shelve that thought for now. However, he suspected he'd revisit it later, probably again and again (and with a smile each time) on the train.

He assumed from last weekend that Rosy was dating. He had hoped it wasn't serious, of course he did. Then today, when he had gone around in that daft cap to invite her back to his, she had been cutting out all those little hearts. His own had dipped. No one did that unless they were pretty caught up over someone. That was a lot of effort – it had looked like there were hundreds of the things. But still she had come to his house, and they'd had a great afternoon. Everything about them had just gelled. They had so much in common; it was as if they had known each other a lifetime, and the chemistry building up to that almost-kiss, that had been undeniable, inevitable even. As if it were not just a natural progression of the bond they shared but the only conclusion. Surely she didn't have that sort of a bond with someone else? He knew from experience how hard that was to find.

To be lucky enough to find it with one person was huge. Could she be so lucky that she had found it with two? Woah, there were a lot of assumptions there. Namely that she also felt they had the bond. Hmmm, maybe that's where the flaw lay? She would, of course, produce this reaction in any man – she was perfect. What was lacking, clearly, was her feeling the same about others as she inspired in them. Stupid arrogant man.

But there was mad chemistry between them. When he had leant in and gone for the kiss, he could have sworn that she was about to kiss him too. It hadn't been one-sided, had it? Had he overstepped, is that why she'd left? He didn't think of himself as predatory, but then who did? No, he was pretty sure he wasn't – he was experienced with women and he knew, he did, when attraction was returned and there was no way, just before that kiss, that she wasn't feeling the same way as him. He had seen it in her eyes, her whole face. So if he hadn't offended her with his intention, if she was as keen as he was, then why had she left just because his sister had called?

The obvious answer, staring him in the face, was that she was seeing someone else, and would not allow herself to kiss him. She was attracted to him, he was sure of it, but she was not going to mess around with him. She may at the moment prefer this other mystery man, but he still had a shot. He knew he did. He was going to have to develop a slowly-slowly plan, stop trying to bloody kiss her and let time and charm win her around.

His bag packed, Matt scrawled her a note, explaining that he just needed to go to London to help Angelina out, but perhaps they could catch up when he was back. There, perfect plan, open and clear that he was looking forward to seeing her again but applying no pressure and not forcing her to face him if indeed he had misread the signs and she had felt the need to escape. Smile on his face, he headed down the path to her house, bag swinging from his shoulder, note in hand and Scramble by his heels.

# Chapter Thirteen

As Matt let himself into his sister's flat, the silence rever-
berated off the walls. Where the hell was she? With no
sound of *Gone with the Wind* or snuffling into tissues, he
closed his eyes and threw the door to the living room
open.

Nothing.

Bloody hell!

He marched from room to room – still no sign –
only pausing as he reached the bathroom door. The most
fearful of them all. Aware speed could be important,
admonishing himself for cowardice, heart beating like a
drum and breath coming fast, he threw that door open as
well. Empty, all as it should be.

Flat checked, he began to list the facts, hoping to quiet
his thundering heart, slow his breathing and bring the sick
feeling that was coursing through his body under control.
She wasn't in any of the rooms, not spread out in some
kind of suicide attempt. She was not their mother. She
wouldn't do that to him. Surely?

He hadn't spotted her mobile in any of the rooms, or
an abandoned handbag. This had to be good. Unless…

Racing to the window, anxiety far from dimmed,
he looked to see if she were splayed on the pavement
below, bag over shoulder and phone in hand. As adrenalin

pumped through his body he could feel himself shaking, his feet restless with energy, panic making him pace up and down in short steps as he figured out what his next step was going to be. *Think!*

*Ring someone.* She wasn't in the flat so she must be somewhere else. *Well done, brains of the nation. Who to ring?* Still pacing, he realized he knew none of her circle; they drifted in and then away again. Skimming surfaces, not getting caught in the depths.

Matt stopped pacing and gently smacked his brow – it was Angelina he should ring, not some stranger. If she didn't answer he would be no further forward… more worried, but that was virtually a default setting when it came to dealing with his sister. But if she did, then problem solved. Although, if she had gone out and was somewhere doing whatever it was she did (it seemed to centre around champagne and paparazzi) then he was going to be livid. Absolutely livid.

He sighed heavily, and again, anxiety quickly replaced by a growing anger as he accepted this possibility. She was the most selfish creature he had ever, ever met!

Then an image of her at nine years old popped into his head, her freckles, the curl of her hair on her shoulder and her utter glee when he had brought her home a rabbit, Hollywood, who soon became her most treasured possession. Dear God, he was veering here from fear, to anger, to maudlin nostalgia. Where was Matt the Man?

Matt the Man took control, squared his shoulders and rang his sister. Much more like it.

'Darling!' came her peppy tones as he answered, although they were hard to make out against the *boom boom* of the background noise, 'Oh fuck! You're in

London, aren't you? I completely forgot. You really are too good to me, Mattie.'

*You're not kidding.* Suddenly he pictured those freckles, that curl and his hands around her bloody neck. When would he learn?

'Oh dear, I'm not there. Well, um… you'll just have to come here… oh… hang on…' There was an even longer pause that coincided with Matt's temper building and building. Was she joking? He was going to do more than kill her.

'OK, that's a great idea… I'm at a club at the moment but I can send a car. Oh, darling, I can't wait to see you, you really are a sweetie. Now it shouldn't be more than twenty minutes max, get yourself a drink as a primer and you'll be here in a flash. We're going to have such a great night, it's years since we partied together, I'm so excited! I can't wait to see you! Oh… you can't turn up here looking like a gardener, um… there are some of Andrei's clothes in the spare room, I was going to cut them up, good job I didn't. You can pop those on. See you in a minute. Ooh!' – squeal – 'Mwah mwah!'

He stared at the phone. He wasn't sure but he didn't think he'd actually got to say a word. Not one. What to do now?

He walked towards the drinks cabinet and pulled out a bottle of whisky. Pouring himself a glass, he looked out at the London skyline from the huge windows of Angelina's swish glass-fronted apartment. Knocking it back, he realized that his breathing, his heartbeat had returned to normal.

A laugh, one of those deep, resigned-to-the-inevitable ones, broke the silence as he shook his head and his anger at Angelina subsided. How had he expected any different? She was a monster, but at least she was a monster knocking back champagne in a club with God knows who, rather than lying lifeless in a bath or sobbing hysterically on the sofa. Yes, she was a selfish, irritating, egocentric, narcissistic, self-indulgent trollop who lacked any kind of empathy or concern but she was his sister and she was right, they hadn't spent a night out together in ages.

Bollocks – he was going to do as he was told. He let the whisky slide down his throat, warming all the way to the pit of the stomach. He was here now, he may as well go out and party! He could leave Scramble in Angelina's room, to sleep on her bed, and the door to her shoe cupboard open. After all, his dog had been far better behaved than his sister and deserved a treat – but there was no way he was changing his bloody clothes.

–

As Matt was ushered through the innocuous-looking door into some chic secret club he wondered if he had had a lobotomy somewhere between home and here. Anywhere that flowing booze and barely clad females were gathered had been a haven in his early twenties, but now, now he liked the garden, a cup of tea, watching the smile in Rosy's eyes turn to a great big cheek-to-cheek grin.

Oof! He felt an unexpected weight unbalance him slightly as he was hurtled into at speed by a very drunk little sister. 'Mattie, Mattie… you're here! I love you! Come, come!' She led him to a table, filled with empty champagne bottles, glasses and what looked to be the upended contents of a handbag, where a scantily dressed green-eyed cat lady with sleek black hair and an intimidating gaze sat.

Angelina pulled him onto the banquette and ruffled through the table to find him an empty glass, which she filled to the brim, so much so it was trickling over the top, and pressed it upon him.

'Matt, I'm so glad you're here, we're going to have fun! Fun! Now drink.'

'You are a pain in my arse, I can't believe you got me—'

'Yeah, yeah, drink!' She started to force his elbow up and he knew from experience if he didn't take a big glug it was going to end up all over him. So glug he did. Angelina clapped her hands and squealed some more. The squealing really needed to stop! More alcohol would help that. He raised the glass again, noting approvingly that someone had approached their table and discreetly left a new bottle there for them.

He gave himself up to the uselessness of chastising Angelina. He had no doubt it would all come out in time, so he threw himself into the party spirit instead. Actually it felt good, this was fun, and before he knew it he and Angelina were giggling like children, clutching at each other and talking nonsense.

Then something shifted; she tensed and a flash of the fear he used to see as a child flitted across her face. The woman with them, Siobhan she had said, who was drinking as hard as they were but not laughing quite so much, narrowed her eyes and focused on a man walking towards them, who was accompanied by a stunning redhead. The girl was all quivery and doe-like, possibly no more than eighteen. Matt himself felt something visceral shudder through him; this was not a pleasant man, and yet he exuded a snake-like hypnotic power that captivated Matt.

Angelina grabbed tighter onto his arm. He could feel the pinch of her anxiety through the fabric of his shirt as she started to laugh and flick her hair about. All Matt's hackles started to rise in defence of Ange, and in protection of the young girl accompanying Andrei (he assumed). This man was unpleasant. He sweated nasty.

Andrei paused by the table and nodded at Matt's sister before carrying on, wordless and not waiting for a reply, heading to a table on the other side of the club. A table he could have accessed easily without walking past them.

'Honey,' Matt cooed at Angelina, whose eyes were now darting about, arms clutching her body, 'do you want to get out of here?'

'Absolutely not!' slurred Ange. 'I'm not fussed about him, I'm too good for him, and...'

'Yep, you are.'

'I know, it's just that... just that...'

'Oh shit... Do you need me to hit him?'

'Oh yes, yes, yes... but do you... um... think you could do it outside in front of the people camera things? You know, kill the bastard! On film?'

Matt's instinct to physically protect Angelina by throwing a punch into the smug, snake-like, child-dating face of Andrei dissipated a little.

'Um, probably not, Ange. But... he didn't... did he... hurt you?'

'Yes, he bloody did! Bastard! He... he...' She started to sob. Oh fuck! Matt was going to have to punch him after all, and after the amount of booze Angelina had poured down his throat this evening he wasn't too sure of his aim.

'He told me gold lamé didn't look good on anyone over twenty!' The tears spilt down her face, plopping into and running down the champagne flutes. Hard to see in the dark throb of the club but there nonetheless.

'But did he hit you?' Matt understood emotional and mental trauma but felt she could, should, learn to live with lamé jibe.

'Oh God no! He wouldn't dream of it. I think he has men for that sort of thing. You silly billy!' She stroked his arm and looked up at him adoringly. 'I do love you, Mattie. Oh look! There's Jonny Selby! Amazing abs, you know!' And with the concentration of a springer spaniel in a field full of pheasants she was up and off and shimmying in as sultry a fashion as someone so drunk could manage.

Matt sat back. Nope, he'd never learn. She was a constant nightmare and yet still he couldn't help but smile at her. It was like being cross with a puppy, just pointless.

The Cleopatra girl slid across the banquette beside him.

'Do you want to go for a fag?'

Matt didn't really. A non-smoker these days, he wasn't mad keen on the smell but knew he shouldn't let her hover outside by herself. Although she looked pretty capable of handling herself. Oh bollocks, being pissed and not wanting to walk the length of the club was not a good enough reason not to be a gentleman. Besides which, fresh air, whether he wanted it or not, was probably a good idea.

'I want to talk to you about Angeleenah,' she drawled. Oh, bloody hell!

'Come on then.' He slid off the seating and offered a hand to help her up. She negotiated the furniture and the club, walking just ahead of him, with grace. He bumped into three chairs, stood on one foot and knocked someone's drink. This whole getting older nonsense seemed to have a real effect on the senses. He was sure he hadn't been this clumsy earlier in the day. Dear God, he'd be having to walk around in bubble wrap by forty if this trajectory continued! He carried on pondering this whole aging process thing as he snaked behind Siobhan and headed towards a different door to that which he had entered through.

The air hit him, making him reel and feel as if cartoon *boof*s and *boom*s had appeared all round him. They seemed to be in a street slightly less salubrious than the one where the club entrance was. Here pallets and bins lined the pavements, the smell arising from them penetrating his nostrils and reminding him how glad he was not to be a city dweller any more. The puff of his breath in the darkness under the street lamp clouded the already thick air in front of him.

'Woah.' He rocked a little back and forth on his toes whereas Siobhan was as collected as she had been with all that weaving stuff she had done.

'So you're Angeleenah's brother then? Matthew, she said. Yah?'

'Yah!' Where'd that come from? Since when had he started talking like an eighties Sloane Ranger?

'And you're visiting London because she's terribly upset about Andrei, yah?'

'Yah.'

'I did warn her, I said it's all very well knowing these people but one doesn't sleep with them, for fuck's sake! Yah?'

'Yah.' Matt put his hand out towards the wall, concentrating on just standing there.

'Line? Yah.'

'Yah. Bloody hell. No. No!' Siobhan had handed him a teeny spoon-shaped implement thingy after taking a very professional snort from it herself. 'No, I don't. Never have.'

'Oh yah. Of course. Entirely up to you. Very welcome. Cigarette?'

'No.' He paused and looked around himself in the darkness. 'Oh, do you know what, actually yes. I think I need to.' He accepted a cigarette from her and they stood there in silence for a second as they both inhaled deeply. He hadn't smoked for years and it was disgusting. He wasn't going to smoke for several more after this. But at the same time, just in this drunken moment, it seemed right. Plus he needed to make sense of what was happening here. Somehow after racing from Cornwall where he had been standing in Rosy's garden in a velvet cap a mere twelve hours ago, he was now outside some club in London with a girl he had never met, who had no qualms about offering him drugs and then doing cocaine very openly in front of him and in a public bloody street. And she was friends with his baby sister. He needed to sober up quick and sort this out.

He stomped on the cigarette and took a deep breath of the morning air.

'Thanks. So, Siobhan, you said you wanted to talk to me about Angelina.'

'Yah.'

'Well, what did you want to say?'

'This Andrei, well, he's vile. But Ange seems really really upset. It took me ages to persuade her to come out tonight, and she's just not herself. Yah.'

'How so not herself?'

'Well, normally she's the life and soul of the party, and tonight, well…'

'She looked fairly life and soul to me.' Matt recalled her slinking around on the dance floor, champagne flute aloft as they had left but a few minutes ago.

Siobhan's response was to look at him pityingly. 'Hmmm. No, really, no. And anyhow…' Her voice began to speed up and her arms became quite animated. ' I want to talk to you about you too. Ange talks about you all the time, about how you just don't really understand the need for a profile, yah. I understand that you have this new programme coming up on terrestrial, gardens and that sort of thing. People just love it, don't they? Love it. Don't understand myself but anyway, going to be huge. Simply huge. I was thinking that really you could do with raising your own profile, your own brand beforehand, couldn't you, get you out to lots of parties, be seen with who's important, yah? Lots of public appearances, networking, really really get your face out there, yah. And of course being Angeleenah's brother could be really useful, yah. She can get you in everywhere. Drop some hints, get you in the paper a lot. Maybe you could date Charlene, from *Celebrity Big Brother*, she's huge right now. Huge. Nice girl. As long as you don't talk to her. Dreadful accent. North or something. But very now. People love her, yah. Well, you and her, and then if we could get Angeleenah back with Andrei, I know he's a shit, but it would only be a short time, we could pitch you as the new showbiz family.

It would be huge, huge! What do you think? Perfect. I knew you'd agree, let's go in and I'll tell Angeleenah that you're on board. Yah.'

'Um.' Matt's head was a whirlwind but he was pretty bloody sure that he didn't want to agree with whatever this woman was suggesting. Not in a million years. Rosy's face popped back into his head: her sitting amongst cardboard hearts, simple, unadorned, smiling. Never in his life had he wanted a *Star Trek* transporter as much as he did now. Two actually. One to disappear bloody Siobhan, who was still standing in front of him, gesticulating wildly and planning, plotting and laughing unnecessarily. And one to beam him up, right back home.

## Chapter Fourteen

Matt woke up the next day with a banging head and a fuzzy memory. He tiptoed into Angelina's swish and never-used kitchen and shoved his head under the tap, gulping like a man trapped in the desert. Last night had been crazy. It had been bad enough being launched upon and fighting off Siobhan in the alleyway – for a laid-back yah-yah gal she had remarkably octopus-like tendencies once she stopped talking – but then when he'd headed back into the club he had been shocked to see his sister, who only moments before he'd left had been doing a great impression of a single independent woman, draped over the Russian gangster she had just broken up with and begging, actually begging, to be taken back. When he had intervened, he was taken outside and dropped on his arse by two henchmen, each the size of Colossus, who made no attempt to disguise the fact that they were armed. It was as his bottom hit the littered frosty pavement, in the exact same place he had escaped from Siobhan, that he had decided his sister needed kidnapping. Just not by some criminal oligarch. As he had shivered outside the club, it appeared that the Russian mobster was not interested in having Angelina back and thus it wasn't much longer before she fell out of the front door of the club, dress

120

ripped and make-up smudged. Siobhan was nowhere in sight.

Sticking his head under the tap one last time, he knew he had to hatch a plan to bring Ange home to Cornwall with him, wean her off gangsters and friends with drug problems and try, yet again, to talk about the importance of boundaries and self-respect. The mere thought was making his head thud harder.

'No! No! No! You evil creature! Arrrrgggghhh! How could you?' Angelina was awake.

He heard her bedroom door open and watched as Scramble screeched out, almost skidding across the floor and heading straight for his daddy with the naughtiest grin on his face.

Matt curled down so the dog could jump straight into his arms and protection. Then prepared himself to deal with Angelina's fury, quickly trying to wipe the smile off his face. Maybe he shouldn't have let Scramble have full access to her shoes but perhaps she shouldn't have... well, that list was far too long to contemplate.

Ange came full pelt out of her room, shoe aloft, reminiscent of the mother in *Tom and Jerry*, and for the first time in years Matt saw her hair as less than perfect. He had always wondered if it stayed exactly in place whilst she slept. Apparently not.

'Do you know what that vile, vile beast—'

'I'm sorry, Ange, that may be my fault.'

'Why? Have you been rolling around in my shoe cupboard chewing my Jimmy Choos? Chewing and spitting on not one, not two, but five different shoes! Have you? No, it's that bloody dog's fault! Why did you even bring him? Couldn't you have left him somewhere, you know, like with that dull woman whats-her-face next door? If he had chewed her sensible bloody shoes he'd have been doing the world a favour!'

'Oh, funny you should mention Rosy, because guess who I was with when you summoned me to London? Where I rushed to with said dog, straight away, may I remind you.'

'Dear God! I don't actually want to talk about her right now! Urgghhh.' Angelina made gagging noises, about as attractively as she was wearing her hair.

'What is wrong with you? Why are you so mean about her?'

'Woof!' Brave now he was in his dad's arms, Scramble also objected.

'Really? I'm heartbroken and your dog' – she shot Scramble a warning look – 'has just trashed over two thousand pounds' worth of shoes and you want to talk about her! You could do so much better than mousey-bloody-moo. I know for a fact Siobhan has a massive crush, and family money…'

Matt's eyes grew huge – where to start?

His sister hadn't finished. 'Now, are you going to put that dog down so I can beat him as he deserves? Five pairs of shoes, Matt!'

'Woof!'

'What do you think? You're not touching my dog! I'm about to take him out to lift his leg and then we can go for breakfast. Can you be ready in ten minutes?'

'Oh God! You know nothing about women, do you. Go on, take your dog and get out. Go eat heart disease on a plate – you can bring me back a soy latte and a mango.

Go. Go on, and make sure that mutt's teeth are removed before you bring him back in!'

–

Matt swallowed the last morsel of black pudding, fed a smidgen of sausage to Scramble and picked up his phone to call Susie. Angelina had very sensibly insisted upon Susie when he was initially offered the presenting job at Penmenna, and he had been touched at the time that his baby sister was so fierce about protecting his interests. That feeling had dimmed fairly rapidly. However, Susie had proved invaluable and was about to help him with his primary job for today. Plus, he knew this call would make his agent very happy.

He had two problems to solve this morning. The first was getting Angelina to Cornwall, but he figured that could easily be sorted by using her number one skill against her: manipulation. Rational debate was pointless. If he dropped some hints about Tom Hardy filming down the road in Roscombe, she'd be packed and at Paddington before he could put Scramble on a lead. The other job at the top of his to-do list, the one he was tackling now, was trickier but manageable. He had the perfect leverage, and what was a little personal embarrassment to help a whole community? He took a deep breath to prepare himself, and just in time.

'Darling! I didn't expect to hear from you today, not after Friday's call. Is everything OK? How are the wilds of Cornwall?'

'Wild. However, Susie, that's not why I'm ringing. I want to discuss some changes to the format of *Green-fingered and Gorgeous.*'

'Eh? You put the kibosh on that name that you're throwing about so freely.'

'Yes, that's because it's ridiculous. But I'm prepared to negotiate. You can let the production company know I'll roll over on the name if they include this new segment idea I have, and allow me complete control over it.'

Ten minutes later, Matt sat back in his chair, read the confirmation email from Susie and beamed from ear to ear. Take that, Edward Grant! #SaveOurSchool.

# Chapter Fifteen

Rosy drove to work on Monday scared that the whole Matt thing was going to distract her from her main focus. He kept popping into her head at the oddest moments.

All that curly-haired boy-next-door charm was a lethal mix, and one she had no intention of being seduced by. They both clearly fancied the pants off each other, and if she didn't stand firm there was only one way that was going. Judging by her diminished strength (both legs and backbone) around him, he was her kryptonite, so she would have to reduce his potency by ceasing all contact. She was not a home-wrecker; neither would she make a fool of herself in a village she was so happy in. Although if they lost the school maybe she could risk a kiss.

No! No, no, no, no.

School was the focus, her only focus, and that, she had a feeling, was going to be crazy. The building lay in front of her, Victorian and built out of the granite that played such a role in the Cornish landscape, with its two separate entrances that were the norm at the time it was built, when girls and boys were segregated. She smiled as she walked into the historic building. It had been a school for over one hundred and fifty years, standing firm through fire and flood, world wars and massive social change; she was damn sure she wasn't going to let Edward Grant and his cost-cutting ruin that now. But she would have to assemble a crack team. She needed people who were good at playing the system, networking and then exploiting those contacts. People who liked responsibility, enjoyed a battle and winning. She needed someone who could motivate and mobilize the parents whilst ensuring it didn't become too militant.

Luckily, she had the perfect person. She couldn't help but smile as her eyes alighted on Marion Marksharp scurrying across the hall, shouting at other less alpha mothers about the correct placement of bunting. Angles were, apparently, of paramount importance for a Valentine's disco. That woman was like a terrier with a rat; there was no escape.

She was perfect.

'Marion, Marion!' Rosy called across the hall. 'That quick catch-up I mentioned on Friday, is now a good time?'

Rosy walked back to her office watching the children as they streamed into school, bags and hair flying around them, the clatter of lunch boxes and high-pitched chatter. Peering through windows she saw them start their pre-register activities: the little ones making fizzy rockets, finger painting and singing about five little ducks; the older ones reading, solving maths problems or putting the finishing touches to their papier-mâché Roman senate.

She knew then that nothing else really mattered to her.

She was going to make the most of this opportunity to ensure the Local Authority realized once and for all that this school was the heartbeat of this village, that these children with their eager faces and naughty smiles needed the security it provided, of walking home with their friends, cutting across the churchyard and piling into the village shop. The security of learning about their community, the farms surrounding them and the beach on their doorstep, not the town some ten miles away with little connection to them, their families and their neighbours.

She felt infused with a feeling of hope, of a purpose. This was something to get her teeth into. This was important. And Rosy recognized that the best person to help alongside her was that neurotic tyrant of a woman, Mrs Marksharp – currently quivering in her doorway with a sense of purpose that would have awed Joan of Arc.

Marion came and settled herself into the chair in Rosy's office, fixing her with that stare and launching straight into things.

'I assume I'm here because Edward Grant wants to close the school...'

'*Possibly* close the school.'

'Quite. There are rumours flying around the playground and they are getting louder, gathering momentum. I have of course done all I can to rein them in, but we will need to address the truth sooner rather than later. And I can't help much more until you tell me the full story, then I can shape the narrative and practise damage limitation. At the moment there are whispers of home educating and online petitions and whilst we need to drum up a campaign of support, on viral levels, we need to be careful as to how we pitch it. Whatever happens we cannot have Harmony involved – she'll have them burning bras and waving sticks at the moon. We'd become a laughing stock. Oh, or Amanda, we'd all be goose-stepping outside County Hall before the week was out.'

'Marion, I think that that's—'

'We need to be approachable, friendly but organized, with a backbone of steel. Luckily I'm skilled at all these things. Obviously, you'll be our campaigns figurehead but I'll be…'

*Goebbels? Don't say it!*

'…in charge of the day-to-day organizing, the running of it. Are you happy with that? Excellent. Now, as you know, I do have my ear to the ground, and I've also heard that Angelina is a new member of the village. Pretty girl. Surely she'll want to be involved. Perhaps you could talk to her? I understand they've moved in next to you.'

Villages… you couldn't breathe in a different manner without someone noticing. And how did everyone know of Angelina except her? Trust Marion to home in on the one woman Rosy would have preferred not to work with. Rosy felt her teeth slide over the top of her lip as she swallowed, a little quicker, a little deeper than usual. This was fine, this was village life. Save the school. Be professional.

'I'm afraid that whilst it is a great idea, I think she is back in London for the time being.' That was the truth, after all.

'But that doesn't mean she won't be back.'

'True, I think the village is her Cornish base as such, but you know how the holiday home situation is down here. I can ask Matt if he can ask her to help, but she's pretty busy from what I gather.' Rosy didn't add that someone who kicks small dogs was unlikely to have any strong desire to help children, but felt it was more politic to keep quiet. Maybe she was learning after all.

'OK, if that's how it is. Hmmm. We can leave it for now, maybe revisit it later. Right then, let's get started! From what I understand from my contacts in County Hall, Edward Grant is tasked with shutting down six village schools in the mid county area – purely for budgetary reasons. He will do it. He is a very ambitious man who enjoys his work. I wouldn't be surprised if he attempts to shut more than necessary. Rosy, I will not see Penmenna School closed, but we are going to need to fight.'

'Marion, I'm going to give it my best shot. There's no way I won't fight for the kids in this school – of course I am. They need this school. Most might survive a transfer and a crazy long bus journey in the morning, but for a couple of them, it could mean the end of a chance of mainstream education and that's so many different types of wrong that I don't know where to begin. But politics, the ins and outs of local government, that game I'm not experienced at playing, let alone winning.'

'Well, luckily, like I said, you can carry on running the school superbly and leave winning the political campaign to me. As it happens I am very good at that sort of thing. Really very good.'

'So, what do we need to do? What's the first step?'

'Knowing Mr Grant's weaknesses.'

'And they are?'

'From what I can see, ego and celebrity. We weaken him by publicly, very publicly, strengthening ourselves and securing the school into a politically unclosable position.'

'OK, that sounds great, but how? How on earth do we do that?'

'We concentrate on our strengths, and we have many; we make sure the whole world knows them too. Our Ofsted reports, for example, let's use that to our advantage. Why close an outstanding school? Then let's look at what makes us outstanding. We have quite a lot of special-needs children on the roll, don't we? You have done wonders boosting the school's reputation in that area since you joined. Don't you have that boy in your class? Let's flag these kids up.'

'Yes, I have Bradley in my class – he's waiting on an ASD diagnosis and has lots of input from external professionals. Katie Holden, the educational psychologist, is due in to see him in a few weeks...'

'Oh, is she that blonde that looks like she'd be more at home wearing hot pants in front of a whirring fan than in a suit and in a primary school? Fabulous for television, let's have her!'

'If you mean the blonde with the PhD and an utter commitment to the welfare of the children in her care, then yes, her. As I said, she's due in soon to check on Bradley and see how he's coping since he started full-time. She would probably be happy to submit a report saying that a move would be detrimental, but I'd have to ask. She sees several of the children here so would be able to include an impact statement for a few of them.'

'OK, that's a great start. Now, seeing as we're talking visuals...'

Rosy thought they had been talking special needs, but then she supposed this was the politics bit.

'Is there any chance we can get that Bradley child to play up in front of the cameras? You know, have some kind of meltdown?'

Rosy's eyebrows shot through her hairline, expressing how offensive this was, and at complete odds with all that Penmenna stood for. But then, bearing in mind it was Marion and subtle never seemed to work, she vocalized her outrage, in her strictest voice just to make sure.

'Bradley doesn't have "meltdowns", Marion. He can struggle with social interactions, situations he doesn't understand, and it's our job to support him, to teach him tools to help him, not to exacerbate him, in any way, ever.'

'Right, understood, sorry. But it's a pity we don't have more disabled children. I don't suppose you'd be prepared to pop a couple in a wheelchair? Just for photos for social media, and television if I can get them involved. Rufus could do it, although it would be better if the children picked looked a little... um, I don't know... poorer.'

'No.'

'Really? It would be very visually effective.'

'No.'

Three hours later and Rosy was feeling breathless. Marion had idea after idea after idea. All of which were accompanied by plans of action covering implementation, continuation and expected conclusion. Rosy had tentatively raised her belief that the schools on the list were selected for personal reasons rather than professional ones, and Marion had wisely reconfirmed that evidence would be needed before action could be taken. She'd also suggested that when such evidence was collected it may be best to take it through the back channels and deal with it that way so that the attack was double-pronged, both by raising the school's public profile sky high as well as pointing out the potential illegality that Edward Grant could arguably be involved in. So far, both Mrs Pascoe and

Mrs Trewithen had confirmed what she suspected and the absence of St Ewer on the list, a school widely known to be failing, located just on the outskirts of Roscarrock but with a man at the helm, indicated that Rosy may well be correct and that Edward Grant's outdated and illegal views on women in leadership positions was in play here. But due diligence was a necessity before making an accusation which, if proved incorrect, would be slanderous.

Marion's plans for raising the school's profile meant that the local newspapers were going to need a dedicated hotline at this rate, and the plans she had for social media were nothing short of frightening. The school's name would soon be known by everyone in the county. Rosy was quite surprised that Mrs Marksharp didn't clasp her hand to her bosom, rise and start singing the national anthem at one point. She was almost beginning to feel sorry for Mr Grant. Yet still Marion wasn't satisfied.

'OK, we'll get the disco out of the way and in the meantime we'll just have to put our thinking caps on. If your theory proves correct that could do it, but either way I can't help feel we need something bigger. Rosy...' Marion clasped the headteacher's hand and stared deep into her eyes. Rosy wished she could just shrink like Mrs Pepperpot and scamper out the classroom and escape whatever was coming next. But no, magic minimization didn't suddenly occur even with all the power of positive thought. 'Rosy, together we can do this, together we're women of steel. We shall save Penmenna!'

Phew, that wasn't too bad. At least she hadn't tried to make Rosy sell a kidney and stream it online. Yet.

# Chapter Sixteen

Matt was turning to drink. It was Wednesday evening, and he was currently standing at the buffet of the Great Western train wondering how much he could down in five minutes without giving an outward appearance of being utterly sozzled. He could have stayed in first class with Angelina but the need for a break was compelling and, whilst not doubting the correctness of his decision to temporarily move her to Cornwall, the maintenance of his sanity was very definitely under question.

Despite all her bravado, being ejected from the club and rejected by Andrei had hit her hard. After he had returned from his beautifully artery-clogging breakfast the other day, he'd found she had finished ranting about Scramble and her overpriced shoes and had sunk right back into sobbing and claiming that she had failed at life.

He had fed her soup, let her sob, watched *Gone with the Wind* after all and secretly booked two train tickets home for today. He had considered doping her morning tea prior to the train journey with any one of the array of pharmaceutical options he had found in her bathroom cupboard but the involuntary shiver he had had whilst looking at them reaffirmed how he could never be comfortable with such an act, even if it would make things easier. He was fairly sure a man such as Andrei Sokolov would have no such scruples.

He didn't, however, have any problem with feeding her a little white lie about the latest big budget production being filmed near Penmenna Beach. He may not actually be able to secure her a spot on set but he had enough faith in her own abilities to slide herself in should she wish. And she did wish. The minute he had dropped hints about the presence of Hollywood's new big thing – a man who smouldered sex so powerfully through a screen that Matt even found himself hypnotized – Ange was racing to her room. It turned out that getting her to pack to leave London was a cinch, no bathroom cupboard needed. Getting her to limit herself to bags they could comfortably carry, not so much.

Knocking back a whisky, he decided that instead of fretting about his sister, he would instead try to concentrate on calm images; images and daydreams that made him happy. So automatically he summoned a mental picture of Rosy presenting him with all the love hearts that had been on her floor as she fell into his bulging muscular arms, panting that she was a fool not to have realized that he was the only one for her. Her eyelids would flutter with adoration and overwhelming sexual desire as he clasped her to his chest and—

'Sir… sir. Sir, your sister is calling for you, it really seems quite urgent, and unfortunately it is somewhat disturbing the other passengers. Perhaps if you could come this way I could organize your refreshments for you.' The green-jacketed train conductor looked frazzled and Matt couldn't simply ignore him. Or push him out of the train door. Maybe these fantasies of Rosy were no good after all, clearly driving him to murderous thoughts. Besides, it was far more probable that she'd be throwing the cardboard hearts at him and telling him to do up his top button!

'Sir! I really must insist.'

'Yes, yes, I'm sorry.' He smiled at the man by his side. 'I'm coming now. I was in a daydream. Is she making a dreadful fuss?' His brow furrowed. Why did he even ask these questions?

The man gulped, clearly torn between saying that she was a gigantic pain and being professional. A shriek from two carriages down pierced all conversations in range. Matt patted the man's shoulder and released a deep sigh.

–

Matt gulped down his orange juice and quickly rinsed the glass. He had not slept well last night, despite being back in his own bed. He had been plagued with dreams about Rosy, but not the sort he had indulged in on the train. He kept losing her, catching sight and losing her again. She seemed to be waiting for him, then, just as he got close, running away, towards someone ill-defined. Everything in the dream was intangible, misty and just outside his grasp. There had been mazes full of Tudor magicians morphing into fog-hidden cliff edges and cold, murky, lurky swamplands. He had not woken up feeling rested.

Yawning, he glanced at his watch and realized half the morning had gone. He had so much to do today. The time in London meant things were piling up and he had a heap of practical changes he would need to make in the gardens now that the production company were happy to go ahead with the new format for *Green-fingered and Gorgeous*. Pulling his wellies on, he shuddered at the new name. Pushing his arms through his coat sleeves, he smiled at the greater good. He had structural changes to implement and oversee in the gardens, and secret projects – one to finish before tomorrow and one to instigate for later – that needed his presence. He glanced up the stairs where he could hear his sister beginning to move and considered making her coffee before he left, but as the clock chimed in the hall he called for Scramble and headed to his car.

Walking down the pathway, Matt couldn't help but glance over the little dividing wall at Rosy's cottage. All neat and perfect and missing her car. She would already be at work; Rosy would be surrounded by children, doing good and generally brightening the world with her simple charm and kind nature. She might be in the middle of the biggest fight of her life but she just seemed to bring calm to all those around her. He had never known anyone do that before.

Smiling, he opened the car door for Scramble to jump in, and reversed down the drive, narrowly missing a determined-looking woman, thin as a rake, make-up trowelled onto her face and clutching a bottle of champagne.

# Chapter Seventeen

Rosy had had a successful few days at school since she'd broken the news to her colleagues, and was gratified to find that the staff were determined to support her in the mission to save the school. It was a rare moment of unity and one she hadn't really experienced before. Following the meeting on Friday, everyone had come into school at the start of the week and put their apathy and their agendas to one side and resolved to work together. She knew that it was going to take more than staff unity and the awesome powers of Marion; they were going to need one grand gesture, something that would really hammer their message home – the value of a village school over a geographically distant mega-beast. She just didn't know what that gesture was going to be yet.

Valentine's Day was looming and parents were teeming all over the school, pulling bunting out of cupboards, dripping glitter hearts and stealing all the wall-staplers. The PTA was akin to a military unit. A unit with an extremely capable leader. A leader who had been canvassing the ranks since the news of potential school closure had been made official in the school newsletter at the start of this week. A leader, Rosy realized, that she hadn't actually seen, or even heard, all day – which was most unusual considering the level of activity. Hmm. However, Rosy had been besieged by parents either popping their heads around her door or stroking her arm as she walked past, their eyes wide with hope, heads nodding and sympathy flowing. All saying things like 'we believe in you' and 'if anyone can save us…' No pressure then!

Plans were all in place to promote the school and all the great things they did. Rosy had reinjected some fire into their social media pages, and had planned to have traditional media, the local newspaper, present at the dance tomorrow. If she could get the message out there that the school was a vibrant hub of community and excellence, that would be an easy start in turning things around, whilst she tackled any areas of the school that needed strengthening a little more discreetly. She knew where the weaknesses were – everyone always did in a school – it was now her job to gently encourage those members of staff who needed to raise their game, a lot, and quickly. Not easy but compared to keeping Matt out of her head, a doddle.

She literally felt her heart dip into her tummy. If she could succeed at school where things were topsy-turvy, then she could cope with one inappropriate crush at home. The house next door had been quiet since their Sunday lunch there but last night she had heard the cottage whirr and buzz as they did when they were occupied. Knowing Matt and Angelina were both home again made it easier, in theory, to shut down any improper thoughts she may be having about her neighbour. It reinforced his relationship status and how he was morally out of bounds. But, at the same time, she couldn't escape the awareness that he was there, just there, a wall away.

Rosy gathered some resources together for the maths assessment she was doing this afternoon, ordering brightly coloured plastic counting bears, blocks and fruit onto a table in front of her. That was it! She could manage Matt and Angelina's presence by having a lesson plan for her evenings, even carry out a risk assessment for potential trouble spots. If she did this every night, just for a short while, then she could train her brain not to respond to their presence, not to think about him coming home from work and jumping into the shower and… oh, for goodness' sake!

Her lesson plan for tonight would be simple: she would cook dinner, with extra left over for tomorrow – disco night! She would be kept busy for some time in the kitchen, cutting, scraping, steaming, frying, which she could do whilst juggling some of Marion's more extreme suggestions in her head. After supper she could have a long bath and make a start on that book Lynne had lent her. In fact, if she had a glass of wine at supper and another in the bath, she was almost guaranteed to fall asleep nice and early, lesson plan complete and next door avoided. Perfect.

She looked up as the children began to pile into the classroom from their lunch playtime. Billy was bowling in with a silly walk and daft expression on his face, lips pulled back and teeth bared comically. Chloe came in squabbling with her friends about the best way to hold a kitten – because she had a kitten and knew everything in the world, ever, that there was to know about kittens and other people who had cats didn't know about kittens at all! Bradley followed in last of all, accompanied by Jack, with whom he was very slowly beginning to develop a quiet friendship. Rosy couldn't help but grin a welcome at them; there was nothing better to take her mind off a man than trying to corral this lot into order and teach them some maths.

–

That evening she arrived home and immediately noticed that all the lights in next door's cottage were out. She felt her shoulders relax a little as she headed into the kitchen, popped the kettle on and sat in her favourite chair. She kicked her shoes off and allowed herself to close her eyes and loll her head as she waited for the water to boil. Lovely.

But Rosy's ears kept pricking up with every car that passed, every clatter on the street. Even with a cup of tea made, a slice of lemon drizzle and a quick episode of her favourite show, the knots in her shoulders were still hovering. Instead of fully loosening up, she felt as if she were waiting for the door to burst open and an accusation from Angelina or a demand from Matt to be hurled at her, probably in tandem.

As she pottered around the kitchen the relief at having her evening mapped out turned into irritation. What was wrong with her? Why on earth did she do this to herself? Why was this teenage version of her taking control? She hadn't done anything wrong; yes, she may have a bit of a crush on Matt but she hadn't actually done anything about it. There were no accusations for Angelina to hurl. And why would Matt turn up and make demands? Was it really time to say it again?

Matt.

Was.

Not.

Josh.

She needed to boot insecure, anxiety-prone teenage Rosy back into her box and let adult, controlled Rosy back out. And preferably before dinner.

A door slammed next door and a frisson shot up her back. She gave the sauce another stir and a glimmer of a smile played at the edges of her mouth. There was a flush of pleasure at the thought of the two of them standing side by side preparing their suppers and settling down for a relaxing night in with only that wall between them. She remembered the roast and his silly sense of humour and allowed her smile to fully develop. He was lovely. Oh, and that daft hat and instrument, and the way he had lent her his jacket on the walk home that very first Sunday. Oh, and how he loved Lou Reed as much as she did. And the way his shirts were rumpled, as if someone had tried to iron them but didn't have a clue how. And that daft dog!

He wasn't a threat. Yes, he was flirtatious but he wasn't a threat. He hadn't tried to take over her whole life, to control her, to hide her away, to ruin her. How had she let herself get so riled up over this just because he was her neighbour? She pictured him tilting his head and looking at her with that quizzical amused look he'd had the day they met.

'That doesn't give you permission to now jump in there and have occupancy,' she said out loud to the image in her mind. Not that she was mad or anything. It was just that speaking out loud when she needed to tell herself off made it more real somehow. Gave it a bit of welly. She couldn't help but giggle as the image of him raised both his eyebrows and nodded slowly, as perhaps you would with someone a little slower than yourself.

'Ange! Angelina!' she heard him calling through the wall, and as she did so the twinkling image popped out of her mind. 'Ange!'

And that was why he wasn't allowed in her head. There was a timely reminder!

The lesson plan clearly hadn't worked; she needed to approach this differently. Glad that her one sharp talk to herself had taken the edge off the fear, now she just needed to concentrate on the lust. Perhaps if she made herself a star chart? What could her reward be? No! She reprimanded herself as her brain quickly flashed an idea at her – that was not appropriate for the problem in hand. Not at all!

–

She heard him enter the garden, which was a coincidence because although she was trying to get him out of her mind she was just about to go and feed the birds. Honestly, she was! She rifled through a couple of drawers before she found the peanuts, and smugly opened her own back door only to hear him mutter a couple of her own favourite words under his breath.

'Hey, good evening,' she called through the fence. There was no harm being neighbourly.

'Oh hey, Rosy. Is that you?' came the upbeat tone back.

'Yep, just topping up the birds.'

'Oh, that's good. More people should do that. You are good.'

She smiled. She was. Should she invite him over for a slice of cake? Oh, for goodness' sake, that had taken all of two seconds. Have some self-control, girl!

'Hmm, not always.' Oh, and bloody hell, that was meant to be truthful self-deprecating judgement, not flirty! Maybe she should just jump over the fence in nothing but a G-string and make a complete fool of herself, just get it all over and done with and out of the way quick.

'Really?' It was hard to tell if he was being sarcastic or interested. *Doesn't matter*, she told herself, *just be grateful he didn't respond with some icky comment about promises or some such nonsense. Lucky escape.*

Rosy spotted a little mound of mud near the fence. That was odd. Could she have moles? She remembered them from her mother's garden, neat, sifted piles of earth appearing overnight on the lawn. Perhaps she had a beginner mole who had made a wrong turn and banged his head on her fence.

Smiling, she headed towards the fence to investigate and started the conversation afresh.

'Hmmm. How are you, anyway?' She wasn't sure she'd ever had a conversation through a fence before, it felt a little bizarre. Very *Pyramus and Thisbe*. Well, maybe not quite, but still.

'Yeah, good. No, actually a bit stressed. I've come home and bloody Angelina has disappeared, not a sign of her.'

What? Was she not supposed to leave or something? This was an interesting insight into his psyche. Dear God, had her subconscious been right all along? Clearly not a lovely twinkly-eyed gardener after all, but some kind of girlfriend-imprisoning control freak. Had she recognized this on some deep level despite his exquisite surface game? She had been through this. And yet again it needed repeating. Matt was not Josh. Hear him out, then examine the evidence and draw a conclusion. Stop always leaping to the worst-case scenario. But despite her inner rationalizing, Rosy remained rooted to the ground, frozen, as something began moving by the fence. Her concern didn't seem to reach Matt; indeed her silence seemed to encourage him.

'Seriously, she was told not to go out and now I come home and poof, nothing! She never does what she's bloody told! Never. You'd think I would have learnt by now!'

*Woah! OK. Imprint this on your brain and remember. Imprint now!*

'And what's really weird, I mean *really* weird, Rosy...'

Really? This wasn't enough for him? 'Go on.'

'Someone's been here, I know it's a bit *Columbo* but there are two empty glasses here, both covered with lipstick, and she doesn't have any friends here, not that I know... oh bloody hell...'

Rosy's concerns about Matt and Angelina vanished, spiralling into the night sky as the confused baby 'mole' emerged from the pile of mud by the fence and bowled straight into her arms, licking her face and wagging his naughty Scramble tail.

# Chapter Eighteen

Despite her overwhelming workload, her strict intent not to engage and the recent discovery that Matt didn't like letting Angelina out of the house, Rosy found herself with his dog in her arms, knocking on his door.

As she waited for him to answer, Scramble squirming against her, she considered whether she needed to reconsider her judgements. Maybe instead of disliking Perfect Hair she should feel a bit sorry for her. Was Matt that type of man that liked a vacuous celebrity girlfriend for the prestige, the power it gave him? Did he like his women scantily clad and stripped of control? That just didn't make sense, it didn't sit right, regardless of this new evidence.

Matt answered the door with a grin as wide as the Nile, reaching for Scramble and shaking his head. As usual, the sheer physicality of his presence made Rosy breathe deep. When had she become so shallow? Was she really thinking of throwing out The Rule for a pretty face and tummy flips? No, pretty was the wrong word, but those jeans, all muddy and really quite tight! His arms, patterned by dark unruly hair and the definition that physical work brought them. She would do anything to run a finger down them and then they, in turn, they led to his hands…

'Rosy, hello in person. I thought you were still in the garden. I've been chattering away to you and instead you were on the doorstep. You'd better come in. Although you' – he pointed at Scramble, already pulling out of his arms – 'you are a disgrace!'

Thank God for that, he hadn't picked up on her silent lust-filled staring as he opened the door. She stared a little longer. This was all such a puzzle – he really didn't emanate menace in any form. The only vibe he chucked out in buckets was irresistible all-round good guy.

'Thanks, I was in the garden, and then before I knew it your pickle of a dog was in my arms! I did toy with kidnapping him but decided even I couldn't handle his level of naughty.'

Matt's face crinkled as he gave up the fight and placed Scramble on the hallway floor where he scampered kitchen-wards. 'We used to say that about Ange when she was little – that any kidnapper would kick her out the car after three minutes.' He laughed at the memory.

'When Angelina was little?' Rosy queried. 'Have you known her forever then?' That would certainly explain the bond that led to their relationship. Of course he wasn't into inane celebrity. She was an idiot.

Matt looked directly at her, eyebrow raised. 'Rosy, she's my sister! Why else would I put up with her nonsense?' He laughed again. 'Now you're here, though, do you fancy playing detective?'

His sister? His sister. He wasn't in a relationship – she was his sister!

'Rosy?' He wasn't giving her any time to process this, and she was not prepared to make more of a fool of herself than she already had.

'Yes, detective, let's do that. Show me these lipstick-covered glasses, you can be my Watson.' She tried to keep her voice as close to normal as possible.

'Oh, well, I always rather fancied Moriarty myself. Not fancied, um… wanted to be.'

*Oh, cute! See, he stumbled just like me.*

Her other voice kicked in. *Cute! He wants to model himself on an arch villain who has killed countless people!* A third, louder, triumphant voice piped up – *she's his sister!*

*Oh, shut up, head!*

'You wanted to be the baddy?'

'He's super clever, super cool and baddies have so much fun. Anyway, you told me only a minute ago in the garden that you weren't such a good girl.'

Great, trust him to remember that. Rosy tried not to look at him, but the frisson between the two of them standing so close in the narrow hallway was palpable. More than palpable – loud and booming. Bordering on sonic.

'Let's see these glasses then, Columbo-Moriarty-whoever you are.' Rosy smiled up at him. It felt fake but she needed to get out of this hallway; another room may be less suffocating. And movement would break the mood.

'Come on then.' He smiled and she relaxed. There, just friendly; she was imagining all this sexual chemistry nonsense. Clearly she was just a bit desperate. The revelation that Angelina was his sister had knocked her – combine that with the fact that it had been a bit too long meant that she was picturing what wasn't here. She needed to get a grip of herself. Maybe log back into her dating account when she got home.

She followed him through into the kitchen where he produced the two glasses with a flourish. And indicated the two empty bottles of champagne next to them. She looked closely and took one from him. The shade was reminiscent of someone, she just couldn't think who. *Come on, brain.*

'It might be nothing…' Matt had come and stood right by her elbow, examining the glass as she twirled it in the air, her brow furrowed. 'But it did occur to me that there was a woman who looked like she might be coming to the house this morning. Blonde hair, lots of make-up, some kind of birds on her dress. But what she'd want with Ange baffles me.'

'Birds on her dress? That's impressive detail.'

'They were lime green.'

'Oh my God! Blonde? Looked a bit like she could snap at any moment?'

'Ha, yes I guess so. Why, do you know who it could be? Sherlock, have you surpassed yourself?'

'I may well have done, Watson, I may well have done. I think Angelina is with Marion. She wasn't in school today and I'm sure I saw her boys being hustled out of school by one of her minions. I knew I recognized that shade of lipstick. Yes, it all makes sense. Angelina must be with Marion.'

'Well, do I need to worry? Who is this Marion? What does she want with my sister?'

His sister! Rosy shook her head. That was insane, and yet so obvious now.

'Oh my God, why are you shaking your head? I'm serious. Ange is really vulnerable at the moment. Who is this Marion?'

'Hey, it's all good. She's not going to come to any harm with her. Marion is the head of the PTA and my rather unlikely ally in the Save Our School fight. By the looks of it they've got super pissed, hatched up some evil plan – sorry, not that Angeli— not evil, um, fun plan that involves more drinking and securing world domination. They'll be together and having a lovely time. Trust me. I think we can both stop worrying. Maybe treat ourselves to a drink as well and put our feet up until Marion brings her home?'

'Do you reckon?' Matt's shoulders relaxed. 'Do you think this is what having kids is like?'

'I really hope not. Tell you what, why don't we both give them a ring if you're still worried and see what they're up to.' Rosy felt saintly. The last thing she wanted to do was engage with Marion this evening – her bath and book were deeply preferable – but that was clearly what Matt wanted to do. And she didn't like seeing him worried, although that little furrow on his brow was kind of endearing.

'Yeah, OK, maybe I should do that. I'm not normally this, well, this wussy but Ange, she needs keeping an eye on.' He shrugged his shoulders in a helpless gesture and again Rosy couldn't control her face as it broke into a sympathetic smile. Maybe her judgement wasn't so off; he wasn't a nutty control-freak like Josh – he just cared about his sister and wasn't afraid to express it. That's how relationships should be.

Matt pulled his phone out of his pocket, tapped it a couple of times and they both stood close, listening to it ring out.

'Voicemail.'

'That's fairly meaningless down here. It could mean her battery is dead, but more than likely means she has no signal, which is pretty common. In terms of phone service we're still stuck somewhere in the mid–nineties, but it can be a bonus.' She felt the smile creep onto her face. She had frequently used the no or patchy signal excuse when speaking (or not) to her mother. 'But obviously not right now. Um, tell you what, I'll try Marion, just in case. Seriously, sometimes it can be so poor that one person at a table can receive a call but not the person sitting across from them. It happens all the time.'

She managed to compose her features back into concerned mode and pulled her own phone out of her pocket. She didn't like seeing anyone perturbed, especially when she could do something small to help. Even so, she couldn't believe she was actually trying to track down Marion and Perfect Hair. She deserved canonization for this!

'Sorry, voicemail too. Look, they'll be fine, really. They'll be having fun. I was cooking supper, just pasta, but instead of staying here fretting why don't you come share it with me? I do owe you a dinner, and now is as good a time as any. What do you think?'

Matt looked back at her and smiled, although in that smile she could see a hundred emotions flit across his face. One of which was a definite 'fuck it, why not?' That was something she could identify with; in fact it was one of her own favourites. Particularly in reference to cake, and clothes shopping.

'And I've got lemon drizzle.' She sealed the deal. There was no way he was going to resist cake, that much she knew. Within seconds they were on her doorstep.

# Chapter Nineteen

The enticing smell of garlic and oregano in the pasta sauce hit Matt the second Rosy opened the door to her cottage. Which was great because he was really hungry, really liked food and was mad keen on spending more time with her. The fact that whenever there was the potential to make some kind of romantic move she spooked and fled was of concern but not a problem that couldn't be sorted. And in the meantime there was pasta.

Scramble settled on the sofa at once and Matt followed her through to the kitchen, secretly thanking him and his wayward sister, who, albeit entirely unintentionally, had secured yet more time for him with his sexy next-door neighbour. He had been so worried when he'd got home, but with the fact revealed that she hadn't run off alone and that Rosy had categorically identified her companion meant that harm was unlikely to befall her. It also meant that he had the evening off and that he got to spend some of it here. Bonus!

He needed the evening off. The pressure of the last few days – from jumping on the train, getting thrown out of a nightclub and dragging Angelina back to Cornwall – was immense. It was no surprise that his head felt like exploding and that the large bowl of pasta that was currently being popped before him, and accompanied by that smile, felt like the best thing that had happened in ages. On top of which he had some news of his own to deliver. Although when he had first devised his idea it had seemed genius, now it came time to share it he was suddenly nervous. What if she didn't throw her arms around him and thank him? What if she felt it was inappropriate and interfering? Perhaps he should just watch for the opportunity to bring it up, quietly and without fanfare and in the meantime switch his mind back to spaghetti and that smile.

They were certainly the best things that had happened since Sunday lunch. There was a theme developing that he was not unaware of. Indeed, was acutely aware of, as she finally came and sat with him, accompanied by Parmesan and grater. How great would this life be every day? Was there anything she wasn't good at?

Scramble's snores came from the other room. He was wiped out from a busy day at Penmenna Hall. Normally the smell of food would have him sitting at Matt's feet, grinning his most winsome doggy grin – but not tonight.

'This is amazing, thanks, Rosy. I can't tell you how timely this is or how much I need it.'

'Rough few days?' she asked, leaning over him and grating cheese. 'Tell me when.'

'When.' The smell of her reminded him of those penny chews, Fruit Salads, that had always been his favourite. Then his gardener's nose kicked in and he could identify rose, rhubarb and a hint of something else. It would come to him later, he knew it. She smelt delicious and, like every part of her, this scent appealed to the child and the adult within him.

She plopped back into her chair and smiled broadly at him.

'So, what's been happening?'

'I couldn't make it up if I told you. But since I saw you on Sunday, I've been beaten up by the Russian mafia, and thrown, actually thrown out of a club. I tell you my arse is still sore – pavements are hard! On top of that I was offered cocaine, which I didn't accept by the way, in a grimy alleyway by a rather frightening woman. Although not in that order. How about you?'

He couldn't help but grin at the way neither shock nor judgement flashed across her face but instead Rosy erupted in a proper deep belly laugh.

'Just a regular couple of days then. Mind you, I would have paid to see the throwing out bit. Was it a proper back of the neck and hurl like they do in movies? Did it hurt as much as it looks like it would?'

'Yes, why are you still laughing? About me being in pain? Humiliated and in pain? You have a bit of a mean streak, don't you? Clearly I got you all wrong!'

'Clearly you got it all wrong about a whole host of other things as well. What on earth did you do?'

'Why do you assume it's my fault?' Matt aimed for the air of an aggrieved child who'd been caught out. Any minute now and it'd be hand against forehead à la Victorian heroine. He was enjoying this.

'You're an idiot! Your face fools no one,' sputtered Rosy.

'The insults just don't stop coming, do they. Here I was thinking I was coming over for a civilized, neighbourly bowl of pasta, but no, it's just attack, attack, attack with you, isn't it?'

She held her hands up and bowed her head in a gesture of apology. 'OK, straight-faced now. How? Why? To all of it. Was it not your fault?'

'Well, it's a long story and I don't want to be disloyal, but…'

'Oh my God, it was all about Angelina, wasn't it?'

Matt smiled one of those what-do-you-expect smiles and spread his hands, and Rosy shook her head.

'I'm a glutton for punishment?' He shrugged.

'Clearly, and that's not all.' She leaned forward and completely unexpectedly drew her fingers across his cheek, just in the corner of his face. 'You're a glutton for my cooking too – you've got pasta sauce everywhere! There, that's it.'

He didn't really hear her words; it was almost as if it were one of those bad film moments that make you wince at the obviousness of it, as everything around the main character is suspended in time and slows down to a near halt, whereas the main character himself is highlighted, sharpened, in focus as he moves forward, hyper-sensitized, and in this particular case grabs the wrist near him.

He wasn't trying to be aggressive and he didn't grab her roughly; it just kind of happened, and he held lightly onto her wrist as she attempted to move away. He looked into her eyes. Her action, its level of intimacy, had shocked him and he wasn't quite sure what he was doing. It was instinctive, intuitive, not at all thought out and he didn't want to look away. He wanted to pull her, gently, determined, even closer still.

'I'm so sorry!' Rosy spoke and the spell was broken. 'I didn't realize what I was doing, I'm sorry. It's inherent, a work thing, I guess. Forgive me.'

Matt dropped her wrist immediately. What *she* had been doing? Was she joking? What about what he had done! That was so unlike him.

'I'm sorry too, I didn't mean to grab you. I don't know what came over me.'

'Oh, don't be daft, you weren't aggressive in any way. Everyone would raise their hand to protect themselves if some mad woman came at their face as if they were six.'

He didn't feel particularly like he was six right now.

'And anyway, I quite liked it.' Her face looked as surprised as he was as she realized what she had just said. He watched as the flush rose from her neck to the roots of her hair. That didn't look like it was something she had meant to say out loud. Matt held her eye contact. Something was fizzing all over him, and he found himself pushing his chair out and standing up. Slowly and deliberately he walked around towards her. He took in every last detail as he went: her dark hair as it fell across her shoulders, curtaining the curves of her neck. Her big eyes, wider than usual as she watched him move nearer; her mouth, slightly ajar as if surprised or, as he watched her tongue flick across the lips, as desirous as he was for what was about to happen next. One hand held on to the table, the other awkwardly on her lap as if she weren't quite sure what to do with it, how to position herself.

Whilst it took a matter of seconds to cross from his chair to her, it felt as if it were all going one slow frame at a time, a compulsion, a black-and-white movie but without the desperate kind of flinging at each other.

A more heightened, modern, slow and silent realization of what they had both been working towards since the night they'd recognized a mutual attraction. That first meeting as they'd bickered on the pavement, then the night they had stayed up laughing, drinking, talking, learning. This had always been going to happen and as he looked in her eyes he knew she had known it too.

He reached her and held his hand to hers, pulling her out of her chair. They remained wordless, and just stood there for a second or two, staring at each other, almost cementing the moment on their brains, wanting it to be clear for future recall. This could be momentous.

She quivered in front of him, as a baby rabbit in the hand of a man. Her tremble though was not with fear; she maintained his eye contact, daring him on. Tongue still flicking across her lips, unaware she was doing it, nerves fully on show. Yet she did not step back and he lowered his head to meet her lips in a deliberately measured way, offering her every chance to step back, scream no, slap him. Yet she didn't. She instead moved almost impercep-tibly closer, willing him forward until he could bear no more.

This was an entirely different way of doing things than he was used to; this seemed full, rich, fertile and bursting; this seemed like one of those life-defining moments where a decision was made; this felt to him like more than kissing his neighbour. This was big.

He could bear it no more. He had to feel her lips on his, just taste them and then pull back, that was the plan. He didn't want to suddenly be swishing pasta bowls off the table – well of course he did, really did – but this was too momentous, this he wanted to secure every step of the way. He had scared her before; he wasn't repeating that mistake.

She met him and as their lips touched he felt the frissons shoot through him. What was supposed to be a simple kiss became much more intense; he had felt her shudder as their mouths initially touched and he needed to feel more. He pulled her closer still as the kiss became deeper and deeper and one hand travelled up to support her head, the other resting in the small of her back, to protect her, to hold her there. She was matching him depth for depth, no hesitancy, no holding back, she wanted him as badly as he wanted her, she was moving from responsive to more aggressive as the heat he was feeling was clearly consuming her too.

He was almost too scared to stop; he didn't want that second to happen when his mouth left hers, when they were separate, even if it were just for a moment. He didn't want any chance of sanity – hers – kicking in and making her stop. He wasn't sure what had been holding her back before, but he had known something had, confirmed on Sunday, but whatever it was, she had given it up now.

He hitched her up onto the table, hands wandering, taking in her whole body. A body that was leaning in to him, encouraging him to go further, to feel more, and he didn't think he was going to be able not to. He wanted to lose himself, he wanted to make her feel the depth of what he was feeling, he wanted her to gasp, to scream with pleasure.

Her hands were also frantic, pulling at his shoulders, up and down his back. He could just lose himself here forever.

But no, as strong as his desire was, and it was, he needed to check properly. He wanted to hear her give her consent. He wanted it made as clear as could be – this could not be a crazed bulldozing of lust, this had to be more.

Matt pulled himself away, hands still on her waist as he took a breath and forced her to as well.

'Rosy?' He was scared to ask. Scared her answer would be no, petrified her answer would be a yes, for he knew this was a Pandora's box, one he wouldn't ever want to close. He had never given anyone such power over his emotions before and he was alternating between trepidation and that feeling of never-so-sure-of-anything-in-his-life. It all hung on her.

Her lips were swollen, her pupils huge as she gazed back up at him, and nodded.

As he felt the smile take over his face, she arched up and pulled him back down. This was really happening; this woman was amazing in so many different ways. He knew, at this moment there was no doubt in his mind, this woman was the one he was meant to find.

He closed his eyes and leaned in, happy, renouncing his fears and committing in this one movement to all the future had to hold as he felt her kiss imbue his whole being. Then he heard a car door slam.

# Chapter Twenty

Rosy felt Matt tense above her and heard an engine starting and moving away. She froze as the sounds of stumbling up next door's path followed. There was no mistaking it – with her cottage out on the edge of the village with very little traffic or street noise, she was attuned to everything.

It had to be Angelina and Marion, and if it were Marion… oh dear God! The realization of what she had just done – and she wasn't sure how she had got there, but she knew she had been very, very willing – hit home. This could be around the village in seconds! Penmenna was speedier than Twitter when it came to the spreading of news.

Aghast, she looked up at Matt and pushed him off. She needed to get him out and home before Angelina noticed he was missing and Marion worked out that her headteacher was spending a Thursday night practically straddling her neighbour.

*Bang. Bang. Bang.*

Too late! They were at her door. How could either woman think this was OK? Neither had ever felt the need to visit before! She stood stock-still.

She heard Matt muttering at her, but could do nothing but stare at him blankly.

*Bang. Bang. Bang.*

'Look, we'd better let them in before they wake up the whole of Penmenna. Rosy, Rosy, are you OK?'

Rosy shook her head (less as a negative response, more a clearing of fug), came out of her catatonic state and launched herself towards the front door.

Marion clattered through into the house, bringing Angelina with her and shrieking in tongues. Well, middle-aged, middle-class drunkenness, but it sounded like much of a muchness. So much so that neither stopped their braying to greet either Rosy or her guest.

She looked across to Matt to catch and assess any expressions on his face. How he behaved here would be key. Suddenly he had gone from being knee-shakingly tempting to possessing the power to shape how the village viewed her. A familiar feeling quickly swooshed through Rosy's stomach, only this time it wasn't based upon desire. She felt sick. Her breath was deep and rapid and her heart was beating so loud and fast it was bound to explode out of her chest any minute now.

Head in the game! She needed to focus herself, and quickly.

A quick glance at Marion saw her teeter on her heels and grab onto Angelina, both still cackling, interspersing it with a stream of babble so loud and incoherent – like a fairground, blare jarring against blare – that she began to wonder if she could get away with this. Could they not have noticed? Could she be free and clear if she just got them out? What about Matt, could she persuade him to keep quiet?

She glanced around: no obvious clues to what had happened, just two settings for supper and a couple of half-eaten bowls of pasta, innocent enough. She turned to Matt and as she studied him assessingly he smiled at her, all reassuring and affectionate and so tummy-flippingly sexy. Damn him! Lust almost replaced fear, curling up from the tips of her toes and whooshing all the way through her, the two combined emotions making her feel weak. Literally dizzy.

She scowled at him. How brazen could a person be? Smiling as if nothing had happened. As if they hadn't just been about to make love on her dining table. On her dining table! Still, that was exactly what had happened and for now her best plan was to smile, say nothing and guide them all towards the door, whilst praying he had the wit to keep his mouth shut.

She forced her brain to try and take control of her physical responses, which were clearly not to be trusted. But her brain was struggling; all it could tell her was that regardless of what happened here, it was a lose-lose situation for her. If Matt told the world, or even just his sister, she'd be straight back to where she was ten years ago – all her hard work forgotten – under the micro-scope and judged for her choices. Arrgggh! She suddenly fully understood what people meant when they said they wished the ground would open up beneath them. If only life were that merciful.

She sent another scowl at Matt, just to make sure he got the message to keep schtum.

It failed. He smiled again, stood next to her and reas-suringly squeezed her shoulder. Reassuringly! Was he insane?

She pushed his hand off and stalked towards the women to properly greet the combined force of her head of the

PTA and Ange-bloody-lina. Both of whom were still tottering slightly on heels and clinging to each other, almost joined, a bit like butterfly chicken.

'And then they said… bwahahahah,' Angelina nonsensically cawed at Marion, who responded with maniacal laughter.

'Marion, how lovely to have you here.' Rosy approached the-parent-from-hell-recently-made-ally and laid her hand on her arm in greeting.

'Bwahahahahah,' the two drunken women cackled together.

Scramble opened one eye, finally woken, and moved deftly under the couch.

'Marion.' Rosy heard her own voice, louder and sharper this time. Marion's head snapped up as she looked at Rosy, furrowing her brow with what looked like confusion before being distracted, within a microsecond, by Angelina launching herself at her brother.

'Mattie! Oh, Mattie, I do love you!'

Mattie, clearly practised, caught her as she teetered in his direction, tried to plant a giant kiss on his cheek and slowly slid down him.

'Whoops, I'm a silly billy.' She nestled into his chest and he, hand placed in the small of her back, tried guiding her to a chair.

Matt shrugged his shoulders at Rosy and shot her a broad what-can-I-do grin, but this was all becoming a bit too difficult for Rosy to take. The grinning, combined with Marion being in the room and Angelina fawning all over her brother, who only minutes ago had had Rosy pressed against the table with her skirt hitched up, was making everything a bit claustrophobic. And this was her house, supposedly her refuge, invaded.

'Ooh, so this is your Matt?' Marion said, suddenly sharper than she had been, standing a little straighter and zooming in on the only man in the room. 'Well, you said he was a sweetie but you didn't say how very attractive he was.'

Oh God. Marion could not have put more emphasis on the 'very' and was now in predator mode. Rosy had seen this before with unprepared fathers who made rare appearances in the playground. Marion had form for purring and stroking men she fixed upon, at school functions, sports day, pretty much anywhere, regardless of marital status or indeed spousal presence. Her overtly flirtatious behaviour had meant that in the past Rosy had witnessed desperate glances from bewildered fathers unsure how to escape and knowing their wives weren't brave enough to haul her off. She was not voluntarily watching this today, not with this cast.

Rosy silently turned and headed to the kitchen where she slammed the door, stamped her foot and violently wrestled the lid off a cake tin and started to eat the contents. Cake might calm her long enough to work out how to throw them out without drawing attention to her fear that her carefully controlled world could collapse around her at any minute.

It was proving hard to think with the noise seeping under the door – even chewing as loud as she could, particularly difficult with a sponge cake – there seemed no escaping the drunken guffawing of Angelina or Marion's purring. She probably had her hand inside his shirt now. If Angelina or Matt weren't going to slap her off, then Rosy sure as hell wasn't. She'd just stay in here a bit longer, let her breathing get back to normal, maybe find some crisps.

She had just perched herself on the worktop and had started a second bag of cheese and onion when the door was pushed open.

'Hey, I think I need to get her home. Apart from anything else she's beginning to turn a funny colour, which experience has taught me means she's best removed. But I do need to speak to you – I've not just been getting thrown out of clubs in London, and there's something we need to discuss.'

*You think!* Rosy would've smiled sarcastically, but she had a great big bit of crisp wedged between her teeth. Plus maybe a clear message needed to be sent here, now there was just the two of them. She concentrated on giving him her most evil look instead. One that had four-year-olds quaking before turning to a life of obedience. It didn't seem to put him off.

Instead he had the temerity to approach her, smiling that oh so charming aren't I adorable smile that he should probably patent, and stop mere millimetres in front of her. She narrowed her eyes even further, so far that it began to hurt her forehead. He just laughed and popped his hands between her knees in an attempt to widen them so he could stand as close as could be.

She clamped her knees as tight as they would go, and carried on scowling. Using all these muscles, with such force, could well be some kind of workout. She should make a DVD. It was taking some welly and she wasn't sure how long she'd be able to hold out. Not because her determination not to break The Rule again was wavering, no – that was very firm – but because it was quite a lot of physical effort, all this frowning and clasping.

He initially laughed and leaned in to stroke her face, but she flicked out of his reach, and his smile turned to confusion. She still hadn't spoken a word but it would appear her body language was doing all the communicating she wanted.

'Um, OK. Well, like I said I'll get her home. But this evening has been special, Rosy, and I'm not entirely sure what's going on but um… I'll leave now. Maybe we could meet up tomorrow evening. I know it's a bit clichéd, but I'd really like to and, Valentine's Day aside, I really need to talk to you. It's about the school and what you said about maybe it closing.'

It was the school dance tomorrow – what exactly did he have in mind? French kissing and a fondle in front of nearly one hundred kids and their parents?

'I'm busy.' She arched an eyebrow at him in a challenge. 'I have a prior commitment, and I don't think this is a good idea. Do you?' Oh shit, although if he did want to talk about the school maybe she should hear him out. But tomorrow – he must be mad. Suddenly she had a solution. 'The school, though, um – is it important?'

'Yes, I think it could be, I think I've got something that will help. Why? Is it definitely being shut now?'

'Looks that way, although we're fighting to save it.' *Stop! Don't get lulled into conversation; he has crafty skills, this man. Stand firm!* 'But you are right, we do need to talk. We should talk about how this can't happen again.'

She felt two sides of her having the most almighty battle. She didn't want to do this; she'd quite like to relax her glare and soften right into his arms but that was never going to be an option for her. Not with someone who lived bang smack in the middle of her community. No, this was not about what she wanted to do, it was about what she needed to do to keep things on the beautifully smooth and even keel that she had now. Certain things needed to be said.

'What? Why?'

'I just feel... um... I feel it's for the best.'

'But... we... but... we're...'

'I don't want to, Matt, is that clear? I don't want to.'

It felt cruel, watching him deflate before her. But what else could she do? She certainly didn't want to hurt anyone's feelings, and she and Matt did have something, something she had never really experienced before, but this was too complicated; she was not allowing herself to get involved in this level of mess. Dear God, this was how TV dramas started – one minute everything bubbling along and then one poor decision, usually influenced by lust, and boom, before you knew it, it was all body bags and prison time. Well, it wasn't happening to her. Not again. Although to be fair there hadn't been body bags or prison last time... but there could have been. There could! She wasn't getting sucked in again, no way.

She deftly slid off the side, angling her body as far from Matt's as she could.

'I'll show you out.'

'OK.' He nodded slowly, stepping back and accepting his cue to leave. 'But maybe we should talk about the idea I've had for the school later, and it does need to be soon. If we forget it's Valentine's Day tomorrow could we talk about it then, in a purely professional capacity?'

Back in control, she pasted her most competent smile on as she considered his tenacity. Despite her previous crush – previous? Who was she kidding? Her up-until-five-minutes-ago-crush – she suddenly looked at him with a new clarity. Yes, he was gorgeous. Yes, he was kind and generous and all those things she had on her wish list. And he obviously wasn't Josh, she knew that; it was just her most basic level that went into panic. But since university she had made decisions about how her life was going to be and so far those decisions had led to a carefully planned but smooth and content life. She had a great job that she loved, she had some good friends and right now, with the school being threatened, this was not the time to throw everything that had guided her well up into the air. She was not the gambling type.

She may have been shilly-shallying around this fact for a fortnight now but something had clicked, like her four-year-olds learning to read, and everything fell into place. She knew this feeling, and with it came a sense of relief. This lady was not for turning.

'I'm sorry. As I was saying, I can't see you tomorrow – I'm far too busy – but if you have an idea that could help please get in touch with Marion, she'll be in school tomorrow and she's the correct person to talk to about this, not me.' And then, just in case twice wasn't enough, 'I'm busy tomorrow, all day. Let me show you out.'

# Chapter Twenty One

It was a bleary-eyed Rosy who drove into school the next morning. She had spent very little of last night sleeping, although she could hear Angelina next door snoring so loudly the windows rattled. It hadn't helped the confusion whirring around Rosy's head. A mishmash of emotion that hours of analysis hadn't helped clear.

She knew that she shouldn't have kissed Matt. The Rule was simple enough – it stated that you didn't involve yourself with anyone with ties to your life, ever. That way, when things went wrong they could be neatly erased from life, and social media, without major fallout. Without them entangling mutual friends or colleagues. Without them broadcasting to everyone who knew you what your flaws were, real or fabricated. Without them painting a picture of you so dark and unexpected that you lost all of your standing in the community, your job and your friends. She knew that most men weren't delusional psychopaths that manipulated the world around them as if it were a personally designed board game. She also knew, through bitter experience, that it only took one.

However, when Rosy had been busy defining The Rule and then practising it over the course of her lifetime, she had applied it rigorously, as if all were black and white. As it should be. It was unfortunate that, up until now, Rosy had forgotten all about the existence of grey. As much as she may not think it should exist, as much as she may not want it to exist, yesterday grey had stood up and announced, no, shouted its presence. *I am grey. I will not be ignored. Stand up and count me and all my shades of gorgeousness.*

Grey said that it didn't matter about what may seem sensible. Grey whispered that there was more to be thought about. That intuitively Rosy knew that walking away was not the sensible option, that she and Matt had a bond, a something unique to them that should be, had to be, explored. Grey reminded her that intuition was what had saved humanity time and time again. It was both part of evolution and existence. Grey had to be listened to. Not to do so, to only see black and white, was foolhardy.

Rosy would have liked to cosh grey over the head and bundle it into a sack with black and white and hurl all of them over a cliff, but instead she got up and went to work. And whilst she loved her job, and usually was happy entering her classroom in the morning, today – despite being exhausted and emotionally wrung out – the primary colours of Class One, the red, the yellow and the bright blue, had never been so welcoming. She might stay here forever.

Sitting at the playdough table fashioning hearts and relieved that for the past twenty whole minutes she hadn't focused on her own, Rosy played alongside the children. 'Played' was a misnomer; she was of course being terribly professional, modelling behaviour as well as shapes, observing social skills and fine motor control. Just in case anyone asked.

'Miss.' She felt her sleeve being tweaked and smiled to see Billy standing at her arm, being very bashful. Billy was not a bashful child; Billy was a rough and tumble ball of joy that had no qualms about shouting out everything he knew all of the time. A shock of blond hair, a swoosh of freckles and a constantly cheeky grin, he was a child to be constantly watching. If the room was quiet and Billy was in it then that was a red flag.

'Billy, good morning. How nice to see you.' This was true; she had a sneaking fondness for the sparky ones, although they did make group reading rather tricksy. She turned on her teeny-weeny chair to look at him.

'Good morning, miss, I've… got… got somefink… I love you, miss!' With that he gave her a card and sped away to his friends in the construction area, blushing as red as any Lego block, legs falling over themselves in his haste to escape.

Rosy smiled and, turning back to the table, opened the envelope. Inside was a hand-drawn card filled with lots and lots of tiny heart shaped sequins, admittedly now all over the floor, and lots and lots of scrawling inside as he had tried to go over the letter shapes his mother had traced out. Billy was not keen on writing, and was far from ready. Rosy knew from experience that he would much rather put a pen up his nose or his friend's nose than hold it in his hand and press it on some paper. This card was special.

Smiling, she got up from her chair and started to herd the children together so that the day's formal teaching could begin.

The day dragged a little but it didn't take long to lose herself in the children. It didn't matter what she had going on in her personal life – the minute she was surrounded by her class nothing else took priority. It wasn't mere professionalism, though; it happened without thinking, she just loved them. Hence it took until break-time before her mind was dragged back to the happenings of last night, as she saw Matt's face, that funny, sexy face flash into her mind, and she swore she could feel the pull of his hand on her leg as he had lifted her onto the table. She decided to escape to the staffroom for lunch, where the babble of the rest of the staff and the extras in the shape of the PTA would drown out any inappropriate imaginings – *memories now*, her irritating internal voice piped up. Oh bloody hell, she was lost. Was rehashing last night's TV over bad coffee really going to work?

It seemed it would have to. There was the usual buzz throbbing out from the door as Rosy approached. She managed to secure herself a cup of coffee and lose herself in the swirl of babble about what had happened last night in Walford.

She had been worried that with all the upset in the school recently, the insecurities would make the staff funny with her. She had seen it happen before and was expecting but dreading it. Surprisingly it hadn't come; she was still treated as warmly as before. But then the realities of the changes hadn't begun yet, so she was concentrating on keeping the school buzzing, the children and their parents happy and their profile high locally. Marion Marksharp opened the staffroom door and the mood fell, the happy but silly babble deflated. There wasn't a single member of staff that hadn't felt the sharp edge of her tongue at some point and as for the parents, membership to the PTA was almost like a biker gang. The hoops they had to jump through to gain entry and move up the ranks were insane. Rosy suspected most of them would rather take the punishments a set of bearded and armed middle-aged bikers might mete out than the public humiliation of one of Marksharp's famous verbal attacks.

For a second Rosy felt a flash of sympathy for her. There was no ignoring the fact that the room had fallen silent and people began shuffling papers and scraping chairs back to leave. It must be horrid to know that you were so disliked. Rather like being prime minister; you were never going to please everyone. Then she remembered that with the power of a single whisper Marion could tell the whole school what she had walked in on last night.

'I need to speak to you, Rosy.'

'Yes, of course.' Rosy made a gesture to leave the staffroom – if Marion was going to say anything about yesterday then it didn't need to be witnessed – as the rapidly emptying room was punctuated by the phone ringing in the corner.

'Oh, just let me grab this.' Rosy turned to answer it. Maybe there was a fire in one of the classrooms? Or the school hamster had escaped again – anything would do! Sheila was on the other end and informed her that it was a call for Marion. Miraculously, she managed to do so without mentioning her grandchildren or forgetting why she was on the phone. Was progress being made?

Puffed up with importance, Marion took the receiver from Rosy and then proceeded to put on her telephone voice.

'Marion Marksharp here. How can I help?... Lovely to hear from you so soon... Yes, yes, it was great to meet you last night... Oh really? Yes, I had heard a whisper about that, such an interesting project, I didn't realize you were involved, your sister never said... yes, quite... well, community is at the heart of all successful endeavours... Really? Are you serious? That would be wonderful... Well, some of the parents may not be keen but in my role as head of the PTA I'm sure I can address any concerns and as you say this would be a wonderful opportunity for the children... How many... All of them, the whole school! That would be quite some undertaking but I don't see why not. I would have to run it by Rosy but I think she'll agree with me that this could be exactly what the school needs. You could talk to her over the weekend... or come in and meet the children, perhaps have an assembly and outline your exciting plans to everyone, although as I say I can't see any problems, but then it isn't entirely my decision...'

Rosy drained her coffee as she listened to Marion's conversation. This couldn't be happening. She knew that she had told Matt to call Marion but she hadn't expected him to actually do it. This was getting serious now. He had just, with one phone call, encroached upon her professional life. How the hell was she going to handle this? See, it confirmed her worst fears; one kiss and he was already at stage two of the psychopath's playbook. Whatever he was saying was certainly making Marion very animated – remarkable for a woman who must have a hangover so monumental it could become the eighth wonder of the world. He was clearly a master at this game. How, how had she managed to attract another one? She knew people had a type but she had worked so hard to actively ensure this never happened again. Whatever happened she needed to deal with this one step at a time, with thought, and precision and a plan. However, this was not the time for that. She needed to get back to class, finish teaching and then work out what she was going to do to make sure this went no further. She raised her hand up to Marion as a goodbye and left her to it.

She hadn't got far when a breathless Marion caught up with her. It was the first time she had looked anything other than immaculate. Well, still immaculate but rather flustered.

'Rosy, Rosy, do wait a moment. You're not going to believe this but Penmenna School is going to be on television!'

Rosy spun on her heel. Was this what Marion had come to see her about – press for the disco tonight? What about the phone call? That was what she wanted to know about! Don't push, Marion would tell her when she needed to. The worst thing Rosy could do was seem over-keen on what Matt had to say.

'Well done, Marion, quite astounding. Although I'm not sure why the local news would want to cover the Valentine's disco, goodness knows how you pulled that off, but well done.'

'No, no, you misunderstand, it's even better than that!'

'What do you mean? Walk with me, or I'll be late for class.'

'It's not the local news. National television want us!'

Oh dear, had the pressure been too much? Was Marion finally cracking? National news were sending cameras to the dance tonight? That was crazy!

'The restoration project at Penmenna Hall, the garden restoration… Matt, lovely Matt that I met at yours last night, he wants the school to be involved. He wants us to help and be included in the programme, a segment a week with the children. If you agree, and why wouldn't you, the school will be on national television, prime-time, every week. Mr Grant's going to have his work cut out now! Can you believe our luck!'

# Chapter Twenty Two

Matt was confused. Not an unusual state of being, but in this case he was not comfortable with it. Women had been a mystery all through school and certainly in his late teens. Yet as he had become an adult they had become less so; he got on well with women, they were attracted to him and he seemed to have a knack for knowing who was genuinely interested, who was playing games and who just wanted to be a friend. He had been told that he was a rarity in the fact that all of his exes and he were on good terms; two had even named him godfather to their children. He didn't think it was big-headed (although he knew he could easily be wrong) but he accepted this was rare, and that he was lucky.

But yesterday, yesterday had confused him. He knew he was attracted to Rosy, he could argue that he didn't know why but then would find himself listing her qualities at great speed and with true belief. He knew this wasn't the mere lust that clouded judgement, that kind of attraction that all of us experience at one time or another, managing to convince ourselves that it is indeed true love, souls meant to be, before using it as justification for ripping each other's clothes off regardless of whether it's a good idea, or really quite a bad one. He knew this wasn't that. Although he was very keen on the ripping clothes off bit.

He knew that Rosy was attracted to him, really attracted to him. This was not ego; he was frequently laced with self-doubt about all number of things, but this he just knew. It was in the way she would look at him; her eyes would smile as she did so. When they had first met those glances had been assessing, amused. Now they veered from confused to more knowing, secure and then whoosh, back to confused again. The way they spoke to each other – they teased and they laughed, she even kicked him periodically, but they spoke to each other with respect. A respect he knew he felt and again believed she did too. The two of them just made sense together, it was that simple. Parents, those wiser than us, and social media all say that when you know you know, it's indefinable but it exists. He knew.

And then last night, completely unplanned, he had been in a bit of a flap about Angelina, the only thing that caused him to unravel, and Rosy had somehow materialized, stepped in, made everything right and cooked dinner. All quite naturally. And then the two of them had… well, he wasn't sure how they had got there. Things just seemed to follow a natural progression and before he knew it, they were kissing. There was no way in the world anything could convince him she wasn't as keen as he was. His mind had kept flashbacks in his head throughout last night and this very lazy morning. One minute he was brushing his teeth, the next his mind would burst into colour with images of Rosy grabbing his head and pulling him back down to her. Knocking on Angelina's door to see if she was awake and in need of coffee, and *boom*, a close-up of Rosy's face, pupils dilated, lips swollen, took over his mind. Maybe he shouldn't drive the car today.

However, drive he must. He needed to get to the nursery – with February in full swing, he needed to step up. Not just to go over his plans again, but also get on with the basics. Seeds needed sowing and he had a feeling that a day with his hands deep in the soil would bring him the calm he needed. The solitude of the gardens and the nature of the jobs planned for today might help shed some clarity on what on earth was going on with Rosy. He had thought things would be quite simple; they had accepted they were both attracted to each other, gone beyond mere acceptance on that table, and would have gone further had they not been interrupted. So why had she behaved so oddly, yet again, once the other two had turned up? He had wanted to stand proud next to her, hand in hand, and declare to Angelina and that strange woman that whilst it was lovely to see them (not quite true), they needed to sod off next door for a bit and let him and Rosy carry on doing what they had been doing. Cementing the nature of their relationship. In the most pleasurable way.

But she had been weird. There was no other way to describe it. She'd stomped off into the kitchen, and then become really arsey when he had followed her. It was similar behaviour to Sunday when he'd had to visit Angelina and she had just fled. This high-maintenance madness did not fit. It didn't fit her personality or what he knew of it; it just wasn't right. And he was fed up with it. There were only two reasons he could think of to explain it. The first was that his radar was massively off, and he was making a big mistake or that, as he had thought when he first moved in, she was seeing someone else. This latter could make sense; he may never have seen him, it could even be a her, but that didn't mean he/she didn't exist. It would explain her reticence perfectly. It tied in with her character – yes, she was attracted to him, Matt, but if she were seeing someone else then the Rosy he thought he knew would be eaten up with guilt. Would push him away until she had all loose ends tied up. Assuming she chose him, that was; she might not.

'Are you not getting dressed?' Angelina wandered into the kitchen where he was standing, staring out at the garden, clutching his coffee.

Oh God! He could see Rosy sat on the countertop, coldly informing him she was busy tonight. Valentine's Day! Then his brain switched to watch her shuffle across the floor on her bottom in her living room, surrounded by cardboard hearts.

'Oi! Earth to Matt!' He felt something whip his arm and turned to see Angelina standing there grinning with a tea towel all twirled up, and *whoosh,* in she came again, *crack,* right against his leg.

He grinned. She wasn't getting away with this. He grabbed another tea towel and battle commenced, a ritual that harked back to their earliest days and in which neither gave any quarter.

*Thwack!* 'So, oh brother of mine' – *flick* – 'why' – *bam* – 'are you not' – *snap* – 'dressed?'

'Ouch!' *Thwack.* 'Ha, that was a beauty, and maybe it's pyjamas-to-work day, you rude cow!' *Snap.*

*Flick.* 'Oh shit, that was nearly the coffee, we should stop.'

'Sensible, Angelina. What has happened? Who are you, and what have you done with my sister?'

'Sensible enough to know you're still a twat.'

'Nice. Do you win celebrity awards with that mouth?'

'Did you want your coffee to survive this morning? Anyway, why aren't you offering me breakfast? You're normally desperate to get me to stuff my face with fatty breakfast food.'

'Good to know I'm appreciated. You normally very rudely reject. Did you want breakfast?'

'No. What I want to know is what was going on with you and Miss goody-two-shoes last night?'

'Before or after you were sick all over her garden path?'

'Nice try. Don't change the subject.'

'OK, I'm not sure. I think I need to go see her later tonight and figure it out. But before you open your mean mouth – don't make that face, you can be very mean – I'm going to tell you to back off this one. I mean to fight for her. I think she's... well, she's special to me.'

Angelina leant over and made a very graphic gagging noise, before whacking him with the towel one more time.

–

Walking through Penmenna Hall towards the nursery always lifted his spirit. As he wound his way down the ancient curvy paths he could feel the pull of history, of all those gardeners who had worked here before, hands deep in the soil and backs sore from shovels. It called to him; he loved that feeling of being part of a great tradition, and maintaining that tradition with the seeds he would sow and the methods of soil preparation that were key to a garden like this. And now, thanks to Rosy, he had a chance to continue all of that with the next generation.

Children adept with tablets and gaming could enjoy a chance to escape technology and feel the primeval joy of sowing, growing and harvesting.

The nursery was his favourite place and he just wanted to run through all the soil improvers he had lined up before the filming started next week. They wouldn't need much, they just wanted to be able to film a short segment on how the ground had to be prepped and the traditional methods of doing so. He ambled down the long Georgian driveway, noting how everything was out a little bit earlier down here. It may only be February but the drive was a colourful riot – daffodils and miniature irises lining the ground, and the pinks and whites of full bloom camellias brightening up the deep green of the shrubbery. He could grow to love Cornwall. Everything here was so laid-back – with the exception of spring, which bounded in like an excited spaniel.

So laid-back that as he reached the nursery he appeared to be the only person in today. He guessed that the other gardeners on staff were all taking advantage of the season to spend or make plans with their loved ones.

He had never really embraced the romantic gesture for Valentine's Day before, subscribing to the view, seemingly common, that it was merely a tacky ploy to generate sales through playing on people's emotions and expectations. This Valentine's Day he saw it somewhat differently. Now he saw it as an opportunity to reinforce his own personal message – and if Rosy was too busy today then tomorrow would do. He had already made a start, the same day he had fashioned his Tudor cap, knowing that he didn't want to take the garage-forecourt-flowers-and-chocolates route.

Before he began work in the gardens he rang the school and spoke to Marion as Rosy had suggested. He had been disappointed not to be able to outline his plans to her in person yesterday but at least progress was made, and Marion had sounded so excited that at one point he was worried she may explode.

He then mixed up potting composts, organized, planted and labelled seeds, and as he headed to the small section he had cornered off to develop his orchids in, he couldn't help but smile as Rosy popped back into his head again. She may be confused but he wasn't; he knew exactly what he wanted and was in no mad hurry to get it. He would simply wait for her to work out what she wanted. He wouldn't push the issue but he would make it clear how he felt. And he would make it clear with these orchids.

An orchid was the perfect Valentine's expression. They were elegant and beautiful. He wasn't sure if Rosy, frequently covered in playdough and glitter, would describe herself that way but he certainly would. Her elegance of spirit, amplified by her patience, was one of the things that attracted him most. They needed tender deliberate care to flourish and that he was happy to provide. Their beauty contributed to a feeling of calm, of awe in the world. With any luck they wouldn't die (he hoped) in a matter of days, but would stay in her house as a symbol of him. This particular one was a hybrid he had developed himself, and struck him as being the exact match to Rosy's colouring – pale but flushed with a little pink. Could he get any more romantic? He thought not.

He realized that it was slowly getting dark, and as his ruminations had taken place over the course of the day he already knew what flowerpot to choose for Rosy: a plain terracotta one that provided the perfect foil to the intricacies of the flower he had chosen. He went and fetched it and then headed off to source the most perfect ribbon he could find.

# Chapter Twenty Three

It was early evening and Rosy had managed to survive Valentine's Day and the disco, and was preparing to head home. Not that she wanted to. This made her quite cross; she loved her little cottage and returning to it and all its little sloping-wall quirks at the end of the work day was usually one of her joys. But after last night, it no longer felt like her little safe space, and she knew she was going to struggle to look at her dining table without seeing herself on it, Matt above her. Matt, who, like Josh, had moved into her neighbourhood and then stretched his tentacles out into her work. As if him meeting Marion last night wasn't bad enough, now he had somehow involved the school in the Penmenna restoration. Her rational self believed he was genuinely trying to help, but her damaged self – and she knew she existed and was getting louder by the minute – was in screaming panic. How was she supposed to reinforce firm don't-touch-or-interact-with-me boundaries when she was going to have to turn up in his workplace with all the children? On top of which, she was then going to have to control that bit of her that just wanted to run her hands all over him and stick her tongue in his mouth. It was a nightmare waiting to happen. She had no idea what he was going do next and going home was no longer a cocoon of man-free safety. Oh, bloody hell!

She toyed briefly with heading over to Lynne's, but knew that she couldn't do that, not tonight. It was only today and birthdays that Lynne actually got to wrestle Dave away from the sixteenth century. Alice had gone away for half term straight after school and everyone else had plans.

She decided to give the school one last look over and then just suck it up and head home. As she headed back out of her office, her head a little bit full of pity-me, she stubbed her toe on the door.

'Oww!'

'Who's that?' came back a shout. What the hell was Marion still doing here? 'Is that you, Rosy?'

Marion appeared in front of her, wearing a rather plunging red sequinned dress, and Rosy almost catapulted into the door again. What on earth? As if yesterday wasn't eye-opening enough now she was exposed to Marion in evening wear! What had happened to the florals and the sensible navy striped boating tops?

'You're here rather late.'

Rosy tried not to let her resentment show on her face. Was the woman suggesting she had more right to be here than the headmistress?

'Yes, I was just heading home.'

'No plans for Valentine's?'

*That's it. Stick the knife in.* Rosy made her face smile neutrally. 'No, nothing special.'

'Well, that won't do.' Marion drew herself up to her full height and gave a little shake of her head. Rosy half closed her eyes; she had seen that look before and knew it signified a grand plan. Oh God! 'I know, why don't you come with me to a party! That's a fab idea, you'll meet all sorts of useful people and we could have a lovely time.'

'Oh, thank you. I did think you were looking very glam...'

'Yes, but I left my phone here so I rushed back to get it. It's going to be a great event, I've helped organize it, do come. There's champagne fountains and the most, simply the most, delicious canapés. The host is also terribly dishy and single, you'd be very welcome.'

'I'm afraid that whilst it's very kind of you...'

'Rosy, it's Valentine's Day and you're going back to an empty house – come!'

Rosy's empty house, table and all, reared its head in her mind and she started to waver.

'Really, come!' Marion's eyes had taken on that sparkle that few dared defeat.

'But I don't have anything to wear...'

'Nonsense. I know for a fact you have that blue dress hanging in the staff loos. That would be perfect. I can't stress how much fun this will be. It'll do you good after all you've been through recently.'

Did anything escape this woman? Mind you, more notable than her knowledge of Rosy's wardrobe was the fact that she appeared to have just demonstrated empathy. That had never happened in living memory. And champagne fountains did sound exactly what Rosy needed right now.

Before she knew it, she was sitting in a car with Marion Marksharp, wearing a dress that was too tight, questioning her sanity and clutching to the side of her seat, both hands almost white-knuckled as Marion appeared to have become a rally driver the minute she got behind the wheel.

Rosy had lived in Cornwall for several years now, but had never been down any of these lanes that Marion was now hurtling along, occasionally reversing at speed and singing Celine Dion louder than a whole school assembly. With the hedgerows high and joining like fairy woods (but with a bit more menace – the dark February evening did not lend itself to dreams of midsummer), Rosy began to long for the reassurance of satnav, although she knew that using it around this part of Cornwall was a daft idea – you always ended up in the arse end of nowhere, surrounded by cows or out to sea wondering why you hadn't stopped at the obvious. Locals used old-fashioned directions and tried to get holidaymakers to do the same, but it was usually a losing battle. Right now, though, satnav would have reassured her that she wasn't being kidnapped and held to ransom until she too promised to dress only in Cath Kidston. Her empty house was beginning to look like the better of the two options.

She closed her eyes and prayed as Marion hit some very sharp bends and careered down one particularly heart-twistingly steep hill before she realized that the driving had suddenly levelled out and the singing – if you could call it that – had stopped. Opening her eyes, she saw heart-shaped lights sparkling down a very long driveway. This must be it!

Marion drove down very slowly as Rosy stared out of the window, slightly awed by the beauty of the approach, the artful nature of the lighting twisted through the trees illuminating the way. They reached a horseshoe driveway with some truly swish cars parked on it. Half of her wanted Marion to reverse back out and take her home; it was a little intimidating. Only half, though – the other half was itching to get inside and see what else there was. This house was truly modern, and designed to be hidden. And effectively so, seeing that she had never heard of or seen it before. It must be one of the area's best kept secrets. Her interest was piqued. She could hear that nasal voice in her head: *and who would live in a house like this?* That was a question she was interested in answering.

She wandered through the front door and just stood in the foyer drinking it in. It was all very modern and open plan, with lots of clean lines and glass. The entrance hall was vast, and full of people milling around. Waitresses meandered through the crowd offering drinks and hors d'oeuvres, and there in the centre was a pink champagne fountain. Wow! She had never actually drunk from one of those before, only ever seen them on television. The whole space was artfully decorated with hearts and cherubs and seraphim but in an attractive way, not an in-your-face garish way. No wonder Marion had avoided cutting out millions of card hearts this year; she clearly had an extravaganza to organize. The woman must be mad doing this alongside the school disco. Talk about opposite ends of the spectrum. Speaking of which... Rosy scanned the room – where was Marion? They had exited the car together and wandered in through the entrance hall and then *poof*, like the Scarlet (sequinned) Pimpernel she was gone. Surely this was her perfect dream – shouldn't she be somewhere in the crowd, making friends and scaring people?

'Hello. Pleased to meet you.' Rosy was taken by surprise as a young man, beautifully dressed, approached her and introduced himself. 'I'm Chase. You look lost. How about I take your coat and give you a tour?'

'Thanks, that would be really kind.' Rosy smiled up at him and his American accent and slipped out of her coat, praying that he wouldn't spot the Asda label inside. She doubted supermarket clothes had ever graced this house before. 'I'm Rosy, I did come with Marion Marksharp but she's disappeared. I was just scanning the room for her and can't see her anywhere.'

'Oh yes' – Chase also had a quick glance about – 'that's odd, she's normally at the centre of everything. Honestly, she's a marvel, I've never met a woman who can organize like she can. If she had been born a couple of generations earlier you guys really would have won the war and been home by Christmas.'

Rosy choked on her drink and spat all down herself. Great.

'I wasn't being rude, I've known her for ages – she is an amazing woman. Amazing. I don't know how she does it!'

Rosy managed to keep her eyebrows in place rather than letting them shoot up to her hairline and decided to go with a non-committal smile and nod. She was going to take a bit more convincing.

Chase held his arm out for her jacket, which she handed to him, carefully folded over, taking advantage of the moment to look him up and down.

He was handsome enough – actually, he was bordering on devastating. Could love be like buses, none for ages and then *whoosh*, they all come at once? Blond and tall and built, he looked like some Norse god. A smattering of hair on his chin contributed to the look and there was no escaping his eyes, a bright but deep cornflower blue that looked as if they could see right through you. He shone with confidence; there was no way this man didn't get what he wanted, and you wanted to be the one who gave it to him.

Then a flash of Matt's dark curls and scrunched eyes whizzed into her head. She shook it to try and get rid of the image quickly. Now was not the time to be daydreaming about him, not when she had a perfect specimen of manhood right here, bang in front of her, holding her jacket and smiling a welcome.

Alas, as she looked at him she could see that his eyes didn't quite crinkle like Matt's, and his hands were beautifully smooth, manicured perfectly, not covered in scratches and wrinkles and dripping with mud. So much for boundaries and The Rule. As much as she wished she were attracted to beautifully smelling, perfectly groomed Vikings in swish houses, it seemed the unconscious part of her was not prepared to make life that easy.

'Right, let's go and pop this away then and I'll introduce you to everybody, Rosy.'

'OK. Do you know everyone here?' she asked as she followed him to a door leading off the main room. She hoped that was a cloakroom and she wasn't just being swept off to a secluded room with a stranger! She figured she'd know when he opened the door, and she could always run for it.

'Not everyone, I didn't know you, but nearly, yes. It's my house!'

Rosy watched as he turned the handle and combined watching with blushing, not out of attraction but embarrassment at her stupidity. He and the house were a perfect match – it was so obvious. And he wasn't leading her somewhere to hit on her, he was being a great host and making her welcome. When would she learn? Perhaps if she just never uttered a word again, that could solve all problems. Although maybe not so good for her working life, but at least the children would learn how to sign.

She was so lost in embarrassment she had stopped paying attention to the cloakroom only to be alerted again by Chase suddenly blurting out in surprise, 'Oh my God… right, OK…' and slamming the door shut again with Rosy's coat still in his hand.

'Um, perhaps we should put this somewhere else.' He turned towards Rosy, hunching his shoulders and beginning to walk away. Rosy, however, was stuck to the spot. Surely she hadn't just glimpsed what she thought she had? But she had, and there was no unseeing it now. She would forever have the sight of Mrs Marksharp in flagrante with her husband in a cupboard. It would appear the way she drove had nothing on the speed with which she tracked down her husband!

Rosy followed Chase. He still had her coat after all, fand there was no way she'd be opening that cupboard door and hanging it up herself. She felt a shudder at the thought of it.

Once they had placed some distance between the cloakroom and themselves, he turned and gave her a look and that was it, the two of them collapsed into contagious giggles.

'It is Valentine's,' Chase snorted.

'I know but still, I never thought that was a sight I'd see.'

'Well, they have a strong relationship, that's a good thing.'

'You don't have to look over the table at them during the next governors' meeting. How will I keep a straight face?'

'That I can't answer. So you work at the school then?'

And from there the conversation flowed. Rosy found herself opening up to him about all sorts through the course of the evening. Her new role, and the school's concerns. That then spilled into telling him about Matt, and what a fool she had been, partly because she wanted to make quite clear that she was being friends and not flirting and partly because she just couldn't help herself.

# Chapter Twenty Four

Chase led Rosy outside to a huge tree hung with white lights and surrounded by a circular bench. Rosy could feel her heart flutter. She had always been a soft touch for trees this old, her romantic self swooning with the incalculable numbers of people who had shed emotions around its trunk. Thwarted lovers, grief-stricken parents and laughing children all could have leant against its steady girth and shared their worries, their heartbreak and their adventures. And then to have a bench around it, this was the sort of thing romantic dreams were made of. She could see picnicking lovers seated at its base, and secret trysts. She wished Matt was here. And then quickly checked herself.

'This is beautiful.'

'Thank you, I am really lucky to have found this place. My taste tends towards modern but I also appreciate a little history now and again and this tree would have sold me the house had I not already made up my mind.'

'Oh my God, is that path leading to a private beach?'

'It is.'

'Wow, you have the perfect seduction palace here. How are you not overrun with playboy bunny types?'

'Who says I'm not?'

'Well, so far the closest I've come to seeing evidence is Mrs Marksharp fornicating in your coat cupboard! That would have been a threesome, at the very least, at Hugh Hefner's house.'

'Eugh! What are you suggesting?'

'Um, nothing! And now I feel queasy again.'

'You started it!'

'I know, oh shush. Shhh! Here she comes now.'

'Chase, darling! Mwah. Fabulous party.'

'All thanks to you, as you know only too well, Marion.'

'It's your gorgeous house. I've been desperate to get in here for years, and now, such luck you've bought it.'

'Ah, but you've done all the hard work, I only opened the door. And you know you are welcome any time.'

'Thank you, such a sweetie.'

Oh God, Rosy was going to gag any minute. Watching Monster Marksharp on her full charm offensive was a bit much.

'And you've met Rosy too. Such a darling girl. Such a huge asset to the school.'

*I am here*, Rosy wanted to shout but managed to smile weakly instead. Two glasses of pink champagne in and she was beginning to feel too whooshy to be difficult.

'I'm sure she is.' Chase's social skills were clearly excellent. 'Let me go and fetch you both a fresh drink, I shan't be a minute.'

'Perfect, thank you. I did want a quick word, Rosy, if that's OK.'

'Of course.'

'I just want to explain.'

Rosy gulped. 'Oh, you really don't have to.'

'I'd prefer it if I could.'

Rosy would really prefer it if she didn't.

'Look, Mrs Marksharp, you can trust me to be discreet and really what happens and where between you and your husband is no one else's business. I have no interest in ever mentioning the coat cupboard again. I promise.'

Marion Marksharp, under the lights of the tree, went seven shades of red. Then she spluttered, and then went even redder, before sitting down upon the bench. Then she stood up again, mere seconds later, and fixed Rosy with her death glare. No shame then or mumbling apology heading Rosy's way soon.

'I had wanted to talk to you about the phone call we received yesterday, actually. I didn't get a chance in the car – always best to concentrate on the road, I feel. Terribly exciting news though and yet you seem remarkably flat. Can I ask why, Rosy? This is such a perfect opportunity – we couldn't have dreamt up a better way of promoting the school.'

'Am I? I'm sorry if it came across like that, Marion' – Rosy didn't often lie but she wasn't prepared to bond quite so honestly with Marion over her reluctance about entwining the school with Matt. Glimpsing the woman semi-naked did not mean she was going to bare herself in return – 'but I think that's a little unfair. You know I'm utterly committed to keeping Penmenna open.'

'Yes.' Marion paused. 'Yes, you are, I know that. I was just surprised that you weren't more enthusiastic about the Penmenna Hall project. This is a golden opportunity that has literally dropped into our laps by a hovering angel.'

Rosy wasn't sure an angel had much to do with it but Marion was right; if she took out her reservations about Matt's involvement, this was better than anything they could have dreamt up between them, and her own plan wasn't working as quickly as she had hoped. Not every head she needed to talk to had returned her calls yet.

'I'll invite Matt into school this week and we'll have an assembly and get the ball rolling as quickly as possible. The sooner our children are on screen and winning hearts, the sooner our battle is over. Now if you could make sure some of the more pathetic ones are wheeled out, that small girl in Class Two, for example, I could see if Andrea could borrow a wheelchair from work...'

'I'm sure I've already said no to that, Marion, let's stick to what is. We've a great school with great kids. But you're right that the Penmenna Hall thing is an opportunity too big to miss. You organize the assembly and we'll go from there.'

'If you think so, plus now I'm friends with Angelina I'm sure we could get her on board. After Lynne mentioned her being in the village, it was too good an opportunity to pass up. I don't know why you were so resistant – she's terribly good fun.'

Marion paused to eye up their host, who was wandering across the lawn with drinks in his hand, accompanied by Mr Marksharp, presumably on the lookout for his wife.

'I wonder... I wonder if we could use Chase... although he's quite reclusive these days. There'll be something he can do, I'll just have to work it out.'

'Should we ask him first?'

Marion laughed, one of those tinkly insincere laughs that really annoyed Rosy usually, but today scared her a little as well. She knew this woman could be politically ruthless but that giggle was bordering on the maniacal. She took it to mean the answer, for now, was a no.

'Hello again, sorry I got waylaid.' Chase passed her a drink.

'Yes, I shall get a reputation for that sort of thing if I'm not careful!' Mr Marksharp boomed as he leant to give his wife a kiss on the cheek. Not a sleazy kiss, or a possessive kiss or even an overtly sexual we've-just-been-caught-in-the-cupboard kiss, just a normal, hello–I-love-you kiss. It was sweet, quick and would have been unnoticeable had not Rosy been particularly focused on romance at the moment – or telling the difference between potential romance and control-based game playing. No one else paid it much credence, but for Rosy it was a window into Mrs Marksharp. She was beginning to realize that there was a lot more than playground terrorist and Machiavellian strategist to the woman in front of her.

'We were just talking about local colour.' Marion immediately extended the conversation to her husband and their host.

'Not the sort you two provided earlier, I hope,' joked Chase. Rosy froze. He was going to get eaten, spat out and stamped upon. She thought he was a friend of the family. Surely he knew this was a no-go? Did he have no self-preservation skills at all? She was tempted to shut her eyes. She did not want to watch this and, to top it all, her forehead now seemed to have formed a permanent stress crinkle.

'Haha, you are such a toad! As if I'm not embarrassed enough!' laughed Marion. Laughed? Had Rosy been transferred to an alternative reality? She scanned around. Everything seemed as normal. And that wasn't one of her usual scary tinkles, that was a deep laugh, a laugh from the tummy. Was this Chase possessed with some kind of magical skills? Maybe they should use him after all. He could surround the school with a no-merge forcefield or something. Unicorns on the gates, that sort of thing.

'I can't take her anywhere, Chase. You know what she's like. Any opportunity and she pounces,' Mr Marksharp added. The laughter grew louder and Marion punched her husband on the arm. What on earth? Rosy decided not to get caught up in whatever this was. There was no way she was going to join in. This was like some kind of *Game of Thrones* trap – one giggle would accidentally escape her throat and she'd be surrounded by triumphant menacing sword-wielding types. She was going to just stare at the floor until the laughter stopped.

'Oh God, sorry, Rosy. I didn't mean to make you feel uncomfortable,' Chase said. 'It's just we've all known each other since uni, so… well, we know each other really well. Tell you what, let's get you mad drunk until all your inhibitions melt away and you too can take the mickey out of Mother Superior, the Monster Marksharp!'

Oh my God, how did they know everyone called her that?

'Rosy doesn't want to get drunk! We're not eighteen any more, she's a professional woman trying to find a solution to a major problem, she wants her wits—'

'No, it's OK.' Rosy heard her voice speaking but didn't understand how or why. 'I think I would really like that.'

'In that case, Richard, you'd better go and get us a couple of bottles, we're going to bed down and bond! Don't look so scared, Rosy, it was your idea! Oh, but

before you play fetch, help us! When you so rudely interrupted us' – she sent her trademark dark glare at her
husband and Chase, which seemed to bounce off without
impact – 'we were just talking about getting Angelina on
board. I put stage one of the plan into action yesterday but
Rosy just keeps looking at me blankly as if she was shaken
at birth. I've already tracked her down, now I just need to
brainwash her into complying.'

'How unlike you, my love,' Richard remarked. Marion
stuck her tongue out at him. Chase smiled and then started
hopping up and down, foot to foot, like one of Rosy's
pupils.

'Angelina? Angelina from all those reality shows? She's
my dream date, my soon-to-be-wife. Well done, Marion!
She's amazing, so beautiful but so vulnerable, you know,
she just needs an understanding man to support her, help
her, instead of those douches she always goes out with. I've
heard she was in the village, and you've spun her into your
web already, good work! What's she doing this evening?
Let's get her over!' Chase looked as if he had won the
lottery, his blond good looks shining with optimism.

Rosy finished her glass in one.

# Chapter Twenty Five

Matt stood nervously outside Rosy's door, orchid in hand. He wasn't sure why he was here; the lights weren't on and her car wasn't in the drive which suggested, strongly, that she wasn't home. However, he had been pacing up and down in his own house for a while now, practising his speech about how he wanted to use today to explain how he felt and so on and so on, until he was compelled to knock and see if he got to deliver his speech in person.

Angelina was driving him potty at home, moping about and throwing herself into Victorian heroine poses all over the furniture. He hadn't realized that not having a Valentine was even more traumatic than having Scramble eat her shoes.

Hence his standing on the doorstep of an empty house on a kind of dry run, just to quell his nerves a bit. He had always seen himself as an alpha male, maybe not a death-defying lorry-leaping James Bond, but certainly a man who knew his own mind, managed his love life easily and wasn't daunted by anything. He wasn't liking this change in personality very much.

Still on the doorstep and dithering, he scolded himself, *Who are you? Just ring the bloody doorbell*. A mixture of relief and disappointment flooded him as he did so and nothing happened. Of course she was out; it would add credence to his boyfriend theory. What the hell was he doing standing on a doorstep like a moping teenager, reluctant to go home? She wasn't suddenly going to appear, all single and full of smiles and cooing over his orchid, perfect ribbon or not. If he didn't pull himself together he'd soon be sporting greasy hair, acne and a notebook full of badly written poems.

He tried one more time, just in case, and then wandered back down the path and home again. As he entered the living room he found Angelina had managed to dress herself in something far too expensive for a quiet night in and had a very determined glint in her eye. Wishing he had stayed pining on Rosy's doorstep, he knew this signalled the beginning of something he absolutely was not going to want to do.

And he was right. It wasn't long before he was being dragged at full tilt by his sister into some sparkling Cornish mansion, thrumming with people and noise, looking like it had been decorated by Hollywood and crammed full with both the overdressed and people in jeans who looked like they hadn't seen a shower in days. He suspected he fell into the latter category. Noticing a gentle four-piece band in the corner, he glanced at his watch and then flashed a smile at a passing waitress as he declined a glass of pink champagne. Angelina grabbed two, knocked one back and then cast her eyes around the house with her this-is-where-I-belong look on.

'Happy now?'

'Don't be ridiculous, Mattie, I'm always happy. Although admit it, it was perfect timing meeting Marion yesterday otherwise we'd both be at home, and frankly your moping was beginning to bring me down!'

'My moping? I don't know how to begin to—'

'Ah, there she is. Marion, Marion.' Angelina stood up on her tiptoes and waved as her friend from the night before weaved unsteadily through the crowd, wearing some kind of sequinned bodycon dress, hair and make-up slightly askew.

'Darling, hello, so glad you're here, I've got so many people ready to meet you! But first of all do say hello to Richard. Oh, and Matt, dear man, how good of you to come. We have such a lot to talk about!' She squeezed his arm so tight he was amazed it didn't pop out of its socket, although the tingling indicated there was a good chance she had managed to stop the circulation. 'And Rosy's here somewhere, I'm sure she'll be pleased to see you.'

'Rosy's here?'

'Ugh, for God's sake, don't mention Rosy to him. Do you know he got her a plant—'

'Did you say Rosy is here?' Matt asked again, attempting to cut his sister's stream off and shake some feeling back into his arm.

'Yes, yes, darling. I think she was outside last time I saw her.'

Matt turned and headed for the vast glass doors that opened towards the garden, ignored by Angelina and Marion, who were still talking ten to the dozen about him as he left.

'…and I said to him, women only respond to diamonds, decent handbags and holidays. A plant, for goodness' sake! There's no hope for him at all.'

The professional in him had to admit that the garden was stunning; as he wandered through he couldn't see a single thing he would have done differently. As at Penmenna Hall everything was in bud, bar the camellias which were in full bloom. It was as busy out here as inside, with groups of people chattering, giggling and swaying. Many were gathered around a violinist playing in the depths of the garden. He was beginning to suspect there would be a harpist in the bathroom.

His eyes lit upon an old horse chestnut, its trunk as thick as three burly men, with lights strung around the very lowest hanging boughs. And there, at its base, on a wooden slatted seat, sat Rosy. He felt his heart still for a second before galloping at runaway-train-on-a-steep-hill speed. She looked perfect, a smile on her face, the lights casting a glow that made her look as if she were framed by starlight.

His feet sped towards her, halted by another man reaching her first. Insufferably good-looking and impeccably dressed, he had features that wouldn't be out of place in one of those men's magazines, all blond and tall like a cartoon hero. He might look like he'd be far more at home in a manicurist's chair than an old bench in a garden but it didn't seem to stop him sinking down with ease as he handed Rosy a champagne saucer and received an intimate smile in return.

Balls! What should he do? Matt couldn't seem to drag his eyes away, and felt a muscle in his thumb pounding. Then his cheek joined in. This was no good. The two looked to be deep in conversation already. His feet felt stuck but there was no way he was slinking back into some bushes. Having already had the man or mouse conversation with himself once today, he knew man had to be the answer. It was just that to approach the two of them, heads together, felt more like masochist than man, a self-flagellating medieval priest kind of madness.

Getting closer he saw that whilst their body language seemed synchronistic, and their conversation was flowing animatedly, there was no overpowering sexuality to their interaction. You could tell when people were sleeping together and his radar was beeping a loud 'no' at this point. Even if he was wrong, and he admitted he could be, he doubted these two were a forever match. He might be back in the game! His face relaxed again, the smile returning to his lips. Maybe Matt the scruffy gardener was more her type after all; she could be left cold by cartoon princes with perfect nails. It seemed there was a distinct lack of spark here, whereas when he and Rosy were in the same space there was a magnetic field compelling them together, sparks electric blue and whippet-quick flying around their every interaction.

Talking of whippet-quick, Rosy's head whipped around, the bond between her and Cartoon Hero instantly dashed. Matt couldn't help but grin so hard that his cheeks hurt and his ears stretched. Rosy leapt to her feet – could this be it? Would she realize how daft she had been last night and hurtle headlong towards him? She was looking a tad hurtle-y actually, swaying a little and raising her right hand and pointing at him. That didn't look like a look of love. In fact, now dead close, his face froze as she raised her hand up again, resting her fingers on her forehead and her thumb just below her lip, her jaw set rigid and her chin jutted slightly. The specific emotion she was feeling was just outside his reach, but whatever it was, it was making him feel less than positive. What had he done now?

He had no choice but to take a couple of steps closer, his grin now fixed and insincere. He may be used to full-on barrages of abuse from Angelina but this was something else. The square set of Rosy's face and silent stare laid heavy on his shoulders. Then, as finally they stood face to face, a few feet apart, the thought of greeting her with a kiss on the cheek was as ridiculous as snow in June.

'Rosy?'

She withdrew her hand from her face; she was no longer static, her arms were sweeping furiously, everywhere, taking in the whole garden, violin, canapé trays and all.

'All three, Matt, all three! Home, then work and now, now this. And today of all days. What is wrong with me? Why do I do this? Why are you doing this? Huh? What is it about you? Why did you choose me to do this to? Surely, the law of averages, it can't be me again, it just can't!'

'Rosy, I'm sorry, I don't... here... let's sit down—'

'Oh no, don't even think about touching me! Do not think about it!' She shook herself, slapping at his hand. 'You haven't left me a single place... you'll be popping up at Lynne's next. Should I give you the name of my GP, my dentist? Make it all a bit easier for you. Just accept it as a fait accompli?'

She was shouting now and Cartoon Hero had moved forward, next to her, shoulders drawn tall in warning to Matt but also shooting looks of complete astonishment at Rosy.

'Rosy, really I—' Matt tried again.

'Just stop! Don't say anything. I can't believe I could get it so wrong again. The bloody Rule, I should have kept

The bloody Rule.' Her voice was breaking now and whilst this made no sense at all, Matt just wanted to draw her in and wrap her up, stroke her hair and make it all right. But her anger was clearly directed at him, and common sense dictated that as much as every bone of him wanted to stay, he needed to leave for her sake.

Her shoulders started to convulse and Hero hovered no more but decisively moved in and wrapped his arms around her whilst looking across to Matt.

'I think you'd better go, buddy.'

'This makes no se—'

'Go! Just go, Matt!' Rosy was now outright sobbing. Shaking and sobbing.

Silently he turned – what choice did he have? – and headed back to the car, passing the guests in the garden who managed to pretend they hadn't been listening whilst shooting him sympathetic looks – those that didn't look at him as if he was a serial killer.

He had no idea what had just happened, what had provoked such irrational distress, but his heart was breaking for Rosy.

# Chapter Twenty Six

Rosy sank into Chase's arms, inhaling the deep lemon scent of him and trying to calm her breathing, rapid-fire gulps slowly morphing into something less frenzied. She watched Matt as he walked away, heavy-footed and with his head down. She wasn't sure what had possessed her as she saw him standing in front of her, but it had sure felt like a least a decade full of rage and fear, and a refusal to be played with again.

'I did it,' she murmured into Chase. 'This time, I did it.'

'You certainly did something.' His hands were stroking her head, as one would to calm a feral cat and this, combined with the sudden feeling of strength she had, was enough to get her to step back and smile at him.

It was as if some tremendous storm had passed, one that had caught her up and whirled her about until she had no sense of where she was. She looked around her and saw, as she re-grounded herself, that she was in his garden, surrounded by a multitude of people, many of whom were staring at her before hurriedly looking away.

Her knees suddenly felt trembly, and without being aware of speaking she realized there was a sound coming from her lips.

'Ooooh… oooooh… ooooh.' A long sound, a succession of them, as it dawned upon her that she may have thrown off her shackles of fear but had done so in front of many witnesses, and that the story of Rosy Winter, held-together headmistress extraordinaire, melting down so very publicly would be around the village quicker than a dose of smallpox.

'Oooh… oooh…' Her sounds were quicker now, higher pitched and she felt herself leaning back into her protector.

'Rosy, Rosy, it's OK. Here, come with me.'

He took her by the hand and led her away from the eyes all around her. She followed him across the garden and down a hilly, stony scrabbly path until she could breathe the salt tang in the air and feel the sand filling the top of her shoes.

'Now breathe deep,' he instructed, his American lilt sounding at odds with the patter of the waves rippling on the shore. And as he spoke he held her hand firmly, but put distance between their bodies until they were both standing upright and square, facing the sea with her copying his breathing patterns, in and out, in and out, until she began to feel the shaking diminish and her breath come back to normal. Rosy wasn't to be fooled twice though and looked around, all around, to ensure that no one was here witnessing this other than Chase. She could hear the murmur of the party a little way up the hill, but here on the beach it was just her and this most unusual man she had met but a few hours ago.

'There. Better?'

'Yes, thank you.'

'Well then, let's sit.' He did so, smoothing the sand next to him, ridding it of the scrunched-up bits of seaweed that were littered all over the beach. 'Now, I'm no professional, but it looks to me like something just happened there that you probably need to talk about. I know I don't know you well, but sometimes a stranger is better than a friend...'

Rosy looked him up and down and the words came tumbling out.

'It was just the final straw, him showing up here and on Valentine's Day. I didn't know you knew him.'

'I don't.'

'You mean he came here uninvited?' Even she could hear the heightened pitch of her voice.

'Woah, woah.' Chase rubbed her shoulders. 'I'm about seven steps behind you right now, but if that is Matt, the man you were talking about earlier, I should say that when you described him to me you left out the bit about thinking he's a psychopath...'

'I didn't say he was a psychopath, but you have to admit, it does look a bit like it, him turning up here uninvited.'

'You know him better than me, but didn't Marion text Angelina and invite her here, when we were all in the garden? And he is her brother, so she—'

'Oh my God! Angelina brought him.'

'That would be my guess.'

'But still, he's displaying all the signs, Chase... he's moved in next to me, then got involved in the school and then turned up here, where I didn't even know I'd be, and heads straight for me.'

'Why don't you start at the start.' Chase smiled in such a way that Rosy didn't feel mad, or judged or embarrassed and, as she sifted the sand through her fingers, she started to tell him the story of Matt moving to the village and the friendship that they had shared. She talked and talked and Chase wordlessly listened, sculpting pictures in the sand alongside her until she had finished.

He fixed her with a stare and, holding her eyes with his, responded to all that she had told him.

'Look, don't hate me, but from all you've told me, he sounds like a pretty normal bloke, who you have a lot of fun with, who wants to help you win your battles at work and you both seem attracted to each other. Like I said, I'm no professional but there doesn't seem to be a whole host of signs of psychopathy so far. Not once did you mention pulling the wings off butterflies, or a sudden up-spike in the disappearance of all the local cats. There's something else going on here, Rosy, and no one is forcing you into anything, but everything you've said, well, I'm trying to marry it with your reaction to him and it just doesn't quite add up.'

Rosy took a deep breath in and looked at the man in front of her. 'It's Josh,' she said and sat back to see his reaction.

'I don't know what that means but I think it's going to make a lot more sense. Tell me about Josh.'

'I met him at university – he was living in the room next to me at halls. He was so so handsome, dark curly hair, sparkling eyes and a way of lighting up a room when he walked in.' She quickly sneaked a peek at Chase, who was smiling and nodding. The world hadn't exploded. She had never told a single soul in Cornwall any of this and it actually didn't feel frightening, right here and now, more like it was something she needed to do. 'I couldn't believe that he was interested in me, plain little Rosy Winter.' Chase didn't interrupt with the whole 'no, you're not' thing, he just kept nodding, his silence encouraging her to continue.

'It didn't take long before we were completely intermeshed, I was so in love, or thought I was.' She couldn't stop the little harrumph that escaped her lips at this point. 'I was so stupid.'

'You were eighteen, away from home for the first time and fell in love. Honey, that's not stupid – that's learning about life.'

'No, in this case it was stupid. Although I did learn a little, I'll give you that. Anyway, we did everything together, he even dropped his course and started mine, in the very first half term. All the friends I had made within the course and in halls were suddenly his. It wasn't until years later I realized that should have been a red flag, that it's not normal not to have friends of your own...'

'But you were young and in love, and you wanted to share your world with him.'

'Yes, yes, that was it exactly. I was so happy. I couldn't believe that life could be this great. He would come everywhere with me. I didn't know what I had done to deserve such huge affection. He wouldn't even let me lift a shopping bag, he was devoted. Or that's what I thought. I didn't even think it was weird that he would drive me to and from work – I was tutoring school kids privately just to top up my student loans – and he would come too, introduce himself and wait in the car until I had finished. It didn't take long before the parents would be inviting him in for coffee whilst I would be dividing fractions and teaching simultaneous equations. At that point I felt so lucky, so blessed, to have this movie star of a boyfriend that everyone adored because he was so charming, and so invested in me.'

'And then what happened? Cos it's real clear that something did.'

'Yeah, it did.' Rosy mimicked his Americanism without even realizing she was doing it. 'To cut a long story short, he hit me...'

'He did what! Oh, Rosy, I'm so sorry, but not all men—'

'I know, but some are. And that wasn't the worst of it – he locked me in our flat for days. I'd banged my head when I went down and came around in the bathroom, locked in. I couldn't get out and when I finally managed to escape, nobody believed me.'

'Oh, Rosy, I am so sorry that this happened to you. Why would they not believe you? Who wouldn't believe that? You seem pretty darn trustworthy to me.'

'It's all right, Chase, it's not your fault, it's not anyone's fault apart from Josh's.' As she said these words, Rosy realized that she had relayed this story without tears, without the iron knot that sat in her stomach when she recalled it to herself, alone as she tried to sleep, as she had done on and off for years. That this time the telling of it was just like telling a story, a story that had happened to someone else.

'It turned out that all the time I had been studying or working or socializing he had been drip drip dripping lies into their ears: Rosy drinks too much; Rosy is a little wobbly, you know; it's not all her fault, her whole family struggles with issues, and so on. Then, when he had me prisoner in the house, he told everyone I was having some kind of psychotic break so when I escaped, ranting like a madman about being his prisoner, everyone believed him. He'd been suggesting this was going to happen for months, and after all no one knew me like he did, and it was no surprise for anyone but me when I behaved true to the type he had cast me as.'

'Well, what happened next? Did you go to the police? That's battery and kidnap at the end of the day.'

'No, apparently it's a domestic, or it was back then. Plus when they asked around everyone backed up Josh's version. I lost my friends, my job – no one wants an alcoholic with psychosis tutoring their kids – and of course my flat, because we were living together by then. Everywhere I went those first couple of days people were looking, talking about me, and how my poor boyfriend had to put up with so much, even the friend I stayed with.' She took a big shuddering breath as Chase put his arm around her and gave her a reassuring squeeze. A much needed it's-OK-you're-safe squeeze.

'Rosy, that's one hell of a trauma. You lost everything. Losing a relationship is hard enough at the best of times, even one so toxic. More so, maybe, because it was such an utter betrayal of all you believed it to be. And then to have all the security you had there, your friends, or those you thought to be your friends revealed to be false as well. Of course it's going to have an impact. What did you do?'

'I went home, home to Mum and Dad, transferred my uni credits and finished my course at the local university, did my teaching qualification and then got a job locally, only finally moving away again once my confidence had been rebuilt. Oh, and I came up with The Rule.'

Chase let out a little laugh, one of those gruff, what-else-can-you-do laughs.

'You mentioned The Rule earlier. What is it? Presumably it's what you came up with to prevent this ever happening again. Also, and you don't have to answer, but what happened to Josh? Do you know? Did he really get away scot-free?'

'I don't mind answering that. No, he didn't, not really. He got his degree, went to Australia and was in a fatal motorbike accident. It was reported in an alumni magazine that came to my parents' house. I almost felt guilty when I found out because of the huge sense of relief. I couldn't stop crying. I know that sounds weird, but I felt like I almost had a responsibility to make sure he couldn't do this again, and I didn't know how to ensure that. Especially with the police refusing to take action. What he did to me was, well, I've told you, but the thought he could do it to someone else, that was such a burden. And now he can't.' She let out a little *huh* noise, one that seemed to encapsulate the whole range of emotions that Josh's death had raised in her, before she continued. 'And yes, that's exactly why I came up with The Rule, and so far it's worked. As long as I've stuck to it. It's simple really. I don't blur boundaries. Everything is kept in compartments – my dating is completely unrelated to any other arena of my life, so when it goes wrong it doesn't blow up every aspect of me.'

'And let me guess, The Rule obviously says no dating your neighbour!'

'Ha! Damn right it does, I won't be caught out twice.'

'So, does it not get lonely living your life in such a fashion? Expecting things to go wrong instead of anticipating they'll go right? And, oh please don't bite my head off for this, but is it possible that not every man that moves next door is a monster' – Chase paused to give Rosy time to throw something at him, but she nodded and waited for him to continue – 'and that just maybe, Matt—'

The sounds of petulant squawking interrupted him as someone hurtled down the little slope leading to the beach, and from the noises emitting from the path, in both high heels and bad temper.

'Who is…?' Chase started to ask. It was hard to make out much more than an outline now the light had gone.

'I knew I'd find you, you evil, shrew-tongued witch! Who the hell do you think you are and what on earth gives you the right to treat my brother like that?'

# Chapter Twenty Seven

'I'm serious, how bloody dare you? That man has done nothing but good his whole life, for Christ's sake, he's even used his big career break to help your poxy school. I swear, I swear you have no idea. The only weak moment in that man's life has been getting some stupid no-sense crush on your dull, mousy—'

'Well, Angelina, I'd been hoping you'd turn up,' Chase drawled, having leapt to his feet, providing a physical barrier between the two women and gently touching Rosy's shoulder in reassurance as he launched into a full charm offensive at Matt's sister. 'I'm Chase, it's a pleasure to meet you at last.'

Angelina's eyes temporarily stopped spitting fire at Rosy as, for the first time since her arrival on the beach, they fell on the six foot two inches of beautiful blond masculinity in front of her.

'Hmm...' Angelina drew herself up from her snarling animal form and grinned right back at him. Hair flicking over her shoulders and deep penetrating you-shall-be-mine gaze turned on full power. Rosy stayed sitting. These two were glowing enough to light a whole village and she was suddenly overcome by waves of exhaustion; her eyes were actually fluttering, but not flirtatiously like Angelina's (whose were going to take flight soon, they were batting so hard) and her chin kept dropping onto her chest, as if it were suddenly lined with lead.

Opening up to Chase had been the last thing she'd expected to do. Only a few hours ago she'd been in school expecting to drag herself home for an ice cream and Netflix binge and instead she'd found herself drinking champagne in a swanky dress and then ended up revealing her deepest secret to a stranger after shrieking at Matt like a banshee on steroids. This evening needed to come to an end.

She knew what Chase had been about to say, that she may have made a mistake by shouting at Matt. That it was utterly possible that all of Rosy's reservations about her neighbour, her sexy, funny, kind neighbour, were her own baggage and nothing to do with Matt himself whatsoever. Indeed, once all her screaming was over and Matt had turned to leave that very thought had arisen, niggling at the back of her mind.

The truth was that her explosion had probably been really good for her, providing a catalyst for disclosing her secret, which once she had done so led to a lightness that she hadn't experienced for years. Admittedly a lightness that this very moment was doing battle with the exhaustion raging through her now. She knew this couldn't be all it took for her to heal, but it was a huge step. She was wondering why she hadn't done it earlier.

Now was not the time to beat herself up. Whatever the rights and wrongs of tonight, something had very definitely shifted. However, trying to explain that to Angelina could be tricky, and not a battle she wanted to take on right now. The woman had been towering over her but a minute ago, quivering with righteous anger – which was probably a first – and Rosy knew she'd need to answer for it. But later.

She flicked a quick look up at her. Matt's sister was no longer screaming abuse in Rosy's face but giggling, simpering at Chase, her hips protruded towards him at such an angle it was a miracle she was still upright.

'It is a beautiful house, I was hoping to meet the host. Have you lived here long?'

Giggle, giggle, hair flick.

Perhaps if she stayed here silent a little longer, Chase could lead Angelina away and she could just lie here as the tide came in and lapped her feet, just until morning, and then she could face the real world.

The two of them continued chatting as Rosy zoned out and concentrated instead on sitting upright until they buggered off. It was not to be.

'The trouble is, Chase, did you say? The trouble is that I really do need to speak to her' – Angelina managed to infuse the word with huge meaning, a meaning that implied Rosy ate babies for breakfast – 'about how she needs to stay away from my brother. How she needs to treat others as she would wish to be treated, such an important rule in life, don't you agree?'

Despite Rosy's heavy eyes and nodding chin, her eyebrows managed to shoot up as she overheard that particular gem. Wow!

'And that she needs to stay away from him...'

'Well, from what I've heard, that is her intent.'

'And I'm sure there's not much you're wrong about, Chase' – giggle, simper – 'but don't be fooled by her. The road to hell, etc. And I'm damn sure I'm not letting her drag my brother any deeper down than she already has.

In fact, that reminds me, I have to call a friend. Maybe now Matt's seen her true self he'll be more responsive to my suggestions.'

Rosy watched through half-closed eyes as Angelina proceeded to strut around the beach, clad in a slip of beige silk that looked like it would fall off any second and heels so tall it was a miracle that they hadn't dug straight through the sand and all the way down to Australia. Chase stood watching her, absent-mindedly rubbing Rosy's shoulder as he did so.

'See, she's not so bad,' he whispered down to her, 'she just really cares for her brother. I always knew she'd have a sweet soul.' Rosy's whole face scrunched up in surprise. Really? He had seemed so switched on when she had been talking to him earlier.

'If this bloody sand scratches my shoes, I'm going to bill you,' Angelina spun around and hissed at Rosy before flashing yet another I'm-such-a-great-person-really smile at their host as she waited for her call to connect.

'Coo-eee!' A loud shriek came from the path and Rosy and Chase turned to see Marion and her husband approaching them. 'I thought I could hear you down here.'

'Where are you? I need you in Cornwall. What do you mean you're in Goa? Goa, for Christ's sake, there's nothing you can get there that you can't have here, other than herpes and a shell anklet. Inner peace? It's not the bloody nineties. I'm telling you my brother needs you. Now is the time!' Angelina failed to respond to Marion and Richard's arrival, so busy was she shrieking yet more rage into her handset.

'Ooh, we're having a beach party!' Marion sank down next to Rosy, whilst Richard hovered above the two, looking nervously at Angelina.

'I say, is that…?'

'It certainly is. I told you tonight was going to be a good night,' Chase said in response to Richard's question.

'Ooh, it has been, hasn't it?' Marion shimmied against Rosy's shoulder in an all-girls-together fashion.

Rosy couldn't help but shoot her a look full of daggers. 'It's been a long night, certainly.'

'Ooh, I heard about that. You being mean to darling Matt. All around the party. I'm surprised Angelina hasn't carved your heart out.'

Rosy whimpered.

'I think that it's all a matter of perspective, Marion. Rosy had her reasons and I think she's a trooper. Seriously, you know better than most how people jump to conclusions about things they know nothing about.' Chase leapt to her defence.

'Well, that they do,' Marion noted knowingly and with vigour, in that way very drunk people do. 'Don't you worry, my girl, we've got all of half term to sort it out. As long as you apologize before filming starts, it's all going to be fine.'

Rosy's whimper became a groan as she buried her head in her hands.

'Too right, you should be ashamed, and you've lost him forever now. Thank God! I've found him someone who'll appreciate him!' Angelina had finished her phone call and turned back to spitting vitriol at Rosy.

'I'll go and get some more drinks then,' Richard chipped in, his obvious go-to plan in every situation.

'Good idea.' His wife grinned.

'No, no, I don't want to drink any more.' Rosy struggled to her feet. 'I need to get home.'

'Don't you go upsetting my brother again!'

'You'll never get a taxi from here at this time of night. Here, woah, Rosy, let me help you.' Marion got to her feet, considerably more unsteady than the woman she was attempting to help. 'Blue room, Chase?'

'Yep, of course. Rosy, I think you should stay here tonight. None of us can drive – let's just get you to sleep. You've had a hell of an evening. I can come and sit with you if you want...'

'Unbelievable!' Angelina's fury at what she perceived to be a raging injustice was encapsulated perfectly in her shrill tone.

'No, no, Chase, that's fine.'

'Yes, I'll take her, you'll never find it otherwise, and we can have a good old natter whilst I do.'

Rosy let herself be led away. Ten minutes ago she hadn't thought today could get any weirder and yet now she was being put to bed by Monster Marksharp. Tomorrow, let alone the rest of half term, probably didn't bear thinking about!

## Chapter Twenty Eight

Half term had whizzed by and the jungle drums of the village had been working overtime after Chase's party, the facts of which were dissected over a dozen different kitchen tables. Yet, to Rosy's amazement, everyone was still talking to her. The woman in the village shop was no ruder than usual, the parents were as smiley and chatty as ever and she'd had lunch in the pub on Sunday, complete with Dave and Lynne and the medieval troubadours, and it was just like every other time.

Half term had only been marred by the death of Sylvie's mum, Margaret. Margaret had lived in the village ever since her twenties and was a cornerstone of the local community. Her death was a great loss and Rosy, along with most of the rest of the village, had attended the funeral. Those that couldn't fit into the church lined the streets to pay their respects.

Sylvie had followed the coffin, holding the hand of her little boy, who was the spit of her and due to start Penmenna next September, and Rosy felt tears rise and prick her eyes. This certainly put her worries into perspective. How selfish was she worrying about how she was perceived when others had to deal with such loss?

However, as shallow as it made her feel, having the first two days back at school and everyone acting normally, and as far as she was aware no online petition had been set up to oust her, was a huge relief. Her private life had exploded in the soap opera that was village life, her behaviour endlessly gossiped about and yet the sky hadn't fallen in. All those years and all that fear about being judged by her community, and it had come to nothing. She didn't quite know what to think.

Now the week was half passed and it was the day that Matt was due in to deliver his assembly and meet the school. Rosy loved watching the school creak to life every morning, and today the children arrived with excitement bubbling out of them like a witch's cauldron full of firework colours. The news that a local man was coming in to meet them in the Wednesday assembly and explain how everyone was going to be on television meant that the children, who had been excited about the Valentine's disco, were stratospheric about this.

She herself was a little more trepidatious. She had heard him coming and going in the cottage over the last week but there had been no hellos over the fence, no contact at all. Half of her was grateful for this – he presumably was respecting her need for space – but it meant that their first encounter since Chase's house was going to be today, in front of a hundred upturned little faces.

Taking the register in class she noticed the clock hands heading ever closer to ten past nine, when assembly would start, and despite impeccable make-up and her most professional suit Rosy was quaking a little. She had a simple introduction planned for Matt and then she would step back and let him take charge. The trouble was her mind wasn't picturing a simple and calm hall full of children listening obediently and adoringly. Instead it kept filling up with images of her screeching at Matt at the party, and even worse, that night he had come to supper, with his hands on her thighs, his lips... oh for goodness' sake! This was unbearable. Perhaps she should lock herself in the staff loo and let Marion deal with it.

But of course, she wouldn't. The children had been practising songs in Matt's honour: 'Five Little Peas' for the youngest and 'Oats, Peas, Beans and Barley Grow' for the slightly older ones. And then the very oldest had written and animated a song about a vegetable alphabet – they had pleaded to be let off including U, X and Z, but Mrs Adams wasn't having any of it.

Rosy was confident that the children would be beautifully behaved in front of the cameras and do the school proud, perhaps with the exception of some of her little ones. Billy, for example, found it next to impossible not to do roly-polies the minute the peas in the song went 'pop'. She hoped an audience would find it endearing rather than a sign of schoolwide subversion – although she wouldn't put anything past Edward Grant when it came to finding ammunition.

'Come on then.' The time had come. She led her own class into the hall, stopping on the spot when she saw Matt and the rest of the school already waiting. He smiled at her, but it didn't reach his eyes and he was running his hand across the back of his neck.

Any nerves he had didn't seem to affect his crazy level of handsome, though. But she knew that after her appalling behaviour she was lucky he had turned up at all. Marion was at his side, no doubt spouting reassurances, and looking like she was going to tuck his curls behind his ear or give him a quick spit-and-scrub on his face. He looked as if he were ready to pass out.

'Hello, hello!' Savannah and Chloe had spotted the cameras set up in the corner and were waving frantically, distracting Rosy from the nerves emanating from the man at the front.

The other four- and five-year-olds realized what the girls were doing and also all started frantically waving at the cameramen that Matt had brought with him.

'Grandma, Grandma, it's me!' Jack called.

'And the pea went POP!' Billy clapped, practising his song and jumping as he did so, pride scrawled wide across his face. 'Clap not roll, clap not roll, clap not roll!' he added loudly, just to make sure everyone knew that he had been trying really hard.

Rosy fought to keep the laughter in as she herded them across the hall and to the front where they sat. The youngest didn't come in often for assembly in the first term and were only now beginning to get used to it. Not laughing but presenting an authoritative face had always been one of the hardest bits of her job. Luckily today the children's spontaneity was a perfect ice-breaker and she felt her shoulders relax as she fought off the giggles.

Matt didn't have such professional restrictions and laughed out loud at the kids' level of cute, waving at them as they walked across and clapping Billy's 'POP!' His anxious expression completely evaporated, leaving that comfortable, relaxed and slightly mischievous one that Rosy knew so well. That she had slid her hand down as he had lifted her to the table. Arrgghhh.

She decided the best thing to do was just to send him her most welcoming smile and maybe try and speak to him later. She was exasperating herself with all the zigzagging in her head but one of the few indisputable facts of this whole sorry mess was that the Penmenna Hall restoration could be the saving of the school and for that she should be thankful.

He beamed back. She felt her neck tingle.

Now all the children were in place – there were ninety-three in total, two of which, the Russell brothers, had only joined the school this week – Rosy began.

'Good morning, Penmenna.'

'Good morning, Miss Winter.'

'Can we please have a Penmenna welcome for Mr… um… Matt, who is joining us today, and his friends from the television.' How the hell did she not know his surname? This was madly unprofessional – any other visitor and she would have checked first. She had let her fretting get in the way. She could have kicked herself.

Reserved clapping resounded through the hall, although a couple of the boys in Class Four made a clattering noise with their feet until a well-practised glare from Mrs Adams made them settle down with hands on laps, heads down and terror on their faces. Rosy herself was in awe of Mrs Adams' looks; they were a nod to the teaching methods of the nineteenth century and seemed to contain the combined power of the cane, the slipper and the guillotine without any recourse to actual items. Mrs Adams was a firm proponent of the 'children should be seen and not heard' school of thought and would prefer classrooms segregated by gender and social class. She was the only woman Rosy knew who still asked 'and what does your father do, dear?'

Rosy smiled and moved her hand down slowly, the international schoolteacher gesture for *quiet*. 'Now, we have been practising a welcome for you, Matt. Class One, if you would.'

Matt listened attentively to all three classes' offerings, clapping and smiling in the right places, and giving a nod and a thumbs up to the older ones for 'ximenia, yam and zucchini'. He thanked them and, as Rosy returned to sit on the floor with her class, he launched into a big hello where he introduced the film crew by name, Bob and Sid, and explained what he was going to be doing up at Penmenna Hall and how he hoped the children would help him.

He launched a quick slide show on the smart board showing what the gardens were like now and his plans for how they would look when he was finished. He pulled children up to the front and had them doing activities; in fact he overran his slot by fifteen minutes, but remarkably managed to keep the children focused, attentive and engaged the whole way through.

The only awkward moment was when the youngest Russell brother stood up and with an imaginary gun took potshots at his brother across the hall. The oldest brother (instead of shushing his sibling) jumped up and took aim back. Matt smiled but didn't miss a beat as Mrs Adams managed to quell them both without getting in the line of fire and removed them wordlessly.

Once he had finished, the children were all excited about going up to the hall, which they would begin doing this very week to start planting and get a feel of the place. Marion had organized the rota and they would be going up in groups of ten, and for the first couple of weeks

Rosy knew she would have to accompany them. If she neglected her professional responsibilities just to dodge Matt and keep The Rule, the very premise of which was so deeply embedded but beginning to lose its hold after the night at Chase's, then she would be disrupting her own life in the very way she wanted to avoid. By going she could make sure everything was run smoothly and that the only outtakes the production company would get would be terribly cute puddle splashing, ladybird conversing and suchlike, rather than the children setting fire to things or slipping things into their pockets to sell later in the playground, Mrs Adams clipping a child around the ear (although after last time Rosy was fairly sure she had learnt her lesson – writing a letter of apology to an eight-year-old was probably the darkest experience of her life), or Hippy Dippy Harmony setting up a crop positivity circle. All the above would be distinct possibilities if Rosy didn't keep a firm eye on proceedings.

The children gave him a heartfelt chorus of thank you and, aping his earlier action, some gave him a thumbs up before trooping back to their classrooms. Lynne, who had come in especially for the assembly even though it wasn't one of her official teaching days, took control of Rosy's class so she could thank Matt and see him and the crew out.

'That was fabulous, thank you. You have a real gift with the children.' Rosy beamed at him. 'I really appreciate you coming in today, especially after... well... thank you. I have a feeling that this is going to be even better than I hoped it would.'

'Did you doubt it?' he asked with an arched brow.

'Of course not! It was just interesting to see you in action with them.' He was right, she should have known. Anyone who could make a Tudor hat out of weed control fabric and teeny bits of gravel was going to be a natural near a primary classroom. Now he was here, in front of her, she felt ridiculous. How could she have allowed herself to spiral so badly and assume he was another Josh? Examining his face she realized, again but with more force this time, that all her upset had been one hundred per cent her, and zero per cent Matt.

'You too! You have that whole mind control thing down pat. One sweep of the hand and a hundred children fall silent. You should market that stuff.'

'Every teacher does that!'

'Yes, but whilst I wouldn't usually dream of being rude about your colleagues, the thought of that scary-looking one controlling my mind could keep me up tonight, not in a good way, and as for that—'

She hit his arm, just lightly, a familiar gesture reminiscent of the camaraderie they had shared before that evening he had come for supper, before she had fallen prey to the crazy attraction she felt and before she'd screamed at him in Chase's garden.

'Ouch! I'm fairly sure you're not allowed to use corporal punishment in schools any more. Where's that one in the tie-dye? I'll tell on you.'

'No, you won't, I'll quell you with my mind control.'

'Ooh yes pl…' He tapered off at the glare she shot him. 'Sorry, not appropriate.'

'Nope. Look, thank you for today but I need to get back to class. I'll bring the first batch up on Friday like Marion arranged, is that still good?'

'Yep, weather looks OK, but wellies and waterproofs just in case.'

'Obviously.'

'OK then, see you Friday, if not before, Miss Winter.'

'Friday,' she said firmly as she handed him and the crew back over to a hovering and intrigued Marion, and started to head back to class. She hadn't taken two paces before she began to feel a bit bad and she turned back to him.

'Matt…' She paused at the door as she held it open. 'Putting the you and me dynamics to one side, I just want to tell you how grateful I am, on behalf of everyone, for what you've agreed to do for the school.' She moved back towards him and held out her hand to shake; she was going to end today on a professional note. 'Thank you, I'm looking forward to working with you.'

He smiled a slightly less Matt smile than usual and shook her hand.

'Here's to saving your school, Rosy. We're going to be an unbeatable team.' And then he was gone.

# Chapter Twenty Nine

Matt was sitting up at the breakfast bar pouring himself a second glass of red when Angelina clattered into the kitchen. He hadn't seen her properly since the party; she seemed to whizz in and out at all hours nowadays and with a purpose he couldn't quite decode. He had stopped asking where she went every day. Experience suggested it was best not to ask unless he wanted to listen to twenty minutes of drawling sentences punctuated with the overuse of 'darling' and still be none the wiser.

So instead he just nodded hello and took another slug. He knew he was a fool to be obsessing over Rosy; she'd barely had the time of day for him since their supper, then she'd had that hideous meltdown that he still didn't fully understand but certainly didn't want to broach and today, although friendly, she couldn't have made it clearer that she was expecting things to be 'professional' only, from now on in. He just wished he knew where he had gone wrong.

Maybe this was what his mates had warned him of when he was younger, that never having a woman say no was not necessarily a good thing. They got knocked back daily, so they said, and all was good. They had always threatened him that one day it would happen and his world would fall apart.

His world may not be falling apart but it was certainly nagging at him. It wasn't as if he was unable to think of nothing else. He was concentrating a lot of time on work, how this project was going to pan out, how involving the children was going to be great, a real USP, doing good for the community, the paying-it-forward thing that people were and should be doing more of. It was a savvy career move as well as the right thing to do. See, that wasn't thinking about Rosy!

'Hey! I said hello, is there a reason you're ignoring me?'

He took a deep breath and felt his eyes roll of their own accord. 'Hello, Angelina. Nice to see you.'

'Well, don't worry about making that sound believable in any way. Are you drinking?'

Matt moved the bottle out of her reach.

'But we don't keep red in the house!'

He gave her a measured, fraternal look. One that stated that he would like her to shut up, and quite quickly. Or he'd burn her Barbie doll.

'Oh my God! You're mooning over Little Miss Perfect, aren't you? Too busy baking to put out? Needs a ring on her finger first?'

Matt arched a warning eyebrow. 'Don't be such a cow and no!'

'Oh wow, I haven't heard that tone since you were twelve! You are, you are. I really thought you had more... I don't know... more taste? And actually after her appalling, appalling behaviour on Valentine's night it's not just a matter of taste but sanity. As in, she's clearly absolutely bonkers and if her outrageous display wasn't enough to put you off then you are too!'

'Angelina, I'm not sure you're the best person to lecture on acceptable behaviour...' Matt grinned at his sister and giggled a little as she gave him a look that stated that she was very clearly the pinnacle of calm and rational common sense and had no idea what he was referring to.

'Clearly, oh brother mine, we need to have a little chat about firm boundaries. That bottle's nearly gone, let me open some fizz.'

He hadn't got drunk with his sister in what felt like ages (well, just over a fortnight ago in London but he couldn't be expected to keep track of such things) and yes, she was a shocking example of humanity – having even less empathy or compassion than your average dictator, and very strong opinions on anything that involved Rosy, or directly opposed her world view – but she was bloody good fun.

She started with the Scarlett O'Hara and the curtains game, moved on to tangoing around the kitchen and then tried to give him a pedicure. She had wanted to tackle his fingernails, but those of a gardener's were pretty different to most and after examination Angelina threatened to have to lie down if he didn't cover them up immediately. Which is why he seemed to be currently dancing around the kitchen with Scramble, wearing a pair of gloves with half a red toenail. The one upside of Rosy's 'professional' relationship with him was that she was hardly likely to come wandering in and catch him like this. Mind you, how much would it make her giggle if she saw him now?

Dancing eventually turned to discussion, as he tried to get to the bottom of Rosy's relationship with the man at the party. Angelina veered between stating that she couldn't bear to listen to such drivelling, self-destructive nonsense, lying on the floor pushing Scramble (who had beautiful red nails at this point) off her, and jumping in on his monologue, outraged by everything he said.

'I think she's dating that guy at the party, did you see him? I wasn't sure at first but she didn't come home that night...'

'That's because she was as pissed as a newt and being very, very needy. Poor Chase had to get Marion to put her to bed, she was spoiling everyone's evening.'

'So they're not dating?'

'Why would he be dating Rosy? He's a multi-squillionaire with remarkable taste-, he's not interested in the country mouse.'

'Are you sure?'

'Oh yes, I happen to know that on the night of the party he was single and very definitely interested in someone else. Someone with style, grace, immaculate taste and a rather wonderful wardrobe.' His sister smirked a predatory smirk, one that made him grateful that he would never be on the receiving end of it. I really think you need to re-evaluate this crazy hang-up you have. She's really not worth it.'

'So, she's not dating anyone?'

'Oh my God, I can't take much more of this!' came Angelina's ever-patient reply as she picked up her phone again.

'But is she dating anyone?'

'How the hell am I supposed to know? Perhaps she's a lesbian? It would explain those shoes,' piped up his sister. This thought was so delicious she managed to switch focus from her screen back to the conversation.

Matt looked at her as if she were insane. He was fairly sure sexuality wasn't something that dictated which shoes one bought.

'I don't think she is.'

'I've never seen any signs to say otherwise.'

'Have you actually seen any signs that she is?'

'She doesn't wear very much make-up, and she owns walking boots and a cagoule!' Angelina was triumphant; it was obviously a clincher.

Oh dear, his sister's views were clearly coming from some pre-World-War-Two era, if not before. He didn't have the energy to challenge this right now.

'See.' Angelina struggled to mask her triumph. 'You need to stop wasting time, mooning about her. It all makes sense now. Start chasing women that actually like you, or men at the very least.'

'She does actually like me!'

'Hmmm, clearly not. She obviously didn't like you very much the other night and you do seem to be here alone.'

'She did at one point! I thought she decided not to see me because she was dating someone else, someone like Chase, but if that's not the case…'

'Oh my God, she's not dating Chase, she doesn't like men! I've had enough of this, I'm going to fetch some more fizz.' Angelina stomped out of the room, phone in hand, and left Matt with the dog.

'I need a really bold idea, a romantic gesture that declares how I feel. But it can't be stalky. That's the trouble, isn't it, Scramble? Some of those old-school romantic gestures are a little bit creepy and I need to be careful. Rosy was so upset the other night, I don't want to make things worse…' He felt he might be slurring his words, but thankfully Scramble was not too harsh a judge. 'What do you think I should do?' The dog, usually so supportive, remained mute, cocking his head and looking at Matt but not actually giving him an answer. Matt was not going to let that stop him. 'Maybe an orchid isn't enough – perhaps a plane with a banner, or a flowerbed with a declaration planted. I could do it on the show. She's such a love…' He saw her in his mind, all petite and furious, and then somehow, the dancing, the whirling, the giggling and the arguing was all forgotten and he found that he was really very, very sleepy.

As he laid his head back, ready to slide into sleep, he heard the living room door thwack open as his sister returned to the room. Opening one eye he could see she had her most determined look on, and that she was holding her mobile aloft with the triumphant stance of a cup winner.

'It's confirmed. All your problems are solved – Siobhan will be back in the country in a few weeks. You can thank me later!'

## Chapter Thirty

Friday dawned clear, which provided more relief than was natural to Rosy as she popped her wellies into the car. Despite her gratitude to Matt for making the assembly go smoothly and not using the opportunity to quiz her over her outburst, today was likely to be a bit of a marathon and she wanted it to go as well as possible. With her overseeing and ferrying groups of children, to and from Penmenna Hall, getting them familiar with the grounds, what they would be doing in the garden and the cameras, it was to be a day ripe with possibilities. But not the sort of possibilities she could get excited about.

The sheer logistics of driving the school minibus with ten small children (fifteen of the older ones) and a healthy smattering of parent helpers to and from the grounds, and then to and from again, and again, throughout the day were tricksy enough. As professional as she was, the thought of pasting on her camera-friendly smile for the entire day, after having to sing 'The Wheels on the Bus' several times on the journey, was of concern. She was really excited about this project but had a feeling she'd be ready for the quiet of her office and the warmth of never-ending coffee way before the day was even halfway over. She had visions of herself being dragged off by three o'clock, head to toe in mud and screeching for buckets of gin. She was a realist, after all.

Throw the presence of Matt into the mix and her ongoing mental conflict that his presence had reignited in her life, along with small children, mud, potentially sharp tools, hovering but well-intentioned parents and a camera catching every mud pie flung, every seed eaten and every micro-expression made was not a relaxing thought.

She pulled up at the school and raced to her office. She had one or two final early morning phone calls to make to confirm what she thought was the motivating factor behind Edward Grant's list choices. Then she wanted to just revel in the calm before the day got manic and whilst she still had the chance. Her peace was not to last as Harmony knocked on the door and let herself in before starting to witter on about animal rights. Rosy wasn't entirely sure where this was going but she knew it was very definitely interrupting the only calm she had anticipated for the day. She also knew it was a head's duty to listen to her staff and their concerns, but she had been finding duty rather irksome of late.

Trying to stop zoning out, she refocused on Harmony only to hear her talking about worms and slugs. God give her strength! This was going to require physical force, and so that was what she employed. Muttering reassurances about animal rights being heavily protected and indeed promoted onsite, she forcibly pushed Harmony out of the room and shut the door behind her. She would try extra hard to be nice to her on Monday.

It wasn't long before she was standing in the playground with Marion counting the first batch of children into the minibus. She had Billy with her, and Chloe. It was tactical; they would be wound up so tight if they were made to wait as the day progressed. By having them in the first cohort, less damage would potentially be done. Seatbelts were checked and double checked, songs were sung and rules reiterated. So far so good.

She also had Bradley with her in this group, accompanied by his specially assigned teaching assistant, Becky. The educational psychologist, Katie, had also come along this morning to monitor Bradley, to assess how the support they had in place for him so far was going and what the next step would be. She would continue assessing him in the classroom once he had returned to school and then would feed back to Rosy at lunchtime. Rosy had already emailed her and given her a heads-up about the Save Our School campaign and was really hoping Katie would come on board. Well-respected throughout the county, her voice could be impactful.

They pulled up in the grounds as close as they could get to the orangery where they had arranged to meet Matt but Rosy could see no sign of him. The camera crew were already set up and waved a hello as the children headed into the kitchen garden area in a crocodile of pairs, all dressed in wellies and waterproofs. The first ten children were only four or five years old and looked so cute; they were going to be TV gold.

'Hi!' Rosy beamed at Bob and Sid.

'Hi, are you all ready?'

'Yep, think so. Are we ready, class?' she turned and asked them. There was a high energy response that couldn't help but make the crew grin. Billy was so ready he high-fived the entire group of children and the parents too. Rosy gently turned him back and popped him into the crocodile again.

'OK, we're not sure where Matt is but we could get a couple of shots while we wait if you don't mind. Perhaps if you would be OK you could all head back to the bus and we could film you getting off, the kids could look really excited, yeah?'

'Well, um… OK.' Rosy wasn't sure of TV etiquette, and had the feeling you were supposed to do what was asked so the cameras had the shots they needed, but really she hadn't planned that this first cohort were going to spend their time getting on and off the bus. She'd do this and then see how things panned out. She turned the children around and they headed back onto the bus.

'I want to do gro-o-o-o-wing!' Chloe grumbled. She had a habit of escalating from a grumble to a grizzle to a full-on tantrum within seconds.

'I want to do gro-o-owing too!' Sophie echoed.

'And we shall,' Rosy stated firmly, popping herself in the middle of the two and holding onto their hands, 'We're just going to help the cameramen first and then we can get busy!'

'Hmmmmm…' growled Chloe. She was good at growling and had learnt it usually got results. But not from Rosy and not today.

'Um… where are you going?' Matt's voice came from behind her.

'We're just doing an off-the-bus shot, Matt,' Sid answered for them.

'Pea-pod-pop man!' Billy spun as he heard his voice.

'Hey, Billy boy, and the rest of you. How's it going?'

'We want to do gro-o-o-wing!' Chloe looked as if she hoped he had a higher authority, and would respond to a crescendo.

'And so you shall! Let's head this way.'

'But they've just asked us for a bus...' She felt her eyes narrow and her lips contract into a scowl as she addressed him, then quickly tried to stop herself. She knew it was embarrassment at not having the courage to talk to him about her outburst that was making her feel tetchy today. Two weeks had passed and she still hadn't explained it. Seeing him reminded her that she was being a bit of a coward, but she wasn't sure she was ready to tackle things yet. Plus, she had a school to save.

Matt looked at her, an indecipherable expression on his face. She looked down at her feet and then shot Katie a quick glance to see if she had caught this silent interaction. Having a psychologist around was unnerving.

'Hello, Rosy, Marion. Yes, but they'd have you doing filler shots all day and you don't want to do that, the kids don't want to do that and I really don't want to wait around so they can film a minibus. They can get the next one as it arrives.' Matt turned and addressed the children. 'We've got growing to do!'

The children cheered and, as if the Pied Piper had arrived, turned and followed him into the huge glass house just ahead of them. Rosy went with them, and sent apologetic looks to the cameramen, but they seemed remarkably unfazed by having their plans scuppered and just followed them in.

Inside the orangery was amazing; it was very warm and equipped with vast wooden tables. There was so much to look at in here, and even with nothing growing just yet, she could smell that warm earth of summer smell that took her straight back to childhood.

Rosy wanted to explore. She saw that there were old drawers that looked as if they dated back hundreds of years over in the corner and wouldn't be out of place in a medieval apothecary's shop, and so many different containers all labelled and looking as if they hosted a treasure trove of gardening goodies. But despite this desire, and it was quite a big one, once her eyes lit upon the table that Matt was now standing in front of, she couldn't drag her eyes away from it.

For there, all lined up neatly, were a collection of little tools, lots of little collections made up of mini trowels and stick-looking things that Rosy knew would have a name but she wasn't sure what it was, as well as a selection of mini brown envelopes and plant labels. The trowels had beautiful pale sage-green handles and startlingly bright silver blades, and along with the other things were tied in bundles with a matching ribbon. She wasn't the only one; the ten children lined up in front of her were quivering with excitement, like puppies waiting for a ball. They looked like they were about to burst, but Matt seemed to have an innate understanding of this as he picked up a bundle and looked towards them.

'Now I know you're all here to do some gardening. And I know you all want to grow your own vegetables and then Miss Winter is going to let you pick them and cook things at school with them. You are going to be just so grown-up with all this growing and the cooking that I thought I should help you out a bit.'

The children stood rapt, even Billy. The quivering had stopped when Matt started to speak, and now they were as still as stone. It was as if they knew what was coming and were not going to do anything to mess it up.

'So I have got every one of you, and you too, Miss Winter, a very grown-up present to make sure you can do your growing as best as you can.'

He looked straight at Rosy as he said her name and she felt a glimmer of the desire she used to have for him, before her old fears and bad behaviour had kicked in and potentially destroyed everything.

He then pulled over a rickety old stool that didn't look as if it would support the weight of a kitten, let alone a well-built man, and sat down.

'Here we have a bundle for everyone, with everything you could need to get these plants started. Shall we look at Miss Winter's first?'

The children all nodded fervent but silent asset. The cameras caught everything: their rapt little faces, Matt's grinning and the gift sets on the table.

'OK, so...' He pulled the ribbon gently and it fell open leaving the contents nestling in his hand. It reminded Rosy of a set of underwear she had, done up solely with ribbons. She felt a little shudder and a flush, but then it was warm in here. And it wasn't as if anyone could mind-read.

'Would you like to come here, Miss Winter?' He beamed at her. Sophie was nodding at her side furiously, as was Chloe, and Rosy had a sense that the four-year-old really wanted to push her forward, but was showing admirable restraint. She let go of both the girls' hands and headed to stand by the stool.

Matt smiled as she took her place and carefully placed the things into her hand, removing only the trowel, which she could see had her name embossed upon it in squiggly silver writing. These really were things of beauty, and glancing across at the table she saw that he had had the names of every individual child in the school embossed as well. It was such a generous and thoughtful thing to do. She felt almost awkward, shy, as she stood there and wasn't sure why such a thing would make her feel such a way. Perhaps now was not the time to analyse it; perhaps she should stop zoning out and pay attention to what was happening in front of her.

Matt raised his hand so both the children and the cameras could see what he was holding. 'Firstly, we have the most important thing, the trowel. This is like a little spade, and the reason it is little is because so are seeds, and we need this to help us dig teeny holes to put them in. Would we want big holes for tiny seeds?'

'No, that would be silly, we need ginormous holes for ginormous seeds' – Billy flung his hand out to demonstrate *ginormous* – 'and little holes for little seeds. Everybody knows that.' He nodded and folded his arms, safe in his knowledge. Rosy smiled at him. He may look like he was one constant roly-poly but she knew Billy was smart and took in far more than other people gave him credit for. He just did it his own way.

'You are exactly right! I think you are going to be great at this. We also need them to help us keep the weeds away, and that's a big job. Now this thing here' – he held up the wooden stick thing – 'is a dibber. Sometimes we don't want to dig a hole, sometimes you might just want to push this into the earth and drop the seed into the hole it makes. You can choose which you prefer – this is great for leeks, for example, but no good for potatoes. Which brings us on...'

Matt carried on speaking for a little while longer, showing them the seeds in their little packets, and still managed to hold his audience's attention. Remarkable considering the average attention span was usually four minutes. Rosy had to admire how he was handling the children. Standing right next to him she could see their little faces turned to him as flowers to the sun.

As well as their gifts he had brought a selection of vegetables to sniff, taste and prod, so they knew exactly what they were going to be growing. It was a nice touch and she wouldn't have expected it from someone who had no experience with little children. He was doing pretty well at this, and she could see that the camera was going to love it, him being all gorgeous-looking and kind to children. Women up and down the nation would be fainting as he filled the screen. And then she supposed he would be fully propelled into the world of celebrity that Angelina inhabited. He would leave the cottage and she could relax again. The thought was actually far from relaxing but she didn't have time to dwell upon it, as he was giving the children their trowels before they headed out to see where they would be doing all this digging and seed planting.

He led them out and gave them all space to play and explore the earth before planting, suggesting that they save the seeds until the next session, and just get used to the tools and the textures this time. The children were more than happy with that and, now immune to the cameras (there was no more manic waving), climbed into the raised beds and gave the earth a good workout. With the exception of Bradley, who just sat down in the middle of the bed and stroked his name on the trowel. Rosy had been keeping a close eye on Bradley, and was surprised that he was happy to get into the raised bed, let alone sit down in it, but he seemed to be coping very well with the change in routine. She was happy for him – this was a great step forward – but at the same time it would have been useful for Katie to see him struggling. As cold as that seemed it meant he stood a better chance of increased provision.

With the parent volunteers hovering over them, Rosy stood back and carried on observing the big picture. Matt wasn't shy, getting into the beds with them and dibbing and digging alongside, demonstrating how to do it without being didactic.

She watched him, his face lit up with enthusiasm, Chloe leaning into him as if she had known him all his life, as he held up a worm and explained to them why gardeners thought worms were magical. If it wasn't so stupidly complicated, Rosy felt she could be falling a little in love with him. By the look of some of the mums she wouldn't have been the only one. Sophie's mum's eyes had practically glazed over with lust, and Sarah, a mum of four, looked like she might quite like to tumble him in the raised beds there and then. Rosy really hoped she didn't. The irony of having to worry about the parents' potential behaviour and not the children's wasn't wasted on her – this hadn't been a problem at the China Clay Museum.

It didn't seem any time at all before their session was over and the children were packed up in the minibus and heading back for snack-time. Rosy would be turning around and heading straight back with the next cohort; no rice cakes and hummus for her. Not even a cup of coffee. She could foresee herself getting a little scritchety as the day carried on.

She realized on the drive back that Matt had barely addressed her directly. He had been very professional and actively engaged with the children and the parents, but with her there had been a polite distance. He had called her up as he had demonstrated the tools he had given the children (damn, she couldn't stop her face breaking into a wide smile, but it was such a nice thing to do, and so entirely unexpected) but other than that he hadn't addressed a word solely to her.

Once her second group was on the bus (she had almost had a fight break out as Sophie's mum was quite determined to do a second run as well, but she was no match for Marion), Rosy decided to see if she was imagining things or whether he really was keeping his distance. She was fairly sure that they were going to be 'an unbeatable team' – his words, she remembered them precisely – and now he seemed to be being so careful around her, almost as if he were scared to get too close. She knew she couldn't blame him, he was respecting her wishes, but irritatingly she kind of missed the relationship they'd had before. Then again, she might just be imagining things, or reading too much into his actions. She just didn't know.

# Chapter Thirty One

This time, as the second group arrived, Bob and Sid were set up and ready, and the cameras were rolling as the children got off the bus, waving at them and at Matt.

Waving is one of the first things babies are taught to do, and as they grow into toddlers and then infants it remains something that is easy for them to replicate and that will garner overexaggerated amounts of praise. Hence the maniacal delight the reception class took in waving at everyone who came across their path. As they grew this would become replaced by other ways to gather praise, sounding out letters perhaps, and then as they got older affecting an air of cool, however it was defined for their generation.

Things didn't change that much as one got older, she reflected, just the manner in which you manifested it. Which is why she had deliberately wiped off the lipstick she had found herself applying on the way here, and then reapplied it. It had been put on as a matter of course, then wiped off in case Matt thought she was making an effort for him and she didn't want to confuse things further, then reapplied because she was going to be on television and God be damned if she was going to appear frumpy. She almost wished she were four again; waving seemed the much easier option.

Her irritation was interrupted by a squeal and then a bawl as Susie slipped in the mud. Susie, who was the youngest child in the school but had had to join this slightly older group because of a dentist's appointment earlier, was already cross that she wasn't with all of her best friends, so falling over in the mud was a case of insult to injury.

Rosy rushed to her side and quickly scooped her up. Assessing her with speed, she saw there were no cuts or anything that needed immediate first aid, just injured pride and embarrassment. Rosy gave her a cuddle, stroking her hair and making soothing noises. She knew that this would only be needed for a second or two until Susie calmed down, whereupon she would jump down and carry on, demonstrating that she was a grown-up four-year-old, not a baby one. If Rosy were to ignore her, the bawling would intensify until no one could be heard over it and punitive measures would have to be taken. Expediency was the key in today's circumstances.

The whole thing took less than a minute and as Susie slid down from her she felt Matt's eyes upon her, and her own shoulders tighten. Did he think she was being too soft? *Come on*, her rational self kicked in, *why would he do that? This is your anxiety raising its head and is far more about you than him.* She would have to get her emotional responses to his presence under better control. Frustration that he made her feel a myriad of ways was *her* responsibility. She could wallow in that later with a big bowl of ice cream; for now her self-indulgence needed to stop.

Matt delivered his welcome and then trooped the children into the greenhouse where again he explained the tools and the vegetables exactly as he had done earlier.

Rosy knew she could watch this all day and each time the wonderment of the different children would keep it special and fresh. She wasn't called to the front this time; he chose Susie instead, who puffed up a good visible few inches as she stood there, in front of all the bigger children, being the helper.

It didn't take long before this group too had had their play in the mud and returned to the minibus, Matt waving them all off as Rosy helped them into their seatbelts. Time for round three.

The rest of the morning sped by. Matt had – and she wasn't sure how he knew to do this without having spent hours understanding the developmental-appropriate nature of teaching – changed the format slightly to reflect their age and abilities. He approached the thing in a more scientific way, still engaging them and making it all a two-way process. She had to admire it.

As they returned to the school, Rosy took her lunch in her office rather than the staffroom. She had the meeting with Katie and a whole pile of paperwork to sort through. Plus, she knew the staffroom was going to be full of parent helpers and teaching assistants cooing over how lovely Matt was. Bleurgh!

Katie knocked and came in, a statuesque blonde with a mind so sharp that Rosy was in awe of her. She was certainly the smartest person Rosy had ever met, and although she could be blunt and incisive, she was rarely wrong.

'So, Bradley clearly needs a lot of support. He did cope very well today, especially at Penmenna Hall, but I think that is because of the excellent care you're already providing in the shape of Becky and his care plan and I don't see why you or he should be penalized for the fact that strong provision is in place. Apart from anything else he'll need a wealth of things in place to ease his transition to Class Two when the time comes. In your email you outlined the potential changes the Local Authority are suggesting, and you're right, a change of schools at this stage to a big, new busier school could well mean he can no longer access mainstream education. I'm happy to write a report robustly stating that, and will include some of your other special educational needs children's details too because it's also going to negatively impact them. Although you and I both know I can't promise it will do any good. Once Edward Grant has the bit between his teeth...' She paused briefly, both women knew the implication, before continuing. 'Anyway, for the here and now I will be recommending that he has a minimum...' She carried on in this vein for some time, outlining the targets they would hope to meet for him, and the best ways to do so. Rosy breathed a sigh of relief. She knew she was lucky to have such strong educational psychologist support; she had worked in schools before where there was no one in post, or the person appointed was completely inept. Having an expert in their corner made such a huge difference to the life chances of these children.

'Now that Bradley is sorted, let's turn to you, Rosy.'

'What?'

'I'm going to cross every professional boundary here because a) my interest is piqued and b) we're supposed to be friends and I can't believe you haven't mentioned the exciting news in your life.'

'I don't have any exciting news.'

'Rosy, I'm an educational psychologist, not a mind-reader, but you'd have to be deaf, dumb and blind not to notice there is a very definite something happening between you and the dishy gardener.'

'Oh, Katie, don't make me doubt your skills now.'

'Oh, Rosy, don't think you can brush me off like a fool. Spill!'

'There's nothing to tell.'

'OK, if that's the way you want to play it, but if I can see it clear as day after being onsite for an hour or so, do you honestly think the children and parents are going to miss it, not to mention the cameras and a national television audience? No, don't scrunch your face up like that, that doesn't make it go away. Nope, neither does picking at that limp bit of salad and pretending I'm not here. All I'm saying is, as your friend, be very careful. Very careful indeed, because this show will raise the school's profile massively.'

'That's why we're doing it.'

'I hadn't finished! It will also probably make a star out of that man. He is ridiculously good-looking and from what I saw a natural with the children; they're going to be swooning left, right and centre.'

'Humpf!'

'And you are going to be the grumpy old cow who shot him a really evil look as you arrived and for no apparent reason. Now which one is going to be vilified in the press? Rosy, I don't know why you have a problem with him but you need to sort whatever this is out, and preferably before the cameras are rolling this afternoon.'

'It's complicated.'

'Ha!' It was a triumphant crow which received a suitably pitched Rosy scowl. 'OK, so we've made progress, you're no longer denying it. What has he done to you? Have you slept with him?'

Rosy watched a bit of lettuce launch from her mouth across the carpet.

'I'll take that as a no, then, but he wants to. Do you know, and this sounds big-headed but I'm not trying to be, I'm just stating fact, he didn't look at me once, not once other than in a friendly nod kind of way. Not that I want him to,' Katie hastily added, 'but they normally do. But you, his eyes went a bit squishy when he looked at you, and then sad. Squishy and sad. You don't stand a chance when that gets aired.'

'Oh bloody hell.'

'So, we've established he fancies you. In my very quick professional and untainted-by-rather-beautiful-arms assessment, I can't see much wrong with him. He seems intelligent, hardworking and bloody decent, if his rapport with the kids is to be trusted – which it probably is. That's the holy bloody triumvirate. Men like that are rare, let's face it, so the question is, what's wrong with you? Why the grumpy face?'

'Thanks for that, Katie. Makes me feel piles better.'

'Seriously, why did you shoot this man a look of pure evil as if you want to pull his fingernails off one by one?'

'Because' – Rosy's voice came out unnaturally high – 'he seems bloody lovely, but, oh I don't know. I'm just being an arse. I behaved badly the other day, I'm embarrassed and I don't think he deserved it, but I'm not sure. I think that's why he got the daggers, guilt on my part, but I did try and rein it in. The truth is, I'm so confused. I think I was in the wrong but I just don't know, it's equally possible that I'm in the right, Seriously, Katie, you're a professional – did you spot any signs of psychopathy or sociopathy this morning? Any glimmers at all? He has been showing all the signs of being keen, but he's just everywhere, all over my life and in a really short timeframe. He lives next door, I get to see him all the time, him and his I'm-so-cute-and-look-I-have-a-bloody-lovely-dog-as-well smile and then if that's not enough, he only wants to come along and save the school. I can't get rid of him, he's at my home, he's now in my work and he seems to have taken up permanent residence in my bloody head. I can't stop thinking about him and yet I know I can't go anywhere near him. Apart from anything else my instincts are all out of kilter and now we seem to be working together. It's confusing, frustrating and it just all makes me want to scream! So, yeah, I guess that's why I may be shooting him looks, but I really do think it was just the one, and it was super quick.'

'Hmmm, the only thing I can tell is something isn't quite right here, and I'm not sure it's because he lives next door. What you're saying is a little bit chaotic and that's not like you. I think this might be a case of you and me and the pub tonight! From what I saw, albeit briefly, this morning, I think there has been some stupid mix-up. Experience teaches us that communication is key. You know that. I know you know that. I suggest you start again. I'm no kind of love guru, my own private life is testament to that, but if I were you I'd hold fire on the evil looks, suck up the humiliation and try and play nice for the rest of the day. We can chat it out a bit more later, but right now I have to shoot, they're waiting for me at

Sanding Bridge school. I'll catch up with you later – six? I'll set the ball rolling re Bradley and I'll see you later. Oh, and seriously, consider what I've said about overthinking, just let the day roll out the way it's going to. Things are rarely as bad as we think they are.'

'Yes, I know. Go on, out! I'll see you in a bit and you can try and sort my head out. But I don't fancy your chances!'

'We'll see.' And Katie and her very knowing looks departed.

# Chapter Thirty Two

It was coming to the end of the day and Matt was exhausted, happy but exhausted. Actually scratch that, yes, he was both those things but baffled, he was very definitely baffled as well.

He looked up at Rosy, who was at that very minute working alongside the eldest children in the school, planting her first set of seeds in some soil. They were going to do experiments with successional sowing, some started early in the greenhouse, some later outside straight into the raised beds. She was making the most of her new tools as she was chatting to some of the kids, a great big beam on her face as they answered just as animatedly.

It was this Rosy that he had got to know over the last few weeks and it was this one that he had been strongly attracted to. He didn't think he had ever used the phrase 'strongly attracted to' before, not even in his head. He could feel his lip quirk even more. She would be perfect girlfriend material – damn, she'd be perfect wife and mother material. Watching her with these children, as he had been all day, was testament to that, if it weren't for that whole Jekyll and Hyde personality thing she had going on.

He could understand Rosy if she was a little insecure, anxious about relationships, scared of intimacy. All that sort of thing would make sense; it was fairly normal and he'd had years of training with Angelina. But this complete split personality was of concern. It seemed to indicate something running a little deeper.

Today was a perfect example: she had properly scowled at him when he arrived, her best and deepest Rosy scowl. The one that always seemed to have her eyes scrunched up and her lips pursed into the sweetest little moue (at least he thought that was what it was called) that he had ever seen. The knowledge that she did not want to be perceived as cute, or sweet, or endearing in any way when she was in this mood, made it kind of all the cuter. Even Sid had asked what he had done to upset the schoolteacher. He had had to shrug and say he really didn't know.

And he really didn't. And this was the trouble; her outburst on Valentine's Day hadn't been explained, and he didn't feel he should push for one. He had to assume when she was ready she'd say, and if she never was, then that was something he could do nothing about.

Before the party she'd been so warm, friendly, open and downright bloody melty. As if she were as attracted to him as he was to her. That kiss – that kiss had been insane. And as far as he was concerned they should be following on from that, and spending this time doing smoochy early relationship types of things. Most of which should be taking place naked. Not scowling and spitting like a cornered cat, which had been her precise reaction when his sister had turned up.

He didn't know which way to turn or what he was supposed to do or think. He quickly glanced at her again and caught her looking at him with deep thought, her head cocked to one side with her brows furrowed in puzzlement.

He felt himself grin broadly back at her. If he was inviting and friendly, ignoring her mood swings, then maybe she would come and ask him whatever it was she was thinking about. That would be the sensible thing to do. Would she smile back, an appeasement of sorts?

She blushed – ha! Victory! If she was blushing just because he was looking at her then he was in with a chance; she must still be attracted to him, otherwise her body wouldn't react that way. It would make sense. Surely the fire they had had between them was not something anyone sane would walk away from. Maybe he had got that wrong; maybe the heat was so strong that anyone sane would run a mile. There would be time to question his sanity later.

As she looked back down at her planting, after flashing him the briefest of smiles back, he decided to grasp the nettle and be manly. He wouldn't embarrass her in front of her pupils but he would go and offer an olive branch.

'Hey.'

'Hi.'

*Great start, Matt, strong and manly.* Now what was he supposed to say? He'd never had this kind of trouble before but his mouth felt really dry. Luckily, he was saved by a child. Which really didn't make his teetering masculinity feel much better.

'Hello, I think it's pretty cool here. I like the feel of the earth. My younger sister was here this morning, she liked it too.'

'Well, thank you, I think it's pretty cool too. You look like you've got this planting down pat, what seeds did you get in the packet?' All the children had a selection of easy-to-grow veg so they could grow a range of different things and compare the different types of vegetables with those of their friends had grown. He looked over the boy's head at Rosy and smiled, trying to include her in the conversation.

'Um, I got some of these carrots, which is great because I like carrots. They're OK as far as vegetables go. Some beans, I've grown those before in Miss Winter's class so I know that they're easy, and I got some of these big ones, which are easy to plant, they're courgettes, I don't like those at all. But my mum does, I think. Miss says I need to push them a bit further into the mud because they're bigger. Is that right?'

'Yep, Miss sounds like she knows what she's talking about.' He managed to flash her another smile; this was returned. But it had an undertone he couldn't quite decode. Never mind, a smile was a smile. 'Which seeds did you get, Miss Winter?'

'Oh, I got some squash seeds. They looked very similar to the courgette, didn't they, James? We thought they might be from the same family.' The boy nodded his head furiously. 'And I've got some tomatoes, and some peas. I've done pretty well really, I'm looking forward to seeing how they grow, but more importantly than that, how they taste.'

'You're right, the squash and courgette are from the same family, both can grow to be massive. And I love cooking with produce from the garden. Are you a good cook, Miss Winter?'

He knew she was, and he felt a bit guilty saying it; it had fallen out of his mouth, almost as if his subconscious was asking her to remember that night. She fixed him with a very Rosy look, not a scowl and not a smile but an are-you-really-going-there look. He felt about eight. Then she perked up and turned back to the child.

'Was there something else you wanted to ask Matt, James?' Rosy may have had her concerned headteacher face on now, but there was definitely something else shooting through her mind. He could feel her mischief as if it were a tangible thing. She grinned up at Matt and he immediately felt as if he was caught in a trap.

'Um... thank you?' James clearly wasn't entirely sure what it was he was meant to remember.

'No, well yes, obviously thank you, but didn't your sister have a message for him?'

'Oh yeah!' James's face broke into a big grin. 'I nearly forgot! She says can she have her hair grip back? She can swap it for another if you like, but it's just that's her favourite.'

'Hair grip?'

'Yeah, my sister's, she said she gave it to you this morning, it's that one there, in your hair, at the front there, the butterfly.'

Matt suddenly understood why Rosy's eyes had taken on that extra twinkle and what it was like to wish that the ground would open up.

And now she just stood smiling, with a triumphant gleam in her eye, almost a challenge as he raised his hand to his head and, sure enough, felt the prongy metal of a sparkly pink and silver hair slide. How had he forgotten about that? It must have been in for hours! What had he been thinking, putting it there in the first place? James's sister had been a bit spooked by a worm so he had had to cheer her up, but to forget it was there... Arggh! So much for his dead manly approach.

He undid the clip and passed it to James.

'Would you thank her for me? It was very kind of her to lend it to me.'

'Yeah, rather you than me though,' answered the boy, clearly more masculine than the thirty-five-year-old man standing in front of him.

'I'm sure she'll be happy knowing you loved it.' Rosy's mischief was all over her face. 'It suited you.'

James giggled. Rosy continued, 'And I'd like to thank you for today, it's been a huge success. The children have loved it. You are so good with them.'

They both turned and walked away from the table now, as James went back to happily rummaging in his seed packets. Was she planning on saying something she didn't want the pupils to hear? He felt his heart beating a little faster. *Play it cool, Matt, play it cool.*

'It's a pleasure, they're a bit of a joy. I can see why you enjoy working with them.'

'Can you?' Her face lit up. 'I do really love every one of them, it feels like such a privilege to be involved in their lives, and yet people can be so disparaging about teaching as a career. But I love it.'

'Which is why you're so good at it. Look, I don't want to push things, and you were quite clear about keeping things professional, but I really think you and I need a talk, a proper talk, not in the earshot of your pupils, and not when we've been drinking buckets of booze and things get confused. What do you think?' *Don't push her, don't say a time and place*, he told himself. *This is a time for slowly-slowly rather than alpha-male-hear-me-roar.* Although how many roaring alpha males sported butterflies in their hair he wasn't sure.

'I think you might be right. Someone very wise told me today that communication is key and I think maybe she should be listened to.'

'I think so too.' He knew he had a grin that stretched from ear to ear, if not wider, and he didn't care.

'OK then, I've got to get these guys back to school, then I've got a staff meeting and then I'm meeting a friend. Can I give you a call when I'm free and we'll arrange something, is that OK?'

'Rosy, that is more than OK, of course.' He couldn't believe it had been that simple. Now all he had to do was work out what he had to say in a way that didn't make her run like a scared rabbit, or bad-tempered ferret the moment he spoke.

They both just stood and looked at each other, and for a minute there he felt his world was perfect.

## Chapter Thirty Three

Matt grimaced as he pulled into the drive of Chase's house. Rosy hadn't rung him yesterday evening as she had said and there had been silence all day today. When his phone had eventually rung it had been an invite from his sister to come to dinner here. He didn't think he'd ever had a dinner invite from her before, plus with the exception of their drunken night earlier in the week he had barely seen his sister since the party, so felt compelled to say yes – but having to come back to this house was not improving his mood much.

Initially he had tried to wriggle out of it, but realized it would be a chance to properly meet this Chase bloke and find out what was going on with him and his sister, and what had been going on between him and Rosy. If anything, the man might even be able to shed some light on why Rosy had screamed at him that night. Matt had a feeling that he wasn't going to like the answers he received and had little faith in the character of the sort of man that his sister liked to date. It was his fraternal duty to speak his mind about the whole set-up but to do so he'd need to establish a few facts first – which was why he found himself on this stupidly ostentatious doorstep, pressing the doorbell and preparing to play nice.

His sister eventually opened the door, swinging it wide.

'Oh wow, you've got a face like thunder! I'm not going to let you in if you don't smile.'

'Seriously, do you know how much I don't want to be here? You owe me for having such a strong sense of sibling loyalty that I turned up at all, so you're bloody letting me in! I've come to find out what's going on and what on earth you are doing spending all your time here, Ange.'

'I thought you were coming for dinner. And don't be rude, I've been cooking for you. I'm sure I smell of onions – did you know that they are next to impossible to cut up? Really hard, slide all over the place, although Chase did give me a particularly difficult one. I don't know how normal people manage.'

'Cooking? Cooking?'

'Yes, it's not that surprising, I am an adult. Chase is teaching me new things. Oh my God, what's that look for?' His sister breathed out so hard he almost felt sorry for her and had to fight the grin that was about to appear on his face, banishing his dark mood. He supposed loud sighs were a step up from thrown crockery. 'I do hope you're not going to be difficult, Matt. I didn't invite you here to be difficult.'

'I'm sure he's not, Ange, let the poor man in. I expect he's just come to check out where you've been spending the last two weeks, and rightfully so. Hi, Matt, do come on in. It's nice to meet you properly at last, I've heard so much about you.' Chase appeared at the door and leant forward to shake his hand in welcome. Matt's innate good manners and the pleading look on his sister's face meant there was no choice. Whatever this guy was playing at, Matt figured going carefully was the way to find out the truth. Making an enemy straight off the bat certainly wasn't going to help anyone. He smiled and outstretched his hand.

'Yup, number one on the list of things Ange loves to talk about is her brother. How do you do?'

'Never stops.' Chase smiled and Matt couldn't help but smile back. 'And Rosy also has some nice things to say, in a kinda complicated fashion!'

What was going on here?

'I doubt that very much, she seems to be avoiding me at the moment.'

'Ah, that I can't answer to, but I can pour you a drink.' Chase led Matt through the huge foyer and then down a hallway into the best equipped kitchen he had ever seen. This man was obviously quite domesticated and, if he had heard her correctly, managed to get his sister doing things in the kitchen. And had mentioned Rosy in front of Angelina and survived.

Chase fetched him a beer from the fridge (down to earth – tick) then made small talk as he threw some steaks on a griddle and asked Angelina to get more salad things from the fridge. This she did, without a grumble. Even further than that, she did it with a smile, so double tick to Chase so far (unless of course he had drugged her or she was suffering from Stockholm Syndrome and then Matt would have to get ready to punch him).

Dinner was served and as they sat at the kitchen table, Chase made the talk flow easily and Angelina managed not to behave as if she were four years old. It was proving to be quite a remarkable evening; he would go as far as to say he was enjoying it. When his sister was pleasant, genuinely pleasant not paparazzi-around-the-corner pleasant, she was capable of being a joy. It was just that Matt hadn't seen it for a while and never in front of someone she was dating. Normally she seemed to assume that histrionics were part and parcel of a functioning relationship and that men were attracted to the drama. Quite clearly Chase wasn't and she knew it.

'So tell me about your first date?' he asked. Normally he wouldn't bother but knowing how Ange liked to brag about chic restaurants and fast cars he thought she deserved a bit of a treat for being so bloody normal this evening.

'It was really nice wasn't it, Angelina?' Chase squeezed her hand as she giggled back at him.

'No, it was vile.' But her words belied the look upon her face. 'He promised me a present and then bought me wellies' – Matt choked on his beer – 'and made me get in a boat.'

'You like boats.'

'No, I like yachts where you can lie in the sun sipping cocktails...'

'You drank a fair amount from what I remember,' Chase teased and received a glower in return. A loving glower. Another first for anyone that wasn't Matt.

'Shush. He made me get in a boat and then he caught fish, and that's not the worst bit because he cut them open too.'

Chase nodded. 'Yep, you have to gut them, Ange.'

She gave a shiver. 'He cut them open and made me eat them; honestly, Matt, I thought I had died and gone to hell. I thought I had been captured by a madman and if I didn't do what he said I'd be next.'

'Really? You thought that was what was happening?' The madman's eyebrow jerked up and then he switched into a European accent. 'You were right. Tonight, baby, tonight I shall cut you into leetle pieces.'

'You met her last boyfriend then?' Matt giggled and received a punch from his sister. 'Ow! What's happened to new mellow Angelina?'

'She doesn't exist for you!'

'Seeing that we're talking of exes...' This was his chance.

'We weren't,' Angelina retorted, kicking him under the table.

'Seeing that we are talking of exes,' Matt repeated, 'tell me what happened between you and Rosy, Chase.' He felt a bit awkward. He liked the man that he had met this evening, but still, he needed to know what exactly had gone on.

'Oh my God. Can you not talk about her for like five minutes? This is my evening. Not bloody goody-two-shoes. I can't believe you!'

'Um... I was never dating Rosy, buddy. I only met her that night and she wasn't interested in me.'

'What do you mean not interested in you?' Angelina rounded on him, half falling off her chair in the process. 'You were NOT interested in Rosy.'

'Well, I hadn't met you yet... ouch! I'm teasing! I met Rosy when she came to the party, we bonded over – well I can't tell you, other than a pretty scary sight. And yes, Ange, fists unfurled please, I thought she was lovely, but just not my type.'

'Because I'm your type!'

'Less so by the minute I should think, shut up, Ange! I want to hear what Chase has to say. Are you telling me you're not the one who's dating Rosy?'

'Yep, I have never dated her, Matt, and from what she was telling me that evening, she only has eyes for one man. It's just… it's not really my place to say.'

Matt felt his heart lift and sink in the space of seconds; this was too much to compute. He had been convinced that she was dating Chase. It had explained everything, especially as he knew she had spent Valentine's night here. But if that weren't the case then who was the guy that Chase was talking about? He realized Chase was still speaking and he hadn't a clue what he had just said.

'Sorry, mate, I missed that, what were you saying?'

'Oh, can we not stop now? This is dull, dull, dull!'

'Shh.' Not completely cured then. His sister was still capable of being a selfish pain in the arse.

'I'm slipping into a coma here.'

'Yeah, but not quietly.'

'Are you two always like this?'

'Nah, normally she's more violent, I think she's on her best behaviour because you haven't been dating that long. Anyway, ignore her. As long as she's not setting fire to anything we should be OK. Now what were you saying about Rosy?'

'Just that whilst I don't like to break confidences I think maybe this needs to be said, cos you kinda got a raw deal that evening. That night I met her, and I agree she is lovely, funny, kind, smart—' Chase's head whipped around. 'Did you just growl?'

'Yeah, she does that, has done since she was about eight. You're right about Rosy, she is all those things, and more.'

'Yep, and as I was saying, and yes, Ange, I promise we'll all talk about you in a minute, anyway, from what I can

see Rosy thinks the world of you but the tricky thing is…
I shouldn't be sharing this… but she has a few demons
from her past that need healing first. That's why she kicked
off at you. She's scared but I think she's making headway.
I think you should stick in there, give her time, be gentle,
get her to talk, and with any luck it will all come good.'

Matt froze. Did he just hear Chase right? Rosy thought
the world of him? She liked him like he liked her? Oh
this was ridiculous – he wasn't some twelve-year-old girl
passing notes in class and crushing on the head of the First
XV. Plus he had enough baggage of his own, most of it six
foot tall, blonde and very demanding. Could he take any
more on? A picture of her teaching him Cornish flitted
into his head and he smiled. The naughtiness of her face
when he was wearing the hairpin widened his face into a
grin. However, getting even soppier in front of his sister's
new boyfriend was not an option; he was going to have
to man it up now.

'Oh right, that's good to know, yeah, I can do that.' He
nodded, masculinely.

'Right, brilliant, are we done now, can we get on with
the evening? Let me show you the rest of the house. The
wardrobe is out of this world! Seriously. Oh my God,
you're going to love the garden! And Chase is taking me
to St Barts next month, aren't you, honeybun?'

'Not if you call me honeybun I'm not!'

And so the evening continued, and yes the house was
amazing, the gardens were to die for and anyone with a
whole bloody beach to themselves was seriously lucky, but
really the only thing whooshing around in his mind was
Chase's statement and the fact that he needed to have a
serious talk with Rosy. A proper one, not a promise of

one that never materialized. He needed her to open up about whatever was scaring her and know that he would never do anything other than keep her safe. Then they could iron out what was looking increasingly like a mess of miscommunication that had done nothing but play with both of their heads.

# Chapter Thirty Four

Rosy was pleased to see Marion; she had just finished on the phone and had some news for her. However, as usual, she hadn't been able to get a word in from the minute the woman hurtled into her office.

'What do you mean we have to throw a party, Marion? Everyone's exhausted. The toing and froing from the garden over the last couple of weeks, the stress of the potential closure, not to mention everyone's out-of-school lives – a party is madness. I'd much rather have a few days in bed with my head under a pillow if I were to have my way on anything.'

'Now, now, Rosy, where's your gumption? And more importantly have you been listening to me at all?' Marion stood in the doorway of Rosy's office in a rather nice green dress dotted about with fuchsia petals, her demanding tone boomeranging off the walls.

'Probably not, Marion, did I mention I was tired?'

Marion smirked and Rosy was taken back to the night of the sequinned red dress and she softened a little. Rosy still couldn't quite believe she had witnessed this paragon of middle-class motherhood in… well… as she had. She realized now that the smirk was not as malevolent as people believed.

'Yes, you did. And I quite understand it.' Rosy was not convinced because still Marion continued at breakneck speed. 'However, this really is important – you do know that the TV show is aired on Friday evening, the first episode? The whole meet-the-kids, when Magnificent Matt handed out the tools, all of that will be aired. You want to hope they've cut your evil stares...'

'Have you been talking to Katie? It was one! One slightly bad-tempered stare.'

'Katie? No, anyway keep listening, this is our time to shine. This is when we capitalize on all the work we've done. We need a launch party, we'll invite Magnificent Matt...'

'Could you stop calling him that, please?'

'Well, he is.' The force of Rosy's glare was so strong it managed to quell even Monster Marksharp. But only for a second. 'He may well have another engagement, I expect he's in great demand. But he seems very committed to the school so we'll invite him anyway, maybe some of the crew, get local news down, make sure that if Edward Grant didn't know about it before—'

'Ah, now I want to talk to you about him. Listen to what I've found out.'

Marion didn't. Obviously.

'—he certainly will soon. This is going to be huge! And this launch is a necessity, Rosy, a necessity. I'll stake my life on it. Don't look like that, you're not getting rid of me that easily. We'll have all the local media there, it may even get picked up by national – I'll have a word with a couple of friends in London. We'll throw a damn fine celebration of the school and all it provides for the children and the community on the night it's aired and

272

then we can all finish by watching it together. I'll send out an emergency newsletter. I have the perfect dress for you to borrow, a beautiful cerise number, Magnificent Matt won't be able to keep his hands... what?'

'Marion, Marion! You need to hear what I have found out. And thank you, but it's a no on the dress.'

'But... OK! I don't want to speak out of turn but those eyebrows of yours can be really quite alarming. Go on, what have you found out?'

'All right, I now know which schools Edward Grant has placed on his list to amalgamate, and when you first look at the list there doesn't seem any obvious reasoning behind it. They're not the closest schools to the new site, nor the poorest performing schools. But as I rang around and played sleuth to find out who had had a meeting, who hadn't, etc., etc., then one thing, my original theory, became very clear.'

'Do come on, Rosy, cut to the chase. I have an awful lot to do, you know.'

'OK, well every single head on the list of closures is female...'

Marion's mouth dropped. 'Are you saying what I think you're saying? Surely not? Surely he wouldn't be so blatant? He must have included St Ewer, everyone knows Mr Doughty is a complete incompetent. That school is in dire need of improvement and new leadership.'

'Well, deeper research shows that Mr Doughty is also a member of the same golf club as Mr Grant. Mr Doughty, interestingly, is chairman there.'

'Are you absolutely sure about this, Rosy? Not a single headmaster's school is on that list?'

'Yep, only headmistresses, but most of them would be over the moon to be moved to a brand new school. Mrs Trewithen says Sanding Bridge is falling to pieces around her ears and she's worried about the safety of the children if they continue to stay there longer than a couple more years. Mrs Pascoe added that she's got a couple of teachers who are so bad at their jobs that the TAs are doing most of the teaching and she's having to invent tasks for the teachers outside the classroom just to keep them busy. An amalgamation would be the perfect opportunity for her to offer them redundancy. Really, it's only us unhappy to be on the list. But it's still a list drawn up based on gender prejudice, regardless of whether they're happy to be on it or not.'

'And you've checked and double checked?'

Rosy stared her down.

'Of course you have. Right, Richard is having drinks with Dave French on Wednesday.' Marion named the chief executive of the Local Authority. 'I will prime him and make sure he slips this information in. You've done an amazing job, Rosy. I can't see how, with this information, combined with the new sky-high profile of Penmenna School, we can't have won this battle. And get Edward Grant's professional practices examined a little closer. You've done it!'

'We've done it, or at least I hope so. We won't know for a while yet, I suppose, but if you get Richard to do his bit, and yes, we launch *Green-fingered and Gorgeous* in the way you want us to, Marion, then I reckon we've got a pretty good chance of getting off that list.' Rosy knew deep down that, despite her desire to hibernate for a day or two, Marion was right, and the school deserved a party.

'Of course we have, Rosy. Who was possibly going to take on the two of us and win?' And with the utter confidence that cloaked Marion from head to toe, she gave one of her most dazzling Marion smiles and waltzed back out of the office.

# Chapter Thirty Five

Rosy was up on Friday as the sun made its appearance. She hadn't slept properly and was tired of repeated thoughts chasing themselves around and across her mind. She needed to shake herself, get dressed and make sure she looked the part. The launch was tonight and Rosy had to concede that the children, who had been beside themselves all week, deserved a celebration of their hard work and achievements up at the hall. The production company had OK'd their early viewing of the first programme during school hours, the idea being that it could then be featured on local news and hopefully help attract even more viewers than it would usually. Both Radio Cornwall and Spotlight South West were heading down. Rosy knew Marion was champing at the bit to get her say on television.

A super-quick shower and she found herself pulling her favourite dress out of the wardrobe. The dark green meant it drew out her eyes and complemented her colouring perfectly. A plunging neckline and silky fabric meant it clung in all the right places before flaring out beautifully in the skirt – she knew it was the most flattering thing she owned. Wearing it elevated her levels of self-confidence to skyscraper levels. And sky-high confidence would be helpful today. She would not be wearing cerise!

She blow-dried her hair and then carefully applied her make-up, taking time to get the lines perfect, the shading just right, making her eyes pop and her lips look film-star gorgeous. Twirling and swirling in front of the mirror, she knew she couldn't look better than she did; she'd cracked it and was now ready for work. And she hadn't thought about Matt once whilst she was getting ready, not once. That had to be a good sign.

There was no point lying to herself. It wasn't the pressure of saving the school but panic about talking to Matt today that had kept her awake. Her drinks with Katie had been eye-opening and she couldn't dispute anything her friend and colleague had said. Which, in a nutshell – Katie was blunt – was that Rosy was her own worst enemy and by allowing her fear to dictate The Rule (which Katie had deemed stupid and self-sabotaging) then she had handed Josh the power to influence the rest of her life.

She had added that fear was preventing Rosy from exploring the basic joys of life and was instead locking her in a self-prescribed box of unhealthy reactions and behaviours. Katie also pointed out that as a psychologist, and not a telepath, soothsayer or magician, she couldn't say with finality that Matt was going to make all her romantic dreams come true but that the one thing that was sure was that if Rosy didn't give people a fair shot then she would be alone forever. Bleak.

Rosy, having heard it, knew Katie's words to be true, especially when combined with what Chase had said that night on the beach. Even discounting Matt, she needed to shake off the shackles she had imposed on herself and start accepting she couldn't change what had passed but she could actively shape her future. She had told two people her secret now in as many weeks and they hadn't appeared repulsed. Her less than decorous behaviour at the party hadn't caused any kind of seismic social catastrophe either. Maybe, finally, the time had come to stop carving out the perfect public persona and just do things she wanted to. Not that she was likely to dance on the tables in The Smuggler's Curse waving her knickers in the air, but giving her heart another chance might be exciting. Or at the very least not letting anxiety about public perception dictate her choices; maybe that was a more sensible place to start.

She needed to talk to Matt and to do so today. The familiar steel chest bands and leaden tummy slunk up on her, but she was not going to be a coward any longer. She would apologize for not getting in touch when she'd said she would, she would apologize for her erratic behaviour and she might even tell him why. She would tell him why. She would explain all her history, Josh, her fears about people getting too close, her fears of judgement, of losing her professional reputation and personal respect – the whole caboodle. Then, when he ran away with the speed of a hungry big cat released on a game reserve, she would know that she had not let cowardice beat her. Oh, green dress, she needed you today like never before.

# Chapter Thirty Six

'And we're here today in the school hall at Penmenna awaiting an early private screening of the first episode of *Green-fingered and Gorgeous: The Cornish Edition* aired on BBC2 this evening at nine and predicted to be the nation's favourite television tipple of the season.' Hugo Sweetling, dressed in tweed and holding his favourite microphone (a type not seen on any other TV programme in decades), gave his trademark wink to camera. A wink that encapsulated bonhomie, cricket and village ponds.

The children cheered on cue, all standing smartly in school uniform (Marion had ensured not a single sweat-shirt was stained, not a single hair out of place and any freckles had been subdued) and waved *Green-fingered and Gorgeous* flags that had been handed out by the production company.

'Matt Masters will be joining us shortly but in the meantime we'll be talking to the headteacher, Miss Winter, and a few of the children all about the grand adventure they've been having over the last couple of weeks, and my understanding is that it isn't finished yet, is that correct, Miss Winter?'

'Yes, Hugo, that is correct. We were lucky enough to be asked to take part in this project as a way of involving the local community in the revival of this great garden, and although the programme airs tonight, the vegetables are still growing and the children are still gardening. We have to crop and cook our vegetables yet, and that won't be happening for a little while.'

'Quite, and I understand that this opportunity has been invaluable for the school. How is that so?'

'If I may jump in, Hugo? Marion Marksharp, school governor and head of the PTA. The school has always been the vibrant hub around which our community flourishes. It has stood on this spot for the last one hundred and fifty years and has seen generation upon generation of families stream through its doors. Many of course went on, in years gone by, to work in the house or on the land at Penmenna Hall. This project has been invaluable for our children, not just teaching them about food production and life cycles but also feeding into their literacy and numeracy work as well as fostering an understanding of the history of this lovely community in which we are all lucky to be a part of, isn't that right, Miss Winter?'

'Quite right, Mrs Marksharp. The children have loved being involved and have found it to be a deeply rewarding experience, from the very youngest in the school to those who will be leaving in the summer.'

'Which is why it is such a shame that we have received the news recently that the Local Authority will be closing the school at the end of the academic year to force a merger with other village schools in the area into a new bigger school that will be located ten miles away in Roscarrock. This will strip the community of its heart and the children of an opportunity to flourish in a school that has served so many generations here in Penmenna. Apart from the practical difficulties of no longer having a school locally, the pressures it will place on parents, of which I am one, having to send their children so far to get an education is immeasurable. It also means that the children will not be able to carry on their work at Penmenna Hall and all the opportunities it brings. It is nonsensical to me, as I'm sure it will be to your viewers, that a school rated outstanding by Ofsted, time and time again, will be abolished in the name of cost-cutting and efficiency.'

'Is that the case, Miss Winter? Is the Local Authority shutting Penmenna School?' The reporter looked less surprised than Rosy would have imagined by the turn of focus, until she realized that this whole thing may have been beautifully orchestrated by Marion.

'Unfortunately it is, and as Marion has said this school is not just a vital lifeline to the community as a whole but is a place where the children feel secure. Their parents, older brothers and sisters have attended, there is a real sense of history here, and with that comes a sense of belonging. The Penmenna Hall project has helped reinforce that and has been especially helpful to the handful of children we have here who need that little bit of extra help to thrive, some of whom will not be able to cope with the transition to another school and as such will lose their opportunity to participate in mainstream education. Although the plans to close us are not written in stone, we have been informed it is more than likely, but we will be fighting this enforced amalgamation in the interests of protecting all our children here and their way of life, but particularly those most vulnerable, those who, without a local village school, will have their security, their friendships and their hope of an inclusive education stripped away from them.'

'These children behind us don't look particularly worried, in fact they look really excited.'

'And that's how we want to keep it. The parents and staff at this school will do the fighting and the worrying in the hope that these children can remain as excited about their education, their school and all the opportunities that it gives them.'

'Well, thank you, Miss Winter, Mrs Marksharp. I'll hand back to you in the studio for now, but we'll be back shortly to talk to Matt Masters, the talent behind the project, and the children themselves to see what they have learnt over the last couple of weeks.'

Hugo turned to Marion and gave her a kiss on the cheek. 'Well done, you. As usual, I have to stay impartial on screen, but like I said, I'll support you as much as I can. Andrew said thanks for the cake, by the way, you know what a sucker I am for your coffee and walnut, and he loathes baking. I don't know what you do to it, but my God it's good. Although not as good as him over there! He's divine. Is that the gardener?'

Rosy froze as Marion turned in the direction Hugo was facing. She was not going to swing round and gawp. She smoothed down her skirt and turned to smile at the children, her thumbs up to reassure them they were doing an amazing job and it wouldn't be long now. Lynne caught her eye and as the cameramen switched focus from Hugo she encouraged them into a quick burst of 'Five Little Peas'. They were all a bit more savvy now and knew a quick shot of this would encapsulate cute if the newsmen used a couple of seconds' snippet.

Her heart swelled with love; they were all so adorable, so excited. She didn't want them to have to go to a much bigger, more formal school, one that didn't know them, their families and their quirks inside out. Of course they would in time, but there was a real familiarity, an intimacy in a village school that large schools, no matter how brilliant, couldn't replicate. As she looked at Bradley, looking at his feet but singing along, her pride went through the roof. It had only been a few months previously that Lynne, who shared the teaching of Class One with her, had worried he would never be able to cope with being in the school hall at all. Now he was not just in it, he was participating, belonging. And then there was the community response to this event; so many people had turned out for this, happily waving their flags and cheering the children on. Even the recently bereaved Sylvie had brought her son, Sam, to help celebrate the school's big day.

'Hello, Miss Winter. Now that is a very big smile on your face there.'

'Oh, hello, Matt.' She turned, smiled and shook his hand, hoping that the lust-filled conflict she usually experienced when faced with those dimples and that twinkle would be absent. Dimple, twinkle. Well, the conflict had gone. 'How are you? My goodness, Scramble, you look particularly fluffy today.'

She thought she deserved a medal for keeping her voice even. She would have made a great spy – no, now was not the time for flights of fancy. She did not want to be a spy, she wanted to be a successful headteacher who didn't make herself look a tit in front of her school, her crush and the local news. Her crush? God help her! But how much better was 'crush' than 'nemesis'? She had made progress.

Scramble jumped up, excited as ever and with no regard for the laddering of her tights.

'I thought a good scrub and a removal of wellies was probably called for today, and Scramble wanted to join in.' That slow smile meandered across Matt's face up to his eyes. 'Down, Scramble, down. He said he liked the look of Angelina's shampoo, some French one apparently, with all sorts in it, grapeseed, rose water and nettle, it said. Do I get top marks for remembering that sort of thing? I read him the ingredients and he was keen. Dead good at conditioning blonde hair, it said, and look, it works on handsome doggy grey hair as well, doesn't it, Scramble?'

'No marks, that sounds like very expensive shampoo!'

'Probably, but look at him, and he smells so good. You know I can't usually say that!'

Rosy picked the dog up and curled him into her arms, burying her face in his coat, giving herself time to deep breathe. He wriggled like fury for a second or two, then licked her face before settling down and shooting a very smug look at his owner.

'He says you smell nice too.' Matt smiled a tentative am-I-allowed-to-say-that smile.

'Hmm, coming from a dog, especially yours, I'm not sure that's a compliment. On top of which, if you were a canine telepath I'm sure you would have bragged about it by now. Come on, I've got to address the hordes, come say hello.' She was very aware, not just of Matt any more, but of Marion fiercely mouthing 'be nice!' and Lynne smirking and giving her the thumbs up. Honestly, the pupils were more grown-up than the grown-ups in this place some days.

'Not just canine, human too. Highly skilled.' He smiled and she thanked God that he was kidding.

'You're a fool. Come on.' Still holding Scramble, she walked around to the front of the children, still all sitting in order, remarkably patiently, and talking amongst themselves. Rosy lifted her arms in a teacher signal, as best she could while holding the wriggly dog, and smiled as she looked around at her charges.

'Good afternoon, Penmenna.'

'Good afternoon, Miss Winter.'

'As you can see I have a friend with me.'

'Two friends, Miss!'

'Quite, Billy, and I know you all recognize them so let's give them a Penmenna welcome too.'

'Good afternoon, Matt.'

'And Scramble,' a few shouted out.

Instead of chastising them Rosy waved Scramble's paw and most of them waved back.

'Any minute now we're going to get to watch the very first episode of *Green-fingered*, not all of it, but the bits we're in.' She indicated the large screen behind her. 'How exciting is that? Matt's watching it with us, and so are these nice people here. Let me introduce them because I know they've got some questions for you after we've seen the segment.'

Introductions made, Hugo explained how he would like some volunteers afterwards and then addressed Matt directly for the camera. The children, now au fait with filming, sat as quiet as quiet could be whilst Hugo did his stuff. Rosy stood by Matt's side, smiling politely, relieved that so far all was going smoothly. She twirled her skirt a little.

'And now for a surprise. Before we head to the revival we have another party celebrating this great community collaboration…' Hugo pointed to the screen and up popped a picture of Angelina and Chase. Rosy turned to look at the screen behind her. Why did she not know about this? The children's we're-so-used-to-telly attitude lost a little bit of cool as several ten- and eleven-year-old girls started swooning over the combined presence of Angelina and what looked like her new boyfriend. Rosy might not like her very much but her megastar support to their project, and her having a new man, could well break the Internet. She turned back to Matt and Hugo and tried to concentrate on what was being said.

'…so the public might not perceive Angelina to be a particularly big fan of gardening, but we understand she is a big fan of you, Matt…'

Scramble had suddenly started wriggling again in her arms; perhaps a larger than life picture of Angelina was not disconcerting for Rosy alone. She had always liked this dog.

'And over to you, Angelina… how come you're supporting the Penmenna Hall restoration project?'

'Hello, Hugo, hello, Penmenna!' Angelina gave her star-quality beam as she raised her glass to camera and waited for the cheer from the children. What did she think this was, bloody Eurovision? Scramble growled lightly, making Rosy banish her uncharitable thoughts and concentrate instead on not dissolving into giggles like an eight-year-old. Matt shot her a look; he clearly wasn't fooled by her sudden interest in Scramble's collar.

'Of course, it's important to support community projects all across the… the… ahem… community but we're here today not just to lend our support to this brilliant little school but to my brother, the ever talented, ever kind Matt Masters. He had this idea for the restoration and then decided to change everything so he could include the school… um, school thing. Everything he does is amazing and I know this will be too. Matt, I can't wait and I bet everyone else feels the same. Trust me, all of you should watch it!'

'Well, well, fancy that. That is a surprise. Who would have thought we would have Angelina tell us to watch a gardening programme? I had heard whispers she was in Cornwall, and this confirms it. And we all know with her, you'd better do as you're told! So over to you, Miss Winter, for the honours…'

'Thank you, Hugo, oh and of course Angelina. It is with great pleasure that I introduce the first ever screening of *Green-fingered and Gorgeous: The Cornish Edition*!' Rosy stood to one side, unable to resist a triumphant look straight to camera. Take that, Edward Grant!

# Chapter Thirty Seven

Rosy watched the screen, aware of how cute the children were looking and how cute Matt was looking, and accepting that she may look a little snarly, but only in one or two shots. The rest she was coming over quite well in, and she would only be in this segment; the rest of the time she had kept well away from Penmenna Hall in her ridiculous attempt to avoid Matt.

The children were captivated, almost silent, with the exception of a little nudge or a giggle as they recognized themselves and their friends onscreen. She had never seen Chloe sit as still for so long before. This was bordering on a miracle. The parents at the back, largely mothers, all made loud *aww*-ing noises as they reached the bit where Matt was handing out the tools, and then got down in the dirt a second later to help the little ones use them. All eyes swivelled lovingly towards him, whereas Rosy, whose anxiety about telling him the truth of her past was beginning to bubble to the surface, felt neither loving or swoony, just a little bit sick.

The rest of the screening passed by in a blur for Rosy. It wasn't until it had finished and Marion stood up to lead a standing ovation for Matt, and then the children, that she fully came back to life. Maybe she should wait, maybe accosting him in a professional setting to bare personal woes wasn't appropriate, green swishy dress or not.

She stood up, having handed Scramble back to Matt, and thanked everyone in the hall for their continuing support and a job well done before the children were allowed to mingle with the adults, and attack the party food the PTA had put out at the back.

Then she wandered back to Matt and tugged gently on his arm for attention. Regardless of her decision to blurt or not to blurt, she still needed to say thank you. Flawlessly he detached himself from the parents and turned to face her, creating a space for just the two of them.

'That went so well, don't you think, Rosy? I should imagine your Edward Grant fellow is going to have a hard job closing you down now. Well done.'

'It did, and I just want to thank you once again for all you've done. You've been amazing. And also, although not here, there are a couple of things I should explain. I know I never rang when I said I would and I think I may have been a bit of an idiot.'

'Oh yeah,' he replied, nodding far more vigorously than he needed to. 'I think that may be true. Is this idiot thing an explanation for that night at Chase's as well? Whatever the reason was, and… look, I know we've said this before but I think you and me…' He paused as he moved closer and picked up her hand with one of his, then used the other to brush a lock of hair from her face to behind her ear. The room stopped for a minute and Rosy looked into his eyes, so close, so intimate, and felt the air whoosh out of her lungs. Was this relief? Was this embarrassment? Was this lo— No, no it wasn't that! 'Yes, we really do need to have that talk.'

Boldly she continued staring into his eyes. Green and flecked with amber, she could see their smile. He was laughing at her, ever so quietly, but he was laughing and suddenly she didn't really mind. He was welcome to; she had been a fool and they had missed out, all because of things that had happened years ago.

'We do. We will.'

'Not here though.' He gestured with his hand around the room, most of it still chattering away but some of it silent, and watching the two of them. Marion and Lynne now had joined forces and were standing rather close, both grinning like lunatics. Oh God, she was embarrassed. And, oh shit, Hugo and the camera seemed to be heading towards Harmony. That couldn't be allowed to happen. She signalled frantically at Lynne, hoping she could interpret her desperate 'stop them' semaphore.

Matt arched an eyebrow as she launched into charades across the room but he seemed determined that this was one conversation they would finish. She was pretty much in agreement with such a sentiment.

'No, not here, but tonight. I promise to turn up this time. I'll come to you. We'll talk.'

'OK, and I'll make it special.'

'Umm... argh... hmmm...' Rosy lost the power of speech at the thought of that. 'Right now I need to head that off at the pass.' She gestured to Harmony and Matt grinned; he had heard enough stories to know why that was necessary and understood the arm-waving now.

'Oh, Rosy Winter, go! I'll mingle and I'll see you later. Meet me at mine this evening. I should be there anytime on from six-ish, no, make that seven. Oh and, Rosy, we're going to get to the bottom of a few things tonight, and do you know what, I think it's all going to be OK.'

The stupid grin was still stuck to her face as she managed to insert herself in between the cameraman and Harmony as she started to answer Hugo's question about the impact the project had had on her, the TV presenter's face glazing over with perplexity as the teacher started to talk about moon cycles and planting.

Suddenly the door of the hall slammed loudly. Being old and heavy it had a habit of doing that and Rosy spun around to see who had walked in. She wasn't alone; several others turned in natural response to the noise.

'Blimey, would ya look at the legs on that!' James from Class Three could be heard to say very loudly and the room suddenly fell silent, with the exception of the odd titter from James's friends, unable to cope with the wanton sexuality of the woman who stood in front of them. A woman with a dark, sleek Cleopatra bob, legs up to her ears, wearing a scrap of red silk and a very predatory smile. Rosy started to head over to welcome their late guest, but the newcomer didn't seem to need to wait for a welcome, slinking across the hall towards Matt and delivering a very public, not-suitable-for-children, X-rated kiss on his lips.

# Chapter Thirty Eight

Rosy arrived home after all the fuss in the hall had died down. Matt had sped out of there as fast as fast can be. In his defence he did not have the look on his face of a man racing home to satisfy raging desire. Rather that of a man who was so completely done with the bullshit that he may hurl himself off a cliff.

Being up close to him again, and especially since the support offered by Chase and Katie, made her realize how desperately she wanted to give this man a chance, how he encapsulated all the qualities she deemed important and how, with his twinkly eyes and beautifully formed upper arms, it had been ages since she'd last had sex. Certainly the melty feeling that zoomed through her when the two of them were together was a very strong reminder of this fact. And she knew the way her body responded to him, the memory of their kiss, was making her puddle with lust.

All this postponing until tomorrow had been cowardice and the arrival of that woman was a reminder that he was not the sort of man that would be available for long. The expression on the faces of most of the mothers had been enough of an indicator.

Bizarrely, although she had felt a little pang of panic when the strange woman walked in and molested him in front of the entire school, she had also been full of a kind of zen calm. She really wasn't used to zen calm. But she was pretty sure that's what it was. It was as if someone had taken her brain and freed it of all its toing and froing and filled it up with unicorns and lilac and lullabies instead. Lullabies that said she was safe and secure with Matt. That it was fact that he had no interest in anyone but her and that he was going to understand why she had acted the way she had, and they were going to make babies and nest build...

Woah! All this surety was fabulous but maybe she needed to hold fire on the babies thing. And whilst it was great that she was now new zen-calm Rosy, the one thing that was fairly definite was that she needed to stop messing him about, tell him the truth and get this great romance started properly.

The clock binged in her hall. It was six now; she should go and see if he was ready yet, and if not, she could knock again later. There were going to be no more mixed messages from Rosy today, she was going to make it clear as could be.

She knew that he knew that what he needed was not a shiny showbiz love but a down-to-earth country girl, a girl who liked to bake, a girl who knew when to step up and apologize. A girl who would shoulder the blame and not make excuses. A girl who happened to live next door.

She put the cake tin down, twitched and twirled her green dress one more time and headed towards the door. She, Rosy Winter, was off to get her man!

# Chapter Thirty Nine

Bloody hell! He couldn't believe his bad luck. He was not the type of man to be rude to anyone — he could see no merit in hurting a person's feelings, as there would always be a way to get what you needed done without recourse to that — but he thought today he may have just hit his limit.

Siobhan was currently sitting in his kitchen making ridiculous demands, driving him mad and embarrassing him to a point of no return whilst he escaped to the bathroom for some thinking time. His poxy sister, the author of this particular little play, no doubt still swilling champagne at Chase's house, should be taking responsibility for this. He had no interest in scary scantily clad women in his home, unless they were Rosy, and this one very clearly wasn't.

It had been a funny kind of day. He had been unsure what to expect at the school. Rosy had been absent of late, failing to get in touch as she'd promised, and prior to that she had blown hot and cold and he hadn't known what the hell was going on in her mind. Chase had been helpful in his encouragement and his words seemed to have a ring of truth today when Rosy had said she had been an idiot. He was relieved she had thought so and been bold enough to say it; it meant that the two of them had a chance at resolving all miscommunication between them, and both understood that a bit of straight-talking and a lot less supposing was the way forward.

Today had definitely looked like it was going to end on a high; her scowling from previous weeks had been replaced with smiles and whispered asides. That high had lessened when he was launched upon by the scary, possibly drug-addled woman currently sitting in his kitchen with next to nothing on. He hadn't dared make eye contact with Rosy as he had whisked Siobhan out of the school hall filled with children and TV cameras. He was going to kill Angelina! However, once he had got rid of her, and that was going to happen any minute now, he was going to make sure tonight went without so much as a ripple. He had big plans, and he needed to get rid of Siobhan so he could do clever things with candles, jam jars and a projector. He would show Rosy that he wasn't interested in anyone else, that they had undeniable chemistry, enjoyed the same things and that it made sense to give it a go. He was going to make it so romantic, an honest gesture of intent. Something to make her see that he was serious. Somewhere that got her as far away from the doubts she had as possible. And bloody Siobhan.

So, bloody Siobhan was the first thing he was going to have to sort out, way before organizing candles, making a romantic declaration, or even the gifting of the Valentine's orchid could occur. He needed that woman back in London very soon, preferably in the next five minutes.

He breathed in deep, unlocked the loo door and headed downstairs to be polite but firm. Very firm. Maybe not so polite.

He approached the kitchen, her coat lifted from the banister in his hand. There – a physical sign of intent. And an aimed shot at the whole 'but I don't know where I put my things' line that she was likely to use.

'Right!' He swung the door open and announced his arrival. 'Now whilst I appreciate… oh, you are joking me! Please put your clothes back on.'

'Yah, but don't you like me like this?' purred Siobhan, who, for whatever reason (OK, he knew the reason) was crawling around the kitchen floor on all fours in her underwear and a pair of uncomfortable-looking heels.

'No, I'm sure lots of men find you very charming but I would prefer you got dressed.'

She curled herself around his leg, and then looked up at him, batting him with what he supposed she thought was her paw. Then she meowed. Then she used her paw to try and pull down the zipper on his trousers.

'For Christ's sake!' He gently pushed her off and then grabbed her hand to pull her up onto her feet. His intent was to get her standing and get the coat on her.

'Ooh, baby. See, you knew it was a good idea.' She came to her feet willingly and curled herself into him, shimmying as she did so, rubbing her breasts into his chest and her pelvic bone against his. All he could think about was that it would be just his luck if Rosy came to the window. He pushed her back slightly and then grabbed her hands and twirled her around as his mother had he and Angelina when they were younger.

'Salsa, baby. I like your style, yah!' She teetered on the heels a little. He steadied her and used the movement to get the coat over one arm and then up on the shoulders.

There was no point draping it on her; she would shrug it off in a second and he would be no further forward.

'No!' she said in a child-like squawk. 'I don't want to.'

'Me neither,' he muttered under his breath.

'I don't want the coat.' She suddenly folded onto him, making her legs floppy and becoming heavy against his frame. Rather like a drunken aunt or uncle needing support late on Christmas afternoon. This was not helping.

'If you slip this on for me I can show you how grateful I'll be,' he whispered into her ear, trying a different tack.

'How grateful?' She looked up to him, eyes lidded but locked on his.

'Very grateful. I think you'll like it.'

'Yah, I'm sure I will.' She slipped her remaining arm into the coat.

He stood back as if admiring her but actually checking the whole Bambi legs thing was just artifice and that she could support her own weight.

'Do you like it like this?' She ran her hands down her coat, legs akimbo, and looked him straight in the eye. He stopped feeling sorry for her. She didn't look vulnerable now, just rapacious. This was a good thing; it would make what he was about to do far easier.

'Mhmm.' He smiled at her, not able to actually say words. He felt pretty lousy doing this as he managed to lure her into the hallway but didn't know how else to get her out the house. Prior to him nipping to the bathroom he had spent a whole hour trying to explain in every way possible that he was not interested and she needed to leave.

She not only refused to listen but just got increasingly creepy about how she knew he was the one. How she had fallen in love with him in London when he had been so kind in the alleyway. It was all a bit of a mystery to him; he had no memory of being kind, just a rather one-sided conversation he couldn't wait to escape from. He felt quite sorry for her. He wasn't convinced her behaviour was driven by any kind of empowered female sexuality, more a kind of desperate sex-by-numbers-for-the-modern-male as seen through Siobhan's eyes. If that male was a fourteen-year-old used to accessing images online.

That may be a bit unfair – many men may find a largely naked woman in stockings and suspenders striking a dominatrix pose in their hallway a fantasy come true, but he was very definitely a bit more apple pie in his tastes. Although if it were Rosy... He suddenly pictured her in Siobhan's gear, hair falling over one eye as she winked – OK, suddenly he could see the appeal. But not with Siobhan.

Now for stage two of the plan. Although 'plan' could be a somewhat optimistic misnomer.

'OK, let's go.' He smiled as winningly as he could muster. She didn't appear fooled.

'Yah, OK, but where are we going?' She looked at him hard. As if she knew that this was not genuine. He was going to be lucky if he pulled this one off. Then he heard footsteps coming down the stairs next door. That meant Rosy was back from school. *Shit. Breathe.* That didn't mean she was coming around here right now – he was sure he had said seven, that gave him just under an hour to get everything sorted. Oh, bloody hell, what if she knocked early? That would be the universe taking bad luck too far. Logic dictated that couldn't happen. No one was that unlucky. But it was a reminder that he needed Siobhan out and fast.

He heard Rosy's front door slam. *Oh shit, shit, shit, shit!* What was he going to do? He looked at his guest, hair mussed, eyes big and face flushed. That, without her attired in a full-on sex kit complete with mac on top and dress dangling from her finger, would be hard enough to explain, and he wouldn't blame Rosy one bit for leaping to the wrong conclusion. Dear God, and he had assumed she was virtually married because of a few daft hearts. Um… um…

He knocked the hall light off and pushed Siobhan up against the wall. Despite the dark he could see her eyes grow bigger and her smile widen.

'Uh-huh, I knew you'd see sense.' She lunged forward to kiss him and he whipped his head back. Maybe she was just going into the village to the corner shop. His movement only inflamed Siobhan further.

'I see, yah, you like to be in control after all. Well, I'm all yours.' She leant back against the wall, opening herself even more.

Then he saw a shadow approaching through the glass in his door. Oh God! Siobhan was still talking. There was only one thing for it. He pressed himself up as tight as he could to her and covered her mouth somewhat aggressively with his hand. He prayed she didn't bite.

Rosy was knocking on the door; if he could just keep Siobhan quiet for a minute or two longer. He turned his head, just a fraction, not enough to relinquish control over his guest, just enough to make out the shape of Rosy against the glass.

She knocked again, cupping her hands around her eyes and peering in. Scramble was barking loudly to notify Rosy, cupping her hands around her eyes and peering in, that Matt was at home and in all probability with Siobhan. He held his breath and prayed. He could feel his heart beating so fast that he felt it was going to explode out of his chest, squishing between him and Siobhan. She must be able to feel it too. It was crazy. Then he realized she was wriggling her arm free to try and feel something else instead. The last thing he needed was their squashed form to make sudden movements, alerting Rosy to the fact that it perhaps wasn't a new hat stand in silhouette that she could see.

Taking decisive action, he grasped hold of Siobhan's hand and secured it fast against the wall. A little moan escaped her lips. Oh, bloody hell.

Finally, Rosy moved away and headed back down the path. Whilst part of him was relieved, surely she should have tried harder? If it were the other way around and Rosy hadn't answered he would have battered down the door to make sure she was safe. And maybe received a restraining order in the process. What was he wishing for? The one thing he didn't want was Rosy seeing him now.

He waited a minute or so until he heard her door bang shut. During the waiting he needed to pin Siobhan's other hand against the wall, but couldn't without releasing his grip against her mouth. Dear God, she was possessed. No wonder she did well in business; she certainly wasn't scared of putting herself forward. Although to be fair they had established that early on in the evening.

However, she was responding far too well to his newfound dominance, and was currently rubbing up and down the wall making moaning noises. This could put him off sex forever!

He leant forward and whispered in her ear. 'I'm going to remove my hand, and then you're going to follow me and do exactly as I say.'

She nodded enthusiastically so he continued to hold her hand, his fingers interlaced with hers, and firmly walked towards the door.

'Where—'

'Who's in charge here?' he barked at her. Angelina had done him a favour after all, banging on about that fellow, Black, Grey, whatever his name was. It worked; she simpered and let him lead her. He cracked open the door; it was only a little way down the path and to his Land Rover outside. If he could just get her that far without her making a noise. Could he be that lucky? He glanced, just quickly, not to give anything away, over his shoulder at Rosy's house. She wasn't standing at the window, pointing, staring or screaming, so all good so far.

He walked Siobhan forcefully down the path. It wasn't just Rosy he had to keep his eyes open for – living in a village had taught him that curtain twitching was an art form, its accompanying jungle drums run with military precision. Could he hope to get away with this?

He got to the Land Rover, yanked the handle and barked at Siobhan to get in.

'Oh, my darling, I rather like this side of you, yah!'

He smiled tersely, started the engine and drove as fast as he could to Chase's house.

# Chapter Forty

Marching to get her man hadn't quite panned out as she had planned. Matt's car had been parked outside the house when she had knocked and she had heard Scramble bark excitedly at the door, yet no one had answered. Which either meant she had misjudged that woman's arrival and that Matt was upstairs, doing all the things she had planned for them to do together this evening or, as her instinct was telling her, there was a perfectly reasonable explanation and she should return home and wait for him to knock.

As she wandered back down the path she realized that this was a whole new feeling: trust. She trusted that he wasn't currently sprawled naked with Egyptian Catwoman and would come for her, Rosy, as soon as he could. Trust. She quite liked it. It might be a gamble and she may feel like a real fool tomorrow but right now she was willing to take that risk. All her fears of being made a fool of since she had met him had come to nothing so far, and the only time she'd felt like an idiot were those situations she herself had created. This time she'd let him lead and see what happened. Trust – who'd have thought it?

As zen-calm and lullaby-like as this new Rosy was, there were limits and she didn't think she could just sit and passively wait. Switching on the TV was no use; concentrating on the drama unfolding in fictional lives was not the medicine she needed tonight, not on the night when she had decided to take action, action that could change her life completely. The local news, which she did want to watch, wasn't on for another half an hour and she doubted zen would last that long. Perhaps if she threw herself into some horrid domestic chore she could scrub out all her pent-up energy and if nothing else at least the house would smell great.

Hence Rosy found herself scrubbing the bathroom grouting – no, she had never known such a job existed until tonight – when she heard her phone ring. Please don't be Matt cancelling, not when she had just made peace with all her demons.

Jumping out of the bath where she had been crouching, she flew to the phone to see that it was an unknown number. Taking a deep breath, she hit accept, her whole face furrowed with worry as she did so.

'Miss Winter?' a deep male voice, humming with authority, asked.

'Yes.' Her answer was tentative.

'Miss Winter, I'm glad I caught you. It's David French here from the Local Authority. I'm sorry to disturb you on a Friday evening but do you have a few minutes?'

Rosy gulped – had he watched the local news? Oh God, had she missed it? How could she? She thought she had set an alarm to remind her! Maybe she could watch it on catch-up with Matt in a bit, if he turned up. What was Dave French going to say? She did hope she wasn't in for a bollocking, although maybe… maybe…

'Um… yes, of course, Mr French. How can I help?'

'I had a meeting with one of your governors this week' – should she play dumb? Pretend she didn't know? If she just stayed silent and waited for what else he had to say – 'and he brought certain things to my attention to do with the new build at Roscarrock, and the schools that had been selected. I had to take some time to confirm things for myself, of course, but I was surprised to hear that you didn't wish to be included in the amalgamation' – oh damn, this didn't sound like a positive outcome – 'especially as Mr Grant had assured me everyone was on board. However, with careful consideration, and a bit of detective work, I have to agree that you may not be the most obvious choice, especially if you are so unwilling. You have been removed from the list and Penmenna School will stay exactly as it is for the foreseeable future.'

Rosy couldn't help but let out a loud squeal and then clasped the phone even tighter to make sure she didn't drop it with excitement.

'Are you OK, Miss Winter?'

'Yes, I'm sorry, I was just excited. Mr French, I cannot tell you how happy I am, how happy everyone involved with Penmenna School will be, to hear this.'

'Yes, quite. I was going to have a press release drafted first thing Monday morning, Miss Winter, as the press do seem to have taken rather a lot of interest in this. However, seeing that you, or rather Penmenna School, have practically taken over the local news this evening I feel I should release one immediately before the Local Authority are lynched on social media, especially after the screening of that gardening programme tonight. Not quite the plans I had for this evening.'

'I'm sorry but yes, yes, thank you. I don't know how to thank you, this is so wonderful.'

'Hmmm.' Dave French didn't sound like it was that wonderful, but then with his next sentence his voice softened considerably. 'I have to say, Miss Winter, you've done a pretty good job. I'll be keeping my eye on you in future. Enjoy your weekend. Goodbye.'

Rosy wasn't sure if that was a threat or a reward but she didn't care, and leant against the wall, dizzy with relief, breathing deeply and knowing she had to let everyone know. She couldn't believe it – it had worked.

First, she rang Lynne, who screamed down the phone so loudly that Rosy thought she may have pierced an eardrum and then – and she was looking forward to this – she rang Marion.

'Rosy, weren't we wonderful? I assume you saw the news. Oh wait, what are you doing calling me? Aren't you meant to be with Magnificent Matt? Get off the phone now!'

'We've done it, Marion! We've done it! Dave French just rang me himself. He's putting out a formal announcement now. He referred to both the list and the media attention but didn't give specifics, just that we were safe.'

'Oh my. Oh, Rosy, that's wonderful...' Marion sounded like she might be hyperventilating, not a sound Rosy had heard her make before. 'I'm so very pleased, we'll celebrate properly next week, with the whole school, I can arrange something outstanding.'

'Honestly, Marion, there is no need. Maybe we can just take the main people who've helped out to dinner.'

'Well, we'll see... really, Richard, stop it!'

'OK, I'm going to go. But, Marion, thank you so much, it couldn't have been done without you.

Ooh, that's the door, I really am going to go. Thank you, thank you, thank you!'

Tumbling down the stairs, she bowled towards her front door with all the energy of Scramble. What a day! Not only did she have the best news ever, but baring her soul was no longer chock full of fear, instead an opportunity to start afresh. It was all a bit surreal.

Wrenching the door open she stood there grinning a welcome, her chest expanding and deflating like a Tudor heroine.

'Wow, hello, those gloves suit that dress beautifully!'

Typical, of course she would destroy the moment with rubber gloves and the smell of bleach!

'Ha! I was doing some chores, but listen, I've just had a phone call.' She was practically jumping up and down on the spot she was so excited. 'The chief exec. of the Local Authority rang and we've done it, Matt, we've done it! We don't have to move and I can't th— aaahhhh!'

Matt had picked her up and was spinning her around with excitement, his grin as wide as could be. Her body pressed against his as he spun, or tried to – the tight hallway meant it wasn't quite as successful as it was in the movies.

As he put her back down he smiled again and looked her straight in the eyes. 'I knew you could do it, Rosy, I knew it. I don't think there's anything you couldn't do if you put your mind to it.'

She smiled back, her head swimming as she stood there looking at him, just the two of them, no onlookers, definitely no children and surprisingly no Scramble, her tummy pooling with lust and her desire to talk about school suddenly taking second place. All she was thinking of now was pulling that T-shirt over his head, undoing that buckle on his belt and sinking against him as his arms encased her body and his lips bent to meet hers.

'I'm so proud, I really am. Well done and hey, I'm so sorry that I'm later than planned. Trust me, it was the last thing I wanted. But I had to deliver Siobhan back to my sister and then stop on the way here. But it does mean I'm now free and yours and I have something to show you. Unless you want to go and celebrate this amazing news with your colleagues — we can do our thing another day, if you'd prefer?'

Rosy shook her head silently. She knew what she wanted. But she would need to clear the emotional baggage first, make sure Matt knew what he was getting into.

'OK, in that case, keep your fingers crossed the rain holds off. Are you ready?'

Rosy nodded, still mute; she was more than ready and very keen on the something-to-show-her bit. She stared right into his eyes, sure that hers were flashing with lustful intent and watched his pupils dilate in response. Ooh, this was going to be good.

'Come on then,' he continued, 'although you probably won't need them.' He nodded once more at the gloves, still somehow on her hands. 'Unless it's your thing, in which case I guess you should keep them on.'

Giggling, she peeled them off and then took the hand he held out for her and walked down the path. It would appear his plan differed slightly from hers; walking to the car was very different to being thrown over his shoulders in a fireman lift and carried up the stairs, but she was going

to go with it. Trust. And a warm hand that was clasping
hers with intent.

# Chapter Forty One

As Matt held open the car door for her, Rosy slid in and felt a warm bubble travel up through her, from her tummy all the way to the corners of her mouth.

'Where are we going?'

'Secret.'

'Are we going to dinner?'

'Not exactly, but there will be snacks. I figured I'd never top the supper at your house that night...' He paused as he held her eyes – oh dear God, help her – before he turned forward again and started the ignition.

'Will there be lots of people there?'

'No, just us two. Is that OK?'

She nodded furiously and he turned once more, and lifting his hand to her face ran a finger down her cheek and across her jawbone. Electricity flushed through her, causing every little bit of her to tingle. This was really happening. She felt the air expel through her lips, far louder and with more force than she expected. She hoped he hadn't heard that, but he just smiled in recognition (at least that's what she thought it was) and turned back to focus on the road.

'I thought tonight would just be about us, and we've got lots to discuss so I figured somewhere private was better. Buckle up, and we can get moving.'

A little deep breathing and she realized they had reached the end of the road. Not that Rosy was looking at the road at all, but was focusing on Matt's profile, the outline of his ear, the marks on his skin caused by shaving, the crook of his nose, the crinkled laughter lines framing his eyes. His eyes which were on the road ahead. This was the perfect time. And once it was said, it was said, and they could get on with the fun stuff.

'Matt, I've something to say.'

'Good. I was worrying that I had the wrong Rosy in the car – you've been quiet for a whole minute and a half. I wasn't sure who this quiet, acquiescent, pleasant soul in my car was. It did occur to me that your recent success may mean that you've gone into some kind of shock.'

'I'm always pleasant. I'm known for it!'

'Hmmm. And your modesty up until about three seconds ago!'

'Will you hush, I'm trying to say something important.'

'Would you not rather wait until we got to our surprise destination?'

'No, I think now is good. You just look at the road and I'll just look at the road and then I can... look, I want to say sorry. I know you must think I'm as mad as a box of frogs. I was mean to you, I ignored you when I had said I would get in touch and I shouted at you, which was very liberating, but... um... very wrong and I'd like to explain why.'

'Rosy, you don't need to explain anything to—'

'Yes, yes I do. Because I don't want you to think of me as anything other than me, and I don't like that I behaved that way. I try really hard to always make people comfortable, and you, who have been nothing short of lovely to me, and the school, well, I made you feel uncomfortable and I'm cross with myself. But I do have a really good reason.'

'Go on then, Rosy Winter, what is your really good reason?'

'Eyes on the road! Thank you. OK, I'm just going to say this, I'm not going to think, I'm just going to blurt and it might not be very articulate but it's probably the best way.'

'You could probably have said it by now.'

'Don't be mean, I'm trying to! Right, when I met you that first time and I was a bit cross because I was late and you were lovely and gave me that plant but more than that you were just so gorgeous that... um... I had a strong physical reaction to you, a reaction that I haven't felt in a very long time and you made me feel like a teenager. Feeling like a teenager should be good...'

'Yup.'

'But for me it wasn't. You see, I haven't felt attracted to someone like I was to you that day – and every day I saw you after – since I fell in love at eighteen.'

'Are you saying you love me, Miss Winter?'

'No, I'm bloody not, let me speak! When I fell in love at eighteen it was a huge mistake and it's affected the way I have dealt with relationships ever since. So for me, when I realized how attracted I was to you, it scared me.'

Matt indicated and swung the car in to the side of the road. Parking up, he turned to her and grabbing both of her hands looked her in the eyes, his mouth set in a little listen-to-me smile.

'No, no! Don't stop the car, don't look at me, this is humiliating enough. Please let me speak whilst you drive or I'll never get it finished, and I really want this to be finished.'

'But, Rosy, we all make mistakes and judgement calls at eighteen that we regret, I mean really regret, later.'

Rosy shook his hands off. 'Please, drive the car, I've got more to explain, and as far as judgement calls go, this one was fairly life shattering.' As he drove off again she continued to speak. 'Now, I know I've just made you drive and what I'm about to say next may shock you so heads up, but keep your eyes on the road and remember this is about teenage Rosy, not adult Rosy, and everything is good now. My judgement call, as you put it, meant I ended up in an abusive relationship with a master of manipulation. It ended with me losing my job, having to switch universities and losing everyone I had assumed was my friend there. I was so in love with him but he beguiled me, spread lies about me and ultimately made me a prisoner. When I finally escaped no one believed me and it has resulted in more than a few trust issues. I was always too scared to tell anybody anything. So you see when I felt those clutches of such fierce attraction again I was terrified. I couldn't trust my judgement so I needed to put you at a distance, and then I'd actually see you and struggle to do so because you were so lovely, and then the fear would strike again and the conflict has been running through my head and driving me mad for weeks now and I just want it to stop. And that night of the party I screamed at you because I felt that you were all over my life, but that had nothing to do with you, it was all about Josh, that was his name, and Chase made me see it.'

Rosy stopped for a second to draw breath. 'And I'm so very sorry I was so hot and cold with you, but I was scared and now I'm not. Well, I am a little bit, but like normal scared not Josh scared because I know you're you and no one else and the you that you are seems pretty great, and I'm worried I've ruined it and I really want to make it up to you, and I want you to understand why I was the way I was and how I'm going to try really hard not to let any of it affect us any more and will you forgive me, and can we not mention it again, at least tonight anyway and ooh, are we at Penmenna Hall? Oh wow!'

Rosy finally stopped speaking as she realized that Matt, who had done a beautiful job of listening and not interrupting, was coming to a halt.

It was dark outside and there was a patter of rain on the car roof, but there in front of her was the long path to the orangery, lit by the twinkle of candles. She squinted but it was hard to see precisely; it looked like tea lights had been laid out in jam jars to illuminate the path. One or two were flickering out as the rain grew stronger and drops caught and extinguished the odd flame. The inside of the orangery was equally illuminated, those candles protected from the rain and casting out a glow of welcome.

Rosy's breath caught in her throat as she realized this was Matt's surprise, and she turned to him as he switched the engine off.

'Rosy, there is so much I need to say about what you've just told me, I knew there was something, but this, this… well it must have been so…'

'Shhh, please.' Rosy's eyes widened in her best puppy-dog look. 'I know we'll need to talk about it some more, but for tonight, just tonight can we forget it now, and accept my apology and know I'm not completely mad. I just have a little bit of baggage which, as sure as dammit,

I'm not going to let influence this chance we've got any more.'

'So we've got a chance? That's good to hear.'

'Well, we might not if you don't stop talking and take me in the orangery.'

'Take you in the orangery? Well, I'd only planned a movie night, but if you insist!'

'You're a fool!' Rosy couldn't help but giggle as she raised her hand to give him a friendly punch on the arm.

The rain was now coming down with the *thud*, *thud*, *thud* of an entire cavalry's hooves on the roof, and only five candles along the path had escaped its onslaught.

Matt caught Rosy's arm before it could land on her target and with his hand on her wrist he spun around in his seat to face her. 'It's pretty vicious out there, listen to it. And it's a bit of a walk to get to the orangery – perhaps we should stay in the car until it passes.'

'I'm quite keen for the movie night you've planned but that does sound like it's about to come through the roof. We could always stay in the car and make out like teenagers.'

'Oh, I like the sound of that, but you know what, we only get one first kiss…'

'Are you telling me you forgot that we had a first kiss?'

'Oh no, never. And I'd thought of loads of big romantic gestures to get us to the next one, like plant you a whole flowerbed as a declaration or get your medieval troubadour friends to do something as an extension to "Greensleeves", make you see how I feel, but the truth is that this next one, this will be a first kiss where we'll have cleared up all the misunderstandings, like when I thought you were dating Chase because of all the red cardboard hearts surrounding you on the floor and then you stayed at his house…'

'You what? That's hilarious.'

'Hilarious? Harsh! But not the point.' They were slowly edging together, eyes now locked and mouths virtually whispering soft breaths directly into the other's as they spoke. 'The point is that you, Rosy, are not just the sexiest women I know, you're the most honourable, tenacious, well, every quality there is and of course I want to kiss you right now, strip you naked and tumble into the back seat but I also want to wake up with you tomorrow and the next day and the next. I want you to understand before we go any further that this is important to me, I want you to understand that I don't just want a quick tumble, I want lots of them, lots and lots. I want us to give this thing between us a shot. I want you to know now how committed I am, I don't want to scare you, obviously take one day at a time, but for me I want this to be long haul and I don't ever want the sort of misunderstandings that have occurred between us to happen again. Straight-talking from here on in. No embarrassment, we just say what needs to be said. Are you in agreement?'

Stunned by this, Rosy nodded. Her confession had been bold but this was real lifetime stuff. Such an admission took guts; she wouldn't have been strong enough to vocalize all this, to lay herself totally open about what she wanted, what she hoped for. He was a good man, and he wanted her and she could feel herself pulsing all over, wanting that tumbling to start right now.

'Is that a yes? Give this a shot long-term? No secrets or worries that we don't share?'

'Yes! Yes, yes, yes!'

'Excellent, and as such our first kiss with this said needs to be romantic, memorable, something we can remember and retell with a smile and the truth is when I think romance I don't think of gear sticks and seatbelts and...'

Rosy moved her hand across her body, down towards her seat belt release, and clicking it she held his eyes and huskily murmured right next to his mouth, so low and soft that it would have been inaudible if it weren't for their physical closeness, as the rain cantering across the roof intensified, 'You're right, I agree, let's make it memorable...' And then with a quirk of her lips and her heart hammering out of her chest she added, 'So... race you!'

She grabbed the handle and thrust the car door open, giggling as she hurtled down the path towards the candlelit orangery, with Matt seconds behind her.

The noise of the rain was broken by their laughter as they both ran full pelt towards the glass house, Matt easily catching her and grabbing her hand as they crashed through the door together.

Rosy saw that not only was the whole place lit by tea lights, but that he had cleared the tables back, hung a projector, somehow sourced and dragged a cosy velvet two-seater sofa in front of it and set up a picnic of Wotsits, pink wafers and Dairylea. Amongst the snacks was an orchid, tall and slim with a smattering of pink flushed petals in a terracotta pot with a scroll, like the very first one she had received, tucked inside it.

Standing there, she felt her breath coming hard and fast, the rain trickling down from her hair, now stuck to her head, with drops rolling down her face, her nose and her eyelashes. Yet the inside of the orangery was warm, the unseasonable warmth of the last few days combined with the mugginess of the rain. The smell that summer usually conjured, of languid days and passion-filled nights, of couples across the years, laughing, playing, loving. She could feel Matt's hands on her shoulders as he stood behind her, so close that she could feel the whole of him pushed against her and making her feel both strong and really quite light-headed. He had done of all this for her and before he had heard her explanations.

'I think I might enjoy movie night.' She turned as she whispered, but carefully, so as to ensure they remained pressed together, so that she didn't lose the beat of his heart against her body, solid, pulsing, ready and so damn sexy, no millimetre of space allowed between them. 'But I think to enjoy it fully, I might need to get out of these very wet clothes.'

Catching a drop from the side of her cheek, Matt looked down at her upturned face and slipped the green strap from her shoulder, sliding his other hand into the small of her back.

'That is, I think, one of your better ideas...' And he leant down and gently, gently touched his lips to hers, inside a glass house strewn with lights, a witness to lovers for centuries.

# Acknowledgements

I can't believe I get to write acknowledgements.

A huge thank you to the lovely Hayley Steed, agent extraordinaire, and the wonderful team at Canelo, particularly Hannah Todd and Louise Cullen who have been an absolute joy to work with.

I also have to mention the Romantic Novelists Association whose constant support and encouragement must make it one of the best professional associations in the world. I've made so many amazing friends within the RNA but would particularly like to thank Nicky for being my rock and Margaret for being my Oracle. You are both marvels.

And of course, Jack and Katharine – you are little toads but no-one makes me laugh like you do, Namdi – practically perfect in every way (and I *shall* deny I said that) and my Mum and Dad for their unwavering faith. Love you all.

## About the Author

Kitty Wilson lived in Cornwall for twenty-five years having been dragged there, against her will, as a stroppy teen. She is now remarkably grateful to her parents for their foresight and wisdom – and that her own children aren't as hideous. Recently she has moved to Bristol, but only for love and on the understanding that she and her partner will be returning to Cornwall to live very soon. She spends most of her time welded to the keyboard, dreaming of the beach or bombing back down the motorway for a quick visit! She has a penchant for very loud music, equally loud dresses and romantic heroines who speak their mind.